DATE DUE

PERMA-BOUND®

JUMPING
OFF
THE
PLANET

DAVID
GERROLD

TOR®

A TOM DOHERTY ASSOCIATES BOOK
NEW YORK

This is a work of fiction. All the characters and events portrayed in this book are either products of the author's imagination or are used fictitiously.

JUMPING OFF THE PLANET

A Tor Book
Published by Tom Doherty Associates, LLC
175 Fifth Avenue
New York, NY 10010

www.tor.com

Tor® is a registered trademark of Tom Doherty Associates, LLC.

ISBN: 0-812-57608-X

First edition: March 2000
First mass market edition: April 2001

Printed in the United States of America

0 9 8 7 6 5 4 3 2 1

for Lydia Marano and Art Cover
with love

MOM AND DAD

I'VE GOT AN IDEA!" DAD said. "Let's go to the moon."

"Huh—?" I looked up from my comic.

"I mean it. What do you kids think? Do you want to go to the moon?"

"Yeah, sure," I said, not believing him any more than I had all the other times he'd dangled promises in front of my nose. In the last thirteen years, or at least as much of them as I could remember, he'd promised me the stars, the sky, and a trip to Disneyland. The only time I saw the stars was on TV, the sky was brown, and I still hadn't ridden the Matterhorn bobsleds and probably never would, at least not until I paid for the trip myself. So when he asked me if I'd like to go to the moon, it sounded like just another one of those things that adults say for no other reason than to use up air.

Is it just me, or is there something about grownups? What happens when you turn twenty-one? Does the brain shrivel up automatically or do you have to have an operation where your judgment lobes are removed? Adults can't stay in the same room with a kid without having to talk. Adults think they have to *relate* to me. But I don't want to be *related* to. I want to be left alone.

Dad shows up twice a year. We get him two weeks at a time. "We" includes me, my weird older brother and my stinky younger brother. Sometimes the older brother is stinky and the younger one is weird. I think they've got some kind of a deal where they have to take turns. I hate being the middle kid.

Weird builds worlds. He never shows anybody what he builds, but he spends hours a day at his terminal. He rents processor time from UCLA, and pays for it by fumigating code for the evolutionarily challenged. He's in the scholarship pipeline, so he's deep into the net. As big brothers go, he's not the worst, but he never pulled a bully off me either, so what good is he? Mom and him had a big fight just before my birthday, about his money for college, and his job, and stuff like that. Nothing was resolved, except that things were more sullen than usual, which is hard to do, because sullen is normal in our house. The two of them avoided each other like they had been magnetized in the same direction. It was fascinating to watch. I think they call it a *gavotte*. That's a kind of a dance where everybody moves slowly and carefully and keeps out of everybody else's way. They didn't even talk to each other at my birthday dinner.

That's when Mom announced that Dad would be coming early for us this year and we'd be spending a month with him instead of two weeks. She said it while cutting the cake, like it was supposed to be an extra present for me. She said it was what Dad wanted and she wasn't going to argue about it, it would be good for us to spend a little more time with our father. But I figured she just wanted us *out*. She looked tireder than usual, and she kept saying she wanted out of the war zone. Like she was blaming us. But we didn't ask to be born. Especially Stinky.

Stinky doesn't do much of anything except whine and wet his bed. Dad thinks Mom is ruining him. I think he's already ruined. I once told him he was an accident—the accident that split up Mom and Dad—and that was another multi-megaton war. Now I know why they call it the nuclear family. Mom spent half the day trying to calm Stinky down, and the other half on the phone with Dad, and I got all the fallout from everybody.

I spent the next three months trying to stay out of the house as much as possible. I would grab some recordings and my headphones and get on my bike early in the morning and see how far I could ride before it got too hot. Weird says I'm stupid for going up topside in the sun, the tubes are air-conditioned, UV-safe, and have more trees, but he doesn't understand. It's *quieter* up topside. People don't bother you. Sometimes, I try to see how far up the mountain I can get. All I want is a place where I can just sit and listen to my music without anybody interrupting. But when I try to listen at home, all of Mom's sentences begin with, "Charles, if you're not doing anything right now—"And when I tell her I *am* doing something, she says, "No, you're not. You're just listening to your music." Hello? Is anybody home?

We live in Bunker City, which is supposed to be part of El Paso, but it's really just an old tube-city built in a hurry to house refugees from the west, and then prettied up a lot when they didn't go home afterward. So now it's another suburb, sort of.

What it is, is a place where a bunch of tube-houses have been buried up to their armpits in sand. When the wind blows, the sky disappears and we get to spend a week at a time staring at the curved walls of our pipe-rooms. Sometimes the lights flicker and go yellow. Twice we've had outages and had to sit in the dark waiting for the wind farms to come back online. I don't know why a sandstorm should put a wind farm out of commission, except it does. Anyway, sitting alone in the dark with no one to talk to except Weird and Stinky is not my idea of a good time. It doesn't take too long before we're all really hating each other. Weird says that during the sandstorms is when most murders happen. I can understand that.

Anyway, Dad shows up every June and the first couple days are always spent driving somewhere. Usually Colorado or Arizona, although once we went to Mexico for two days. That was like a downtown tube-city with hot sauce. I got to practice my Spanish in a restaurant. I understood two words of the waiter's reply.

Dad works so hard trying to be a *pal* that it's embarrassing. He tells us how much he loves us, how much he misses us, how he wishes we could spend more time together, and we all do the obligatory performances of, "we love you too, Daddy," but it's like acting for a stranger. Who is this guy anyway? Weird just grunts and Stinky just whines and it's up to me to carry on the conversation. And that's about as much fun as kissing your brother. Either one.

Eventually, after two or three days of Dad's earnest attempts to be Dad, Stinky usually does something ghastly, like peeing in the back seat or throwing up into the cooler, and Dad loses his temper, and then everything is back to normal. Nobody talks. Dad turns up the stereo and we listen to Beethoven or Wagner or Tchaikovsky and that's actually not so bad. It's better than trying to talk to each other. Sometimes Dad tells us stories about the music, but not very often.

Dad works for a music consortium, so he knows a lot of gossip about composers and what they were thinking of when they wrote this piece or that. Sometimes he really lights up when he talks about his music and I remember we used to have fun times together when he tried to teach me about conducting—but something happened, I don't know what, and it was like part of the fire went out. Now Dad still listens to music, but he doesn't talk about it so much anymore.

So there we were, in Dad's rented minivan heading west toward someplace in Arizona and suddenly he says, "I've got an idea. Let's go to the moon. What do you think, Chigger?" What was I supposed to say? I said what I felt. So of course, Dad got angry at me. And then Weird and Stinky did too.

But if he didn't want to hear it, then why did he ask?

And why didn't he ask when it was important? It was my family too. Nobody asked me if I wanted it split up. They just did it.

A HOLE IN THE GROUND

I **DON'T KNOW IF THE** Barringer meteor crater is at the end of the world, but I'm pretty sure you can see it from there. If there's a lonelier, uglier, more empty place in the world, I'm sure I don't want to go there.

You drive for hours across the desert, and then there's a sign with an arrow, so you turn off and follow a two-lane road across some more desert, but the road still doesn't look like it's going anywhere. The ground goes up a little, but there's nothing to see except a dinky little building. You go through the building because you have to pay admission, and then you walk out the back, and up a path. Then you go up some stairs and suddenly there you are—standing on the edge and staring down into the biggest hole in the world and saying a lot of stupid things that don't come anywhere near to expressing how deep and scary it really is.

Dad said, "Geezis." Weird said, "Oh, wow!" Stinky said, "Daddy, is that a real hole?" And I said a word that got me a dirty look from all three of them.

It was the biggest empty space I'd ever seen in my life. It was *eerie*. At the bottom, there were some buildings and even a couple of scooters and jeeps. That's how you could tell how big it was.

Weird started reading aloud from the souvenir pamphlet, "The Barringer crater is named for the American engineer, Daniel M. Barringer, who theorized in 1905 that it was caused by the impact of a meteor. The meteor struck the Earth almost head-on, 25,000 years before the birth of Christ; it was mostly nickel and iron, 30 meters (100 feet) in diameter—actually, that makes it an asteroid—and weighed 63,000 metric tons. It was traveling 8–16 kilometers, or 5–10 miles, per second. The blast was the equivalent of a 35-megaton nuclear warhead. Most of the asteroid was vaporized, but approximately 30 tons of fragments have been collected. The minerals coesite and stishovite, which can only be formed under very high pressure, have been discovered here.

"The crater is 1.2 kilometers in diameter—that's about three-quarters of a mile. It's 180 meters deep, surrounded by a rim rising 50 meters above the surrounding plain. This wall we're on is 160 feet high. So that makes it 760 feet to the bottom."

I said, "I bet you could put the Empire State Building inside it and it wouldn't show."

"No," said Weird, still reading. "The Empire State Building is 450 meters high—1475 feet. The top half would still be visible."

"You know what I like about you, Douglas?" I said.

"No, what?"

"Nothing."

"Hey, it says so right here, Chigger—" He waved the pamphlet at me. I slapped it away.

"All right. Knock it off, you two," Dad said. We both turned away from each other, annoyed.

The four of us were all alone on that crater wall. If there was anyone else around, we didn't see them. Not even at the bottom of the crater. All around us everything was very hot and very silent and very dark all the way down. There was no wind. It was like being frozen in time. The whole bottom of the crater was one big shadow. And it looked haunted. It made me queasy.

"Look," said Weird, pointing. "There's a path. I'll bet it goes all the way down."

"Where?"

"There." He pointed. It spiraled around and down. The crater walls were too steep to get to the bottom any other way. Stinky started being Stinky almost immediately. "Can we go down there, huh? Huh?" He didn't wait for an answer. He just started running along the path.

Dad hollered, "No, wait—" but Stinky didn't stop. So Dad poked me and said, "Go, get him."

"Uh—" I didn't want to say that the height of the crater and the steepness of the wall scared me. "If I chase him, he'll just keep running. If we just stand here, he'll give up and come back—"

"And what if he slips and falls?" said Dad. "*Go get him.*"

I looked to Weird for support, but he just pushed me forward. "Go on, Chigger."

"You too!" I demanded.

"*Both of you, go after him! Now!*" said Dad. Weird pushed me again, and I was off. Behind me, I heard Dad say, "You too, Douglas!" I could hear him following behind me, but it didn't sound like he was making much of an effort. Apparently he thought this was just a kid thing, not worthy of serious geek attention.

The path was narrow and steep and scary. It was like running down the side of a wall. I tried not to look off to my left, where there was nothing at all except a lot of nothing at all. Maybe it was all that time living in a tube-town, I just didn't like big open spaces—and this was the biggest and openest I'd ever seen. So I didn't look. And if I didn't see it, then it wasn't there. I hoped.

"Stinky, you stop right there!" I called after him, but he giggled and shouted back, "You can't catch me. You can't catch me." He kept running and laughing, like it was all a game. And to tell the truth, it was almost kinda fun running down and around the crater wall. It was all downhill, so it was easy running. You let yourself go loose and then you just keep falling forward and let your feet lump down in front of you. If only there wasn't that big *hole* there—I slowed down automatically—

"Come on, Chigger!" Weird said impatiently. He gangled past me.

I looked back. Dad was following after us, but he wasn't running, just walking fast.

And then Stinky slipped at the first switchback and skidded off the path, which would have been warning enough to any rational person that running down the side of a hole big enough to have its own area code was not a good idea—but Stinky didn't have good ideas. He picked himself up, shouted, "You're a big doo-doo head, and you can't catch me," and headed toward the next switchback.

"Bobby! Stop it! If you slip, you'll roll all the way down. You could get killed—!" But he didn't pay any more attention to me than I paid to Dad. He just kept shouting and taunting.

I wondered if I could cut him off, but that would have meant taking the short-and-fast way down, and I *really* didn't want to do that. So I slowed down for the turn, tried not to look, and kept after the little bastard. Behind me, I could hear Dad shouting, "Go get him, Charles!" as if it was *my* fault he'd run down here.

Eventually Weird caught up with Stinky, and so did I. Weird grabbed Stinky's arm and they skidded along the path for a bit, and for a moment I thought they were going to lose it and just go on down the side, but then their feet caught and they stopped. And then Weird started yelling at Stinky about how dangerous it was to run down the side of a steep hill. "You almost slipped! What do you think you were doing? You'd have rolled and bounced all the way down to the bottom. You'd have been killed!"

"Yeah!" I said. "And then we'd not only have to walk down to get you, we'd have to carry you back up." Weird gave me his weird look. "Well, we *would*."

Stinky didn't say anything, he just did that nasty hate-stare that he's so good at, and we all stood around for a minute not talking, just catching our breath, waiting for Dad to get to us. We hadn't gotten very far down the side of the crater. Most of it was still below us, but we'd come a long way anyway, at least half a klick, maybe more.

It wasn't until Dad showed up that Stinky started talking

again. "I wasn't gonna fall it isn't fair I wanna go to the bottom Dad make him let me go *let go of me!*" And then he did wriggle free and started running down the path again. And Weird and I had to go after him again. With Dad *walking* behind. This time Stinky was running away just to be nasty. "You can't catch me, neener, neener, neener!"

I was so angry, I started after him—which was *exactly* what he wanted. Only, I wasn't going to yell at him like Weird. I was going to gut-punch him like he deserved. No matter what Dad said. Weird came running after the both of us.

The path went back and forth down the side of the crater in a series of switchbacks. The first one turned so sharply, it was hard to stop and turn back the other way. If you're going to fall, that's where it's most likely to happen. And that's where he did slip—

Stinky was shouting and looking back, not watching where he was going, and he stumbled over a bump and bounced face forward and slid down the slope—and for a moment, that queasy feeling in my gut turned into a flash of black fear that he was going to slide all the way down—but then he stopped sliding in a patter of loose dirt and gravel and just hung there on the steep side of the crater wall, caught on a tiny bush. "Don't move!" I screamed. "Don't move!" And I knew even as I said it, that he would do exactly the opposite, because that was the kind of stupid little monster he was.

Except—he didn't move. He was too scared to move. He was screaming as loud as he could. "Daaaa-ddeeee!"

"Just hold on," I called. I was the closest. I looked back and Weird was just coming around the last switchback. What I really wanted to say to Stinky was, "This is your own fault. We told you not to go—" But I was close enough to see how scared he was and as angry as I was at him, I was even more scared *for* him. "Just don't move, I'm coming to get you—" If only I could figure out how.

Stinky had slipped about five meters down the slope. It was mostly dirt, with only a few little things pretending to be plants. He'd caught on a scraggly little bush that didn't look strong enough to hold him. It was already bending precariously, and I was certain it was going to snap before I could get to him.

The problem was that the slope was too steep for me. If I tried to go down it, I'd just go skidding all the way down to the bottom. And it was a long way down. There was that queasy sensation again. Heights. Open spaces. Holes. Everything. I couldn't explain it. And there was no way to get down underneath Stinky either, to catch him. I said a word, the one that Mom always tells me not to say.

"Charles! Go get him!" That was Dad, always full of good advice . . . from a distance.

I couldn't see how—the only thing I could think of was to lie down flat on the ground and try to inch my way downward, and even that seemed like a really stupid idea, because if I slipped, we'd both go rolling a hundred meters to the floor of the crater. Only it looked farther. I began edging myself down the slope, all the time muttering through gritted teeth, "Just hang on, Bobby! Just hang on—" I went from handhold to handhold. There weren't any rocks or weeds strong enough to hang onto.

I couldn't get close enough. I anchored myself as best as I could and unbuckled my belt, pulling it out of my pants as safely as I could. I let the end hang down toward Stinky. He could almost reach it, but it would have meant letting go. "No, wait—I'll try to get lower."

And that's when I froze. I realized I couldn't move either. Not up, not down. My mouth was dry and I couldn't swallow—and the great empty hole yawned beneath us. We were stuck on the wall, just waiting to slide down. I knew it then—we were both going to die here. And it really pissed me off. This was not how I'd planned my life—

"Chigger, wait!" That was Douglas, above me. I turned my head. He was just taking off his belt. He wrapped one end around his hand, then stretched out flat on the ground. He lowered his belt to me and I grabbed hold. There was just enough to loop it around my wrist and grab the buckle. I wanted to beg him to pull me up, but Stinky was starting to lose his grip below me. He was whining and crying the way that he did when all hell was threatening to break loose around him—all that somebody had to do now was tell him to shut up and he'd start flailing and screaming. It was very tempting.

"Okay, Stinky!" I said. "Look at me."

It worked; I got his attention. "Don't call me that!" he cried angrily.

"All right, but you have to look at me. I'm going to lower my belt. Don't reach for it until I tell you, okay? Because you're only going to get one chance. I'm coming down now—"

Still holding onto the end of Douglas's belt, I edged downward, just a little bit at first—I felt myself start to slide—and Douglas caught the slack instantly. Some rocks and pebbles rolled away around me. But I didn't follow them. I might live through this after all. "A little bit more, Doug. I'm almost there." I looped my belt around my other wrist, like Douglas had done, and lowered it to Stinky. It almost reached. I stretched as far as I could.

"Okay, kiddo," I said. "On three—"

"I can't do it!" he whined. *"I can't!"*

"Yes, you can," said Douglas. "Just listen to me—"

That wasn't going to work, Stinky never listened to anyone, "No, Doug, Stinky's right. He can't reach it. *Stinky's just a little baby.* He can't do *anything*—"

It worked. Before I'd finished the sentence, Stinky had swung and grabbed the end of my belt and nearly yanked me off the wall of the crater, he grabbed so hard. Without thinking, I pulled back in response, and Doug pulled on me, and Dad was there pulling on Doug, and somehow we all ended up back on the path, Doug against Dad with Dad holding him tight, and me against Doug with Doug holding me, and Stinky in my arms, hanging onto me like a human death-grip. The four of us just stayed like that for the longest time, all of us trying to catch our breaths at once.

I kept my eyes closed. Because when I opened them, all there was to see was how deep the crater was and how high we were—and all that empty space made me want to throw up more than ever now.

Eventually we untangled ourselves—very carefully. It would have been real stupid to fall down the hole now. Dad looked gray and shaken, but he waved me off when I asked if he was all right. He looked like he wanted to say some-thing, but then he looked like he didn't know what—finally he just waved his hand as if to erase everything and pointed back up the path.

Douglas took Stinky by the hand to follow him—and of course, Stinky tried to pull away. "Let me go!" he whined. "I gotta go to the bathroom! I gotta pee!" That was what he always said when he didn't want to cooperate. And it usually worked, because what if he was telling the truth?

But right now—Weird wasn't letting go.

"Go ahead," I said, coming up to block his other side. He wasn't running away again.

"Where?" he demanded.

"I dunno," I said in that really bland, passive-aggressive voice I'd learned to use on him. "Do you see a bathroom around here?"

He looked around. We were a quarter of the way down the wall of the biggest hole in the world, and we could see forever in all directions. There were no bathrooms, no water faucets, no elevators, no nothing. Stinky started crying, "But I gotta pee!"

"Well, then, just pee!"

"Where?"

"Here!"

"But everybody'll see!"

"There's no one to see! And besides we're so far away from everything, no one could see anything anyway. Just go!"

"I can't!"

"Then hold it till we get back to the top!"

"I can't! It's too far!"

"We told you not to come running down."

"But I gotta go!"

"Then go here!"

"I can't!"

The kid was paralyzed. No matter what anyone said, all he could say was "I can't!" So I said, "Well then, just pee in your pants and stop *whining!*"

So he did.

Now he was wet, uncomfortable, and smelled bad. But this

wasn't as bad as when he threw up in the cooler and spoiled everyone's lunch, and at least now that we'd gotten Stinky's first accident out of the way, we could get on with the fun part of the trip. Ha ha.

By this time Dad had realized we weren't following. When he got back down to us, Weird was yelling at Stinky, "Why did you pee in your pants?" and Stinky was crying full blast that I'd told him to.

That's when Dad did something strange. Stranger than usual. He didn't say anything at all. He stopped where he was and sat down. He put his elbows on his knees and his chin in his hands and he just sat and stared and looked sullen in that way he gets when he's thinking real hard about something—like a bad decision. I was sure he was thinking about turning around and taking us all back to El Paso.

"Now look what you've done—" I began to say to Stinky, but Weird swatted me hard across the chest with the back of his hand and told me to shut up, which actually startled me into silence, because Weird almost never touches anyone, let alone me.

"What's he doing?" Stinky asked.

Weird shook his head and grunted. "I dunno." He sounded kinda faraway when he said it. That's when I figured out that something was going on, but nobody had told me yet. Whatever Weird knew, he wasn't saying.

GEEKS

DAD? ARE YOU ALL RIGHT?" Weird asked.

Dad took a deep breath. "I was thinking about the moon." He pointed out at the big emptiness below us. "On the moon, there are craters this size everywhere. And bigger ones too. There's nothing special about a crater on the moon. Could you imagine living every day of your life in a place like this?"

Weird didn't answer. Neither did I. How do you answer a question like this? We just looked at each other.

Dad took another breath. "Y'know, people say that kids are the hope of the future—that a baby is the human race's way of insisting that the universe give us another chance. But I don't know. Sometimes it feels like a baby is just another chance to screw things up even worse than before. There's so much you kids don't understand, and I wish I could explain it to you, but I can't, because I'm not sure I understand it myself. And I can't ask you to forgive us because . . . well, I don't have the excuse that we did our best, because I know we didn't."

I'd never heard Dad talk like this before and it sort of

scared me. It was kind of like one of those movies where someone knows he's going to die soon and is trying to get all his good-byes said in two minutes. And everybody else is supposed to forgive him for being a jerk. I don't know why they always forgive each other. I wouldn't.

But whatever Dad was talking about, I didn't think he was dying. Instead, he started talking about the world and the mess it was in and all that kind of stuff. Corporate warfare. Chocolate dollars. Sugar dollars. Beef dollars. Oil dollars. Plastic dollars. Kilocalorie dollars. Silicon dollars. Cyberdollars. All of them spreading into new territories, like so many economic disease vectors, leaving a trail of infected and collapsing economies behind them. Governments unable to control their own economies because international corporatism had made all borders irrelevant. Money flowed like water seeking its level. Where it got too hot, steam rose—where it got cold again, rain fell. The economic weather was turning into a tropical storm and circling to become a global hurricane of dollars funneling around and around. According to Dad.

I couldn't see exactly how or why it would affect us, but he said it was "tear-down time." Every so often, people just get tired and frustrated with building—every twenty or thirty years or so, they start tearing down what the last generation built, even if it still works, just to tear something down and rebuild it. So the money was circling like flies, unwilling to land anywhere. Only this time, it wasn't landing. It was *going away.* That was why we didn't have the money for the reclamation projects or the recycling we needed and why everything was getting worse.

"This planet is no place to raise a family," he said bitterly. "It's just a matter of time until the whole planet turns into Calcutta." That part I understood. There were plagues in Calcutta. All over India. And Rome too. Black Peritonitis. African Measles. Europe was shutting itself down in panic, and brushfire wars had broken out all up and down the eastern half of Asia. Fifth World revolutions. Wars and plagues. Craziness everywhere. The planet didn't have the resources to manage itself anymore. Like the guy on TV said, "The machinery is breaking down faster than we can fix it."

"The problem is, we're all in it together, whether we want to be or not," Dad said. "More and more I look around at the way things are going, and I don't want to be part of it anymore. When I was your age, Charles, everything seemed so simple and easy. You don't know how easy it is to be a kid—"

"Yeah, right."

"—but then I grew up and everything got complex, and I just wish I could figure out how to get back to what's really important. You don't understand any of this, do you? And you won't, not until you turn forty." He sighed. "But wouldn't you just like to get up and go away sometime? Someplace new, where you can start fresh?"

Well, yeah. But there isn't any such place. It's all people, everywhere. So it's silly to dream of it. The best you can do is go up in the hills once in a while and listen to your music alone. But I didn't say any of this aloud. Why bother? In three and a half weeks, we'd be back in the war zone with Mom again.

I knew Dad wanted me to say something, but I'd stopped doing that a long time ago. There was no cookie there. When he realized I was simply waiting for him to do something, he stood up and brushed the dirt from his pants. "Well, come on, let's get going." He pointed toward the rim of the crater and we all started hiking upward. It was a difficult climb, not because it was too steep—it was just hard because it was all *up*.

Stinky whined the whole way that it was too hard and kept demanding that someone carry him, but no one wanted to touch him because he smelled so bad. I said, "You shoulda thought of that before you started running down." Then Weird made one of his pseudo-profound observations about how it's easier to cooperate with gravity than fight it, like this meant something, so I called him a techno-geek, and he said, "Yeah, so?"

Dad started to say something about that, one of those comfort-lies that grownups tell, but Weird interrupted him. "No, Dad—everybody's a geek about something. I *am* a techno-geek. You're a music-geek. And Charles is a nastiness-geek because he doesn't have anything else to be geeky for." It was the longest paragraph I'd ever heard out of Weird that didn't have the word gigabyte in it. I didn't have the breath left to tell him what he was full of. I just grunted, "Devour my richard," which is the polite way of saying it. "And Stinky's a pee-geek," I added, just a little louder.

"Daddy—" Stinky wailed.

"Well, it's your own damn fault! Dad told you not to go running down! Now we've all got to hike back up—"

At this point, Dad should have been screaming at all of us to shut up. Instead, he stopped. He squatted down in front of Stinky to look at him eye-to-eye. "There's a lesson here," he said.

"Huh?" Stinky rubbed his eyes.

"Do you know what it is?" Dad asked.

Stinky shook his head slowly.

"Two things. First—*never* go anywhere unless you know how you're going to get back. Look down. Suppose we had let you go all the way down to the bottom. Do you think you could climb all the way back up to the top? Look how much trouble you're having going just this short way."

"It's not a short way!" Stinky wailed. "It's a long way."

Dad ignored him. "And the second lesson—go to the bathroom *before* you go anywhere. Either that or learn to poop in the bushes."

"I wanna go home," Stinky said flatly. "I wanna go home *now*."

Dad responded with that grunt of resignation he does so well, whenever he realizes that whichever one of us he's talking to isn't really listening. Without saying another word, he straightened and started back up the crater wall. If he was angry, it was a kind of anger I'd never seen before. He didn't show any emotion at all. I looked at Weird, but he was pushing Stinky up the slope and no one was looking at me and I wondered why I had bothered to come at all. Here we were, standing inside the biggest hole in the world where a ton of rock had fallen out of the sky and blasted a hole so deep you could put a roof on it and have a stadium large enough for the Godzilla Bowl—and the only important lesson to be learned from our visit was that you should go to the bathroom before you went anywhere. Sheesh.

We finally got to the top and Weird took Stinky into the bathroom and got him cleaned up and into some fresh clothes, while Dad and I sat on a bench and sipped sodas and waited. Dad didn't say anything. He was still off somewhere else. On the moon, I guess.

"We're really screwed up, aren't we?"

Dad looked up. "Eh?"

"Us," I said. "Weird and Stinky and me. We're not exactly the Happy Family." He looked at me blankly. "The Happy Family, like on TV? You know? George and June and all the little Happys."

Dad got it then. "Nobody is the Happy family," he said. "Not even the Happys. It's all pretend."

"Yeah, but we can't even *pretend* to be happy. We're really screwed." I don't know why I said the next part, it just fell out of my mouth. "I don't blame you for hating us."

Dad looked startled. "I don't hate you," he said. "I love you, Charles. More than you realize. All of you. And—" this was where his voice got funny "—I don't think you're screwed up. None of you. I think you're terrific kids. I wish I could spend more time with you."

"Yeah, like *this*—" I waved my hand in the direction of the crater "—is a lot of fun."

"For me, it is. I'm sorry you're not having a good time."

"I'm having an okay time," I admitted. The crater had been interesting enough. Because it was so big. Living in Tube-Town, you never really got an idea of the size of anything.

Dad sighed. "I really do wish I could live with you and be a real father. All the time. Maybe it *would* be better for all of us."

"Yeah, well then why don't you?"

"It's a long story."

"I'm not going anywhere."

"Your mom—" He stopped himself. He said something else instead of what he almost said. "Your mom is a good woman. She works very hard for you boys. I'd live closer to you if I could. She asked me not to. She thinks it would be . . . disruptive."

"Yeah, so? Don't you get a vote?"

Dad shook his head. "It's too complicated to explain." He looked at me sadly. "You really are having a bad time of it, aren't you?"

"I'll do better in my next life, okay?"

"Charles . . ." Dad began carefully, his voice as serious as I'd ever heard it. "I want to ask you something—"

But before he could ask, Weird and Stinky came back, and Stinky started crying immediately that he wanted a soda too. And then he wanted something from the souvenir rack, and whatever Dad had wanted to ask me was forgotten while Weird and Stinky played another round of I-Wanna-No-You-Can't. Dad sighed and patted me on the shoulder. "Later, Charles." I followed him into the souvenir part of the store, where he tried unsuccessfully to steer Stinky's attention toward the cheaper toys.

Finally, they compromised on a programmable monkey—which struck me as being sort of redundant, especially for Stinky, but maybe it would keep him quiet for a while. Dad even bought some extra memory for the monkey. He was chatting with the lady behind the counter while she rang up the sale and suddenly she offered him some old memory cards that someone else had used and returned and she couldn't resell as new, so Dad bought them at half-price. It was a lot of memory, but Dad bought it all. He even paid cash, which for him is *serious*. Credit dollars are a lot more flexible, even though they're not worth as much. Weird offered to install them, but Dad insisted on doing it himself. "Let me prove I'm good at something besides paying the bills," he said as he snapped them into the monkey's backside.

Later, when we were back in the car and on the road again, with Stinky in the back happily trying to teach the monkey how to fart, I asked, "Dad, you were going to ask me something back there—?"

"Never mind," he said. "It wasn't important."

Only we both knew he was lying. Whatever it was.

FINDING THE LINE

MEXICO IS HOT. HOTTER THAN Arizona. Maybe hotter than Hell. And there are these little tiny lizards, small as bugs, everywhere. They flicker across the sidewalk so fast, they look like heat ripples.

The surprising thing was how clean everything was. Everybody in Bunker City says that Mexico is dirty, the streets are dirty, and the people are dirty. But it isn't like that at all. Everywhere we went, everything was hot and bright and clean. Cleaner than Bunker City. Which just proved what I already knew. When people don't know what they're talking about, they make stuff up.

And the Mexicans were friendly too. Dad's Spanish wasn't all that good, but Weird and I knew enough to get by, and where we didn't, there was usually someone else around who spoke enough English to help. So we weren't going to starve to death.

We headed south on the new highway. Dad didn't talk much, not about where we were going. He said it was a *Magical Mystery Tour*, which meant that you weren't supposed to know where you were going until you got there, so the fun had to be in the going, not the arrival; but I was pretty sure Dad had a destination in mind. Every so often I'd catch him muttering about travel times and schedules, so I knew this trip wasn't as random as he kept saying.

We stayed our first night in Mexico at a Best Inn, which is two lies in as many words, but never mind. We were on the eastern coast of the Gulf of Baja, somewhere in the middle of nowhere, with dirty blue ocean to the west and scruffy brown desert to the east and some purple hills in the distance beyond that.

After dinner, there wasn't much of anything to do except stand around watching Stinky playing on the swings with his monkey or look up at the stars. They were a lot brighter here than they were in El Paso. In fact, in El Paso, we could hardly see them at all, so it was something different to just look up at the sky and see how bright it really was. Weird saw a shooting star, and then I saw one too. Dad pointed out Orion's belt and the Big Dipper and a couple of other constellations as if they meant something. I asked him where Sirius was and Betelgeuse and some of the other places where the brightliners went, but he didn't know. Dad said that Sirius was the North Star, so all we had to do was look north, but Weird said no, Polaris was the North Star, not Sirius.

Dad ignored it. Instead, he pointed south. "Look, you can almost see the beanstalk from here."

We squinted into the darkness. I couldn't see anything. Not at first.

"Look for a very, very thin line," Dad said. "Find the line. It'll be high. Up out of the shadow cone. About ten o'clock high. Maybe eleven o'clock."

Weird was the first. "I think I see it," he said. "Is that it?"

"Where?"

"There."

"Oh—oh yeah!"

It was like looking at a razor blade edge on. It shimmered in and out of existence. First it was there, then it wasn't. We could only see a little bit of it, but even so, it seemed to stretch impossibly upward against the darkness. The orbital elevator, a braided strand of monofilament nearly 72,000 kilometers long.

"We should be able to see it better tomorrow night," Dad said. As if that meant something. "It's the stepping-stone to the stars."

His voice sounded so wistful I turned to look at him. I hadn't heard him sound that way about anything for years—the last time was when he guided me through the fourth movement of Copland's Third Symphony, showing me why it was such a masterpiece. It was when I was nine and got to sit in on the rehearsal for one of his concerts. He was very proud that day. He introduced me to everybody. I sat behind him on the podium, and every so often he would stop to explain something to me—and to the musicians as well. But we'd never done it again after that, and I always wondered what I'd done wrong. Not too long after that, the arguments between him and Mom started getting worse, and he'd started staying away more and more, and then Mom moved us to El Paso to be closer to Gramma and Grampa, only they died—

"Would you like to go there someday?" Dad asked.

"Huh?—Where?"

Dad pointed to the sky. "Anywhere. Out there."

"You mean, the star colonies?"

"Sure."

"You'd have to win the lottery. Two lotteries."

"Mm, maybe. Maybe not," Dad said. "Some of the colonies will pay your way if you'll promise to stay for seven years. And if you have a needed skill. And children."

"Indentured servitude," said Weird. "That means you'd be a slave."

"It's not so bad, Douglas. The jobs all fall under the guidelines of the Corporate Treaty of Singapore."

"Yeah, Dad—and who enforces the rules eight point three light-years from Singapore?"

"The Treaty Authority has offices wherever there are indentures. And the locals are very strict about self-enforcement. Most of them were slaves once too, before they worked off their debts."

"I can't believe we're even having this conversation,"

Weird said, suddenly angry. "Mom would drop her load. Are you *seriously* considering it?" I could see him thinking about Grampa and all the stories he used to tell about great-great-umpty-great-Grampa and what it was like to actually *be* a slave.

"It's a way out, that's all I'm saying," Dad said.

"A way out of what?"

"Here. This." Dad gestured vaguely around. "I'm just trying to say something, that there are still plenty of opportunities for a good life. If not here, then out there. You pay the price however you can."

"It's too high," said Weird.

"I just want you to have a good life, son—I want you to know that there might be more possibilities than you've considered."

"Not for me." Weird said, and the way he said it was like a door slamming.

Dad looked at him sharply, as if trying to figure out who he really was. Finally he said, "You grew up too fast. I hardly know you."

Weird didn't answer that. He just shook his head in disgust and turned and walked away from us. I couldn't tell what he was thinking. What was he angry about? Nobody was going anywhere. So why were we arguing again? Probably because that's who we were. The Crankys—not even in the same neighborhood as the Happys.

Dad looked at me glumly. "And what do you think?"

I shrugged.

"You think I'm a pretty lousy dad too, don't you?"

The question caught me by surprise. "Huh, no—I don't think that." But even as I said it, I knew that I was lying.

"Charles, I can see it in your face. You're almost always angry. I can hear it in your voice."

I shrugged again. What else could I do?

You see what I mean about adults and the way they talk to kids? When they finally make up their mind to really talk to you honestly, they want you to be just as honest with them in return, even when you both know that if you tell the truth, it's only going to make things worse. *Really* worse.

The hell with it.

I said, "I don't think you're a lousy dad. How should I know what kind of a dad you are? You're never there."

My words hurt him. I could see that.

"I'm sorry you feel that way, Charles."

"Me too. I wanted a real dad."

I started to follow Weird, but Dad grabbed my arm.

"Hey," he said. "Give me a chance. Please? We don't have a lot of time together, Charles. Can't we make the best of it?"

I shrugged. "Whatever." But I still tried to wiggle out of his grasp.

"What's it going to take to reach you, kiddo?"

"I dunno." And I really didn't. This time, Dad let me go. I knew he was hurt, but I didn't know what he wanted and I didn't know how to give it to him, and even if I did, I wasn't sure I wanted to.

THE GULF

WE DROVE SOUTH, DOWN THE coast of Mexico, and by the end of the second day it was obvious where Dad was headed: Beanstalk City in Ecuador. He didn't have to say anything. After all of his talk about space and the moon and the stars as a way out, where else could we be going?

Weird had been real silent all day, but Stinky had gotten the way he gets and he kept demanding to sit in the front seat so he could watch for the beanstalk, so Weird and I let him. I was kind of interested in the beanstalk myself, but I didn't want Dad to know it.

But finally, I couldn't stand it anymore. I asked, "We are going up, aren't we? At least as far as One-Hour, huh? Huh, Dad? Please?" Weird and I did a couple of rounds of this, until Stinky joined in for the chorus.

Dad smiled, satisfied. "I was sort of planning on it. Actually . . ." His voice trailed off.

"What?" I demanded.

"It's a shame to come all this way and not go to the top. I was thinking of taking you boys all the way up to Geostationary. That is, if you want to go that high . . . ?"

"Geostationary? *Really*?"

"I assume that's a yes. How about you, Douglas?"

Weird just grunted. "Does Mom know?"

Dad hesitated. "I didn't tell her we were going this far. We can call her from the top, okay? We'll surprise her."

"Let's call collect," I said. "And *really* surprise her."

Dad laughed at that. "Your Mom is taking a vacation of her own. At least, that's what she told me. But we can try to call her, if you want."

"Yeah!" Stinky said. "I wanna call Mom from the top."

"Then it's settled."

Weird said, "Dad, we gotta talk. You and me."

"Right now?"

"No. Just you and me."

"All right," Dad said. "There's a beach up ahead. Why don't we let your brothers play in the surf for a while."

"There's no surf here. This is the Gulf of Baja." Weird was like that. If you told him it was 6:30, he'd check his watch and announce, "six twenty-eight and thirty seconds." Like it made a difference.

"Check the map," Dad said dryly. "We're already to the mouth of the gulf, just north of Mazatlán." I guess Weird inherited it from Dad.

Dad pulled the car off the road onto a wide patch of packed dirt that served as a parking lot. There was no one else around, so Stinky and I stripped down naked and went running into the water, screaming. The sand was so hot we danced across it, keeping our feet in the air more than on the ground.

The water was warm and salty and didn't smell bad at all. Stinky and I splashed around and screamed at each other. The sand under the water was as soft as mud, but there were rocks in the sand too, so mostly I floated on my back and paddled gently, just lazing in the sensation of not having to go anywhere or do anything. After that got old, I just stood and watched Stinky. He wasn't doing anything, so I looked up onto the beach. Dad and Weird were talking about something; I couldn't tell what, but it looked serious.

"I gotta pee," Stinky said.

"Go ahead," I said.

"Right here?"

"Right here."

"Shouldn't I get out of the water?"

"I hardly think it matters."

"But I hafta get out of the pool when I hafta pee, why don't I hafta get out of the ocean?"

"Because it's the ocean. Everybody pees in the ocean."

"Teacher says that's why the oceans are so stinky. Because everybody pees in them. And poops too."

"Go ahead. I won't tell."

"I already did," Stinky said. "I made the water warmer. Didn't you feel it?"

"No, I didn't." And I was just as glad I hadn't. I moved a little bit away from him anyway and watched the water lapping around us, wondering how long it would take to dilute his little contribution.

Dad and Weird were apparently through talking. Dad was leaning against the van with his hand over his eyes as if he had a headache, or maybe he was crying. Weird was walking down the beach, kicking at the sand. Every so often, he'd stop and look back at Dad, and then he'd turn around and walk a ways farther. But it was clear he wasn't going to walk too far. He was just angry. That was weird—even for Weird, because he never got angry. And now, this trip, he'd been angry almost since we'd left. What was going on between them anyway?

Stinky started coughing then—he'd gotten a mouthful of water, so I had to duck under and grab him and pull him up. It wasn't really anything, but he started crying anyway, so I picked him up and carried him as far as I could across the hot sand. Dad met us halfway and took Stinky from me. "What did you do to him?" he asked accusingly.

"I didn't do anything!" I protested. "Don't yell at me. He did it himself. He was fooling around and got water up his nose. I pulled him out."

"I'll deal with you later," Dad said, turning his attention instead to Stinky's tears.

"Yeah, right. Tell me again how you're trying to reach out to me too." I grabbed a towel and my shorts and stalked up the beach after Weird. "Hey, Douglas—wait up!"

It was my use of his real name that made him stop. He glowered, but he waited for me. "What do you want, Chigger?"

"Nothing."

We walked in silence for a bit, while I tried to figure out what to say. Occasionally, Douglas stopped to pick up seashells. He'd look at them for a bit, then hand them to me. They were little gray things that looked like cornucopias. "Periwinkles," he said. "They always spiral out the same way. Clockwise. How do you think the periwinkle knows which way to turn?"

I shrugged. "Who cares?"

"I dunno. It's just—how come periwinkles are so stupid but they always know which way to turn, and human beings are so smart and we hardly ever know?"

"I don't know what you're talking about, Douglas." I tossed the shells away.

"It doesn't matter."

"Yes, it does. I'm part of this family too."

"It's not your business—"

"Now you're acting like Dad," I said. Doug gave me the sidewise glower, so I blurted, "Well, just because Dad's acting like an asshole doesn't mean you have to."

Douglas shook his head.

"Well what's going on?"

"Never mind."

"Tell me—"

"It's kinda personal, okay?"

"So?"

He gave me the look. The one when somebody says something too stupid to reply to.

"So?" I repeated, pretending I hadn't seen it. "Who else do you have to talk to?"

"It's not anything I want to talk about."

"It's about UCLA, isn't it?"

"Partly," he admitted. And then after another moment, he said, "I got approved for a conditional scholarship. Dad won't sign, but he doesn't have to. I'm almost eighteen, but—" He stopped himself. "You don't know what's going on, do you? Between Mom and Dad, I mean."

"They hate each other. What's to understand?"

"Mom thinks Dad is crazy. She went to court last month to have his visitation rights terminated. Dad counter-sued. He had some big New York lawyer on his side, so he won. Now he gets us four weeks a year instead of two. But Mom still thinks he's going to try something."

"Like what?"

"Like not bringing us back. Or something stupid like that."

"Dad isn't that crazy. Where would he take us?"

"Well . . . think about it, Chig. What's he been talking about?"

I thought about it. It didn't take much thinking. "Oh," I said, a sinking feeling in my gut.

"Uh-huh," said Weird.

We walked for a while, neither of us speaking, just pushing forward through the sand, while I sorted stuff out in my head.

Finally, I said, "So if Dad isn't trying to kidnap us, then Mom is schizo-paranoid. And if he *is*, then she's right and *he's* crazy. But either way, *we* lose—because either way we've inherited the genes of a crazy parent."

Douglas half-smiled, that funny expression he gets when somebody says something scientifically.

"So, how do you know all this?" I asked.

"Mom told me. She told me not to tell you. She said you'd side with Dad."

"Mom obviously doesn't know me as well as she thinks. I'm not on either of their sides." And then I realized what else Douglas had said. "You didn't keep your promise."

"It's our family too. I'm tired of all this back-and-forth stuff and nobody ever listening. Aren't you?"

I stared at my older brother as if I'd never seen him before. I couldn't remember him ever being so . . . so adult. Finally, I said, "Thanks, Doug." And I meant it. After another minute, I asked, "But what were you and Dad arguing about?"

"My scholarship. Dad doesn't want me to take it. He doesn't like the conditions."

"What conditions?"

Doug shook his head with a sad smile. "It's kinda personal."

"It's one of those rechanneling scholarships, isn't it?"

"You know something, Charles? You're too smart for your own good."

"I *knew* it."

"You don't know the half of it."

"Well, you *can't* do that. You won't be *you* anymore."

"Yes, I will—" He looked like he wanted to say more, but suddenly, Dad was honking the car horn at us. He'd finally calmed down Stinky and put him in the front seat, and the two of them had motored half a kilometer up the road to catch up to us. Douglas nudged me and we headed across the hot sand to meet them.

It was all too much. I didn't know what to think anymore.

GOING SOUGH

AFTER THAT, WE GOT BACK on the InterContinental Express-way. It was Doug's turn to drive, and he immediately pushed the speed up to 160 klicks, until Dad told him to back off a bit. Doug eased back to 150 and Dad began muttering again about estimated time of arrival and beanstalk schedules and stuff like that.

We skipped staying in a motel that night, while the two of them took turns driving and sleeping all the way down to Puerto Vallarta, where Dad turned in the car and we got on board the SuperTrain Express, which would take us south through Central America and straight to Beanstalk City at speeds up to 360 klicks—225 mph. Dad said we'd be in Beanstalk City in less than thirty hours.

Stinky and I slept through Nicaragua and Costa Rica. Dad woke us up at 7 A.M. so we could see the Panama Canal as we raced over it, but it was no big deal. The Colorado River is wider. The canal was just a straight-walled cut through flat green fields, filled with a motionless line of dirty freighters and smaller private boats, all waiting their turn at the next lock.

We spent most of the day gliding south through Colombia. The highway and the train tracks raced each other, swirling back and forth across the mountain slopes in great sweeping loops, hardly ever losing sight of each other. I was glad we hadn't driven the whole way. It would have taken a week or longer. We'd have killed each other.

Late in the day, the train began rising up the western slopes of the Andes and there were some places where the view was spectacular. By now, the beanstalk was a visible presence day and night. We could see it sometimes out our windows when the train went around a curve, but the best view was from the seats in the upstairs observation domes. The beanstalk sliced straight up into the bright blue sky almost from the very edge of the horizon. You'd think it would keep going until it was directly overhead, but it didn't. It disappeared about 11:00 high. Dad said it had something to do with angles and perspective and atmospheric haze. When we got closer, it would reach more toward zenith.

The SuperTrain was a lot wider than the old-fashioned kind—as wide as an airplane, but roomier, and the cars were all two-level. There was even a restaurant car with real waiters. We spent most of our time in the lounge car where there were terminals and even a theater at one end. Stinky wanted to play World Stomper, so Weird had to help him at the terminal. Dad and I went to the other end of the car and plopped down in the only available seats. I stared out the window and he ordered a drink from the table.

There was a fat man in a shiny suit sitting next to Dad; he was arguing across the table with a dark-haired woman. They both looked like Mexicans, but they could just as well have been Texans too. Sometimes it's hard to tell. They were both wearing fancy clothes and expensive-looking jewelry, so I figured they were Internationals, people with world-passports and no countries of their own.

The woman was angrily telling the man what was wrong with his politics, and he was telling her what was wrong with hers.

The fat man was explaining to the woman that money was a liquid, and that the health of an economy could be measured by how fast the liquid flowed through all the different parts. He said that if you gave a hundred plastic dollars to a rich man and a hundred plastic dollars to a poor man, the rich man's plastic dollars would be like drops in a reservoir, and they would move a lot slower than the poor man's plastic dollars. The poor man's money would be like drops in a river. They would flow a lot faster and farther than the rich man's money.

Dad looked uncomfortable. He obviously didn't like having to listen to their political discussion, but there was no other place to move to. He turned on his zine, but it was clear he couldn't concentrate. I smirked at his annoyance and he glowered at me.

The dark-haired woman said that the rich man's money worked just as hard as the poor man's—investments created jobs. But the fat man argued that rich dollars just flowed from one financial reservoir to another, without ever going through the rest of the economy. The poor man's dollars are more liquid than the rich man's, so funding the flow-through—paying people to consume—was good for the economy, because poor people bought things and that created jobs for everybody. The fat man looked at me then; he'd noticed that I was listening to their argument. "Am I right, *muchacho?* Or am I right?"

"I'm not your *muchacho*," I said.

"*Perdóneme.*" He held up a hand. "But you have studied plastic flow-through dollars *en la escuela*, have you not?"

I nodded. Reluctantly. Because I didn't really want to talk about it. We'd had a lot of flow-through kids in school, so the teachers had to explain it that some people's parents were being paid to be consumers, but everybody still called them weasels and thieves—because everybody knew that flow-throughs were the reason everybody's taxes were so high. At least that's what I used to think, until Mom had to sign up for the flow and we moved to the tube-city and then other kids were calling Weird and me and Stinky the same names. Then I didn't know what to think. We weren't stealing from anyone—the government was paying us. But if the government was paying us with the money it was taking from other people, then maybe we shouldn't be taking it, should we? But if we didn't, then how would we live?

I could tell that Dad didn't like the conversation either—because of the way he was holding his zine and glaring at me over the top of it. The fat man saw it too. "*Señor*, I apologize," the fat man said to him. "I saw that the *muchacho* was listening, I don't mind. It's good for children to be curious about issues. Allow me to introduce myself." He held out a meaty hand. "Bolivar Hidalgo, Associate Representative for Baja to the SuperNational Congress. This is my esteemed colleague, *Señora* Juanita Ramirez, Economic Consultant for the Fiscal Alliance. I think they are all greedy reactionaries and she thinks that I am an agent of confiscatory totalitarianism because I do not share her feudalistic views of the world."

"I'm an old-fashioned conservative," *Señora* Ramirez announced to Dad and me, as if this were something to be proud of. "I believe in absolute fiscal responsibility, minimal government, and the preservation of individual freedoms."

Hidalgo snorted. "If we were talking about simple individuals, that would be fine, but you are talking about corporations who do not care if real people starve."

She reached across and poked him in the stomach with a perfectly manicured finger. "You are a fine one to talk about starvation. When the world food crisis finally occurs, you will be able to live off your stored fat long after the rest of us are bones bleaching in the sun."

I had to smile at that. These folks didn't talk like friends, but they didn't fight like enemies either. And . . . it was nice to have adults actually speaking to me as a real person. Even if I didn't understand most of what they were talking about.

She looked at Dad and me. "You see, here is where my porkulent friend's argument breaks down. *Real* economic growth occurs in the development and deployment of new technology. The beanstalk, for instance—I assume you are going there?—do you know that the construction of the beanstalk expanded the world economy by almost three percent? It is the equivalent of constructing a new continent—a vertical continent. You'll see when you get there. And the economic benefit is still growing. What most people don't know is that the technological fallout of the beanstalk has been of far greater value to the economies of the Earth than the beanstalk itself. The money was spent here on Earth, and we built ten thousand factories and created a hundred million jobs. And thousands of new products that could never have existed before. My fat friend here would have you believe that the ownership of wealth automatically disqualifies one from full participation in the human race, as if somehow the possession or control of money is such a burden that it drains all compassion out of the soul. But he has a cure. He will take away the wealth and we will all be equally virtuous."

Bolivar Hidalgo just laughed and grinned, but it wasn't entirely a friendly grin. "Juanita," he said to her. "You misrepresent my views almost as badly as you misrepresent your own. It is not *only* about wealth, Juana. It is about the human suffering caused by economic plate-tectonics."

"Uh-oh, here we go—" she said. "*The* speech."

"And I will keep delivering it until you start listening. You cannot move a trillion dollars more than two inches in any direction without it flattening whoever or whatever is in the way, leaving a trail of broken economies in its wake. The people who'll pay your salary have taken trillions of dollars out of the North American economy and moved it into anonymous Ecuadorian holdings. The economic health of the entire hemisphere has been depressed by the greed of the fiscal underliners. And the ripples are still spreading. But your people don't care about the misery they leave behind, do they?" He eyed her curiously. "That money isn't even on the planet anymore, is it, Juana? It's on its way up the Line, isn't it?"

"Again with the conspiracy theories, Bollie?"

"Thirty trillion dollars has been drained out of the world economy. Where is it? We are heading into a global depression because the money has mysteriously disappeared. Where did it go? Your people are playing with disaster, Juana."

Very quickly, they forgot about Dad and me—which was just as well, because I was afraid that they were going to start asking more personal questions; but an aide came then and whispered something to Dr. Hidalgo. He looked annoyed, excused himself, and headed forward. *Señora* Ramirez followed glumly.

I looked to Dad. "What was that all about?"

Dad's expression was dark and unreadable. "Paper dollars,

plastic dollars, future dollars—none of that exists. But people argue about it anyway—as if it's important."

"Is it?" I asked.

He shrugged. "If you can translate it into spendable dollars, it is. And if you can't . . . you start a war."

"Is there going to be a war?"

Dad frowned. I could see the question troubled him. That meant that it was a very real possibility. But he considered the question fairly and gave a slow shake of his head. "I don't know." He put his zine down and tried to explain. "I guess those people think war is about money."

"Isn't it?"

He looked at me sadly. "I guess some people think so. But it's the rest of us who'll pay."

POPULATION CONTROL

WEIRD AND I DIDN'T GET too much more chance to talk about what Dad was planning. Or why. Or even if he was planning anything at all. Maybe insanity was hereditary—or at least contagious. All we had to go on was what Mom had told Weird, and we already knew that Mom hated Dad so much she'd say anything. Weird said that was why she'd lost in court this time, when she'd tried to deny Dad custody rights. Because the judge caught her lying.

In the bathroom once, I asked Weird what he thought we should do. Should we call Mom or what? He shrugged. What could Mom do? We were over the border. Seven borders now. Eight if you counted Guatemala, even though we hadn't really gone through Guatemala, but around it. By the time anyone could do anything, we'd be up the Line. And besides, Dad hadn't done anything illegal. Yet. So all we had were Mom's suspicions living rent-free in our heads. Just because Dad had mused aloud about going off to one of the star-colonies.

But I could see why Dad and Weird were angry with each other.

It goes back to when Dad and Mom got married. In return for certain tax credits, they'd agreed to have only boy children. The Population Control Authority had determined that reducing the ratio of girls to boys would reduce the worldwide birth rate. The target was to reduce the world population to ten billion people in three generations. That meant we had seven billion too many and everybody had to have fewer children. Or at least, fewer *female* children. In order to get international monetary credits, a lot of the fourth world countries had adopted such strict breeding policies they were almost totalitarian.

What we were taught in school was that in some countries, the people didn't think girl children were valuable, they only wanted sons. So parents would kill female babies before they were born. So letting those parents have two sons, but no daughters, was a popular idea in those places. In our country, the government didn't have that kind of power, so instead they passed a law giving extra tax credits for male births and parents would decide for themselves.

In one of our classes, we were told that some women thought these policies were the equivalent of genocide. I suppose, maybe, they had a point—but it sounded more angry than sensible. They were saying that it was men who were irrelevant and we should be making more girl babies and less boys. I guess, if you were a girl, you might feel that way, but you could just as easily argue the other side of it. With less girls than boys, girls were more valuable now—and a girl could choose who she wanted to marry from the very best. She wouldn't have to take whoever came along. Of course, it might not be so good for the boys if there weren't enough girls to go around, but lotsa guys never get married anyway. I couldn't see myself getting married. I mean, I wouldn't rule out the possibility altogether, but I really didn't know very many girls, and most of them were in separate classes—but the ones I did know, well, they all seemed like they were from another planet or something. Dad said I'd probably feel different about girls when I got older, but if the way he and Mom ended up is any example, I'd just as soon not bother.

But anyway, that wasn't good for Weird. There were now

six boys for every four girls, which was supposed to be okay for economic productivity in some areas, and not so good in others—but since the time he was born and the time he grew up, the PCA had come up with another one of their good ideas for slowing down the birth rate. They had lots of good ideas that way.

This time, they were offering college scholarships or tax credits for guys who went in for rechanneling and had their sexual orientations reversed. That's what Weird had said he wanted to do. Dad was against it, but Weird said it was the only way he could afford school. So that was a big part of why they were angry at each other. Mom didn't have any money, and neither did Dad. At least not enough to pay for college for all three kids. So maybe from Weird's point of view it made sense, selling off what he probably would never get a chance to use anyway. I dunno. The whole thing made me uneasy and I spent a lot of time looking at Douglas when he didn't know I was watching, trying to figure out what kind of difference it would make in him, if he'd look or talk different or if he'd even still be my brother.

And what about me when it came time for me to go to college? Would I have to do the same thing? I didn't know what it was and I didn't like it already.

I didn't want anybody trying to change me. Even for my own good. I didn't even know who I was and already everybody else had made decisions that it was the wrong way to be, that there were too many of us anyway, that there should be more of one than the other, and that I shouldn't even be here at all, but now that I was, I shouldn't be the way I was going to be, whatever it was, we still didn't know, but whatever I was, somebody was sure to tell me it was wrong. Probably Dad. Or Mom. One of them first. And then everybody else.

That's what I hated about all of this. Adults were supposed to take care of their own problems, not pass them on to the kids. But it felt like Mom and Dad and now Doug were all passing the load on to me—as if somehow I should have to carry it too. It wasn't fair. They all kept telling me to act my age. Well, why the hell didn't they act theirs?

And it wasn't just Mom and Dad. It was all adults. I mean,

kids get born into this world, and as soon as we're old enough to understand the smallest piece of it, adults start talking about the mess we're going to inherit and maybe we'll do a better job than they did. That's real smart. Think about it. How the hell are we going to do a better job if all we've got to go on is the stuff *they taught us?* Where's the place you go to get some *real* answers?

And then they wonder why kids are so confused and moody all the time.

So it wasn't exactly a fun trip. This part, at least.

And maybe it was because none of us were feeling very comfortable. This close to the equator, everything was hot and muggy and very bright. Even inside the train, we could feel it. And it was especially bad whenever we had to make a stop and all the doors were opened. We got out once to stretch our legs, but decided not to do that again. How did people live in this heat day after day after day?

Once we got into Ecuador, the train tracks ran down the center of the InterContinental Expressway, so whatever view there was, there were always cars and trucks in the way. Occasionally, we saw a train going the other way—it *whooshed* past so fast that we could feel the impact of the wind like a shotgun blast against the side of the train.

After the fortieth round of "no, we're not there yet," Stinky started whining about not having anything to do at which Dad reminded him of his monkey and Stinky complained that it didn't do anything. Dad looked real annoyed for a minute, as if he was going to lose his temper, but he didn't. Instead he said, "That's right, you have to teach it. That's what makes it fun. Douglas, will you help him?"

Then I said something to Weird about what a waste it was spending all that hard cash for a toy that has to be taught. Weird grunted something about Dad not wanting to use his credit cards. "So what?" I asked. Then he asked if I'd noticed that Dad had paid for the train tickets with cash too. And I said, "Yeah? So what?" And Weird said that if he'd paid by credit card and someone wanted to find us—like Mom—it'd be real easy to look up the account transactions to see where we were going. Dad heard that, and said that it was also cheaper to pay cash because you didn't have international

ransaction fees and you didn't have to worry about flexi-
dollars going up suddenly either, and that way we could save
money and do more. So there I was, with two more conflicting stories and one more reason to be as paranoid as Mom.

Vacations are supposed to be fun—except vacations with
Dad were never fun; they were just this *thing* we had to do
every year, and this one wasn't turning out any different—
so whoever made up that crap about vacations being fun
didn't know what he was talking about, or maybe he'd never
been on a vacation with Dad. And besides, I kept thinking
about what Dad had said back in the crater: "Don't go anywhere unless you know how you're going to get back."

See, that was the point.

I didn't know if I wanted to go back.

What if Weird was right?

If he was, I wasn't sure I wanted to stop Dad—because
part of me was starting to think that maybe Dad was right,
that going to the stars was the only way to get out.

It sure couldn't be worse than here.

TERMINUS

AFTER A WHILE, DAD GAVE up trying to get us kids to talk to him. Even Stinky had figured out something was going on and stopped talking. So Dad scrunched down in his seat and watched the news while we continued to grind southward. It was more of the same old same old. People were dying. Food riots in China. Botuloid Virus in Africa. Comatosis in Asia. Wars in India, Somalia, and Manchuria.

"You hear that, Charles?" Dad asked.

"Yeah," I grunted. "Don't live in places ending with the letter 'a'—especially 'ia.' "

"Never mind," said Dad. He shut up again. Whatever it was he'd wanted to say about all that stuff, it wasn't going to get said while I was in one of my moods. On the lighter side, some girl in Oregon said her horse had been eaten by a giant pink caterpillar. Dad was right. The world was going crazy. But I wasn't going to give him the satisfaction of agreeing with him.

Things got a little better as we got closer to the beanstalk.

Close up—like the last hundred klicks—the Line was almost too bright to look at. Up in the observation domes, you could plug into the telescope channel and see views of it from broadcast stations all over Ecuador.

Dad punched up the coordinates of one of the Andes installations and we all stared at the shimmering view of One-Hour Station. We'd seen it before—but this was *live* and that made it more *real*. Seen from this angle, through miles of atmosphere, One-Hour was just a gray indistinct blob, but we could see all three of the cables clearly delineated, and once we saw a tiny blip slide up into the station and another one drop away.

Most people think the Line is just one cable, but it isn't. It's three independent cables, all linked together for triple strength, so it's really three beanstalks in one. Originally there was only one, but they'd added the other two to triple the capacity of the stalk and provide additional "vertical services."

Eventually, they wanted to add three more cables. All six would touch down as an even bigger triangle than the present one; it would cover four times as much land. The newer triangle would point north, the original triangle would be inside it, pointing south; its vertices at the center points of the sides of the larger triangle.

They didn't know yet if they'd need to expand beyond that, but they were prepared to. Dad told us all this on the train. He drew a diagram and showed that six cables was probably the most you could put down without hitting the point of diminishing returns. Part of it was land area, part of it was economics; it all had to do with something called Elevator Theory.

By the time we got to Beanstalk City—that's what everybody calls it, but that's not its real name; it's really named after Sheffield Clarke, the English engineer who designed and built the whole thing—all of us were excited in spite of ourselves. Even Weird had stopped being a jerk long enough to ask Dad questions. And Dad answered honestly.

I was excited, but I was also getting a little scared too. This wasn't going to be like an airplane. An airplane, you knew what was holding you up. This was different. Nothing was holding you up. What if it *broke?* I knew it *couldn't*, but what if it did anyway—?

We arrived at the beanstalk at ten in the morning. First we rolled across a big plateau with dark mountains all around. There were a lot of warehouses and industrial buildings—and tube-towns too. Everything looked big and new and shiny—except for the parts that were small and cheap and dirty. The last twenty miles we passed a whole bunch of parking areas and hospitality structures and hotels and tacky little side businesses—and then abruptly, that all stopped and we were riding through what looked like a big park. Weird said this was the safeguard zone around the beanstalk.

For security reasons, they don't let anyone drive right up to the elevator. The closest you can approach by car is one of the official arrival areas. These are all at least fifteen kilometers away from Terminus. All traffic from there is by shuttle-train. I suppose a terrorist with a rocket-launcher might be able to do some damage from that distance, but if somebody really wanted to assault the beanstalk, they wouldn't do it with a rocket-launcher anyway. Dad said that almost the entire Ecuadorian economy is based on the beanstalk now, and they're a world power too, and a sponsoring nation of the Colonization Authority, so they don't take any chances with Line security.

The sky had gone all hazy gray and overcast—there was a tropical storm heading in from the Pacific—so we couldn't see if the Line went all the way up to zenith or not. But all of the beanstalk's lights were on and that made it very bright against the grungy clouds. We could even see the flashing lights of vehicles sliding up and down the Line. I started wondering how often lightning struck the cables and what kind of trouble it could cause to the people in the elevator cars. Despite the high gloom, the weather was still sweltering. Dad said they never have cold days anywhere on the equator, but it was definitely windy outside; we could see the trees whipping back and forth, and occasionally big palm fronds would go tumbling by. Weird said there was nothing to worry about; the Line was secure for wind velocities of up to 625 kph.

Dad opened the tour book he'd bought that showed how the base of the Line was surrounded by cargo facilities, ter-

minals, parks, tourist sites, stadiums, theaters, and a whole
webwork of highways, tracks, and canals. The widest canal
circled the beanstalk—Weird said that all of the bridges over
it were retractable, in case terrorists or someone tried a
ground assault. Airplanes weren't even allowed to fly within
fifty klicks of the Line without special permission. He said
the Ecuadorians were very serious about this; they once shot
down somebody's Lear Jet and there was a big lawsuit about
it.

When you get close enough, the bottom of the Line starts
rising up over the horizon like a big white mountain. It
spreads down and out and out and just keeps getting bigger
and bigger the closer you get. And it takes a long time to
get. A half hour at least. The top of the cone part is over
two kilometers high. At the apex there's a ring around the
Line, an observation tower where you can view the surrounding countryside or just watch the Line-cars go sliding up into
the sky.

Closer still, you can see that there are wide gaps along the
bottom of the cone—like a tent just a little too short for its
ropes. The train slides in right under the edge. And then
everything gets *real* bright.

Terminus is more than a launching station, it's a domed
city—bigger than enormous, twenty klicks across. Think of
a gigantic tent that uses the three cables of the beanstalk as
the central mast, the tent fabric is made out of the same
monofilament stuff as the Line, and all of the supporting
cables are actual beanstalk filaments anchored off axis for
additional stability. So once you're inside the tent, you're
actually *inside* the beanstalk. It's a whole other world. Dis-
tances don't look the same. You can't tell how near or how
far anything is. And everywhere, the filaments of the beanstalk spread out like rays of the sun, stabbing into the ground
and anchoring themselves deep in the bedrock.

The top of the Terminus dome goes up so high it fades
away in the distance. It's almost like someone took the meteor crater and turned it upside down over everything like a
gigantic cup, only *bigger* than that. Terminus dome is so big
it has its own weather. They get clouds and fog, and sometimes they even get little rainstorms. But the outer surface

of the tent is painted with solar crystals to generate power for the air-conditioning inside, so it's mostly comfortable.

And of course, the three main cables of the Line are visible from everywhere. They're all lit up like a big bar of sunlight, so everything inside is as bright as it is outside—and that's pretty bright, because it's right spang on the equator. There's a line drawn across Terminus so you can tell where the equator is; you can stand in both hemispheres at the same time if you want to.

The actual cables of the Line were a lot thicker than I thought they would be. And they were spaced quite a distance apart; it looked like at least a kilometer, maybe more. There was a lot of traffic on them too. There was always at least one car inside the dome going slowly up or down on each of the strands. They don't really get up to full speed until they get out of the dome and out of the thickest part of the atmosphere.

I guess we did a lot of gaping. Everyone did. That's because Terminus dome is like no other place in the world—at least not any place I'd ever been. It's like an amusement park and a shopping mall and a factory all scrunched together. Everything was stacked on top of everything else. Towers and balconies and gardens and waterfalls everywhere. And rides and restaurants and all kinds of theaters and stores and clubs. And signs and lights and music and a constant roar of noise. We could even hear it inside the train.

The train station is elevated, so as the train pulls into the tent you can see the whole interior of the station spread out below like a big jumbled toy box, and everybody all over the dome can see the SuperTrain too. It's really impressive. But when you get off, Weird pointed out, you're still in a holding area. You have to go through multiple security gates where you get scanned and photographed and inspected, and then only when they're satisfied that you're not some kind of terrorist or madman do they let you go down the ramp into the city. Stinky was already pulling at Dad's arm. "I wanna go on the rides—" But Dad shook his head and said, "We're about to go on the biggest ride of all, kiddo."

We were each responsible for our own luggage. Dad had insisted that we travel light. When we turned in the rent-a-car in Mexico, we left behind everything we weren't going to need for the trip up to Geostationary and back, and that meant most of Stinky's toys—not the monkey, though; Dad insisted Stinky bring it after he'd spent all that cash—and the rest of the stuff like bathing suits and towels and dirty clothes and extra jeans. We just put it all in a big box and shipped it home.

Weird and Stinky and I had all our stuff in backpacks. Dad had his stuff in a rollaround. Stinky had half his clothes in his own backpack and the other half in a smaller one on the monkey; he held its hand and chattered at it like they were married. It waddled beside him like an obedient child with a full diaper. It was almost cute. I said they looked like twins, which got a laugh from Weird and a dirty look from Dad. "Well, it looks just like him—" I started to say, but Stinky heard that and started crying, and suddenly he didn't like his monkey at all anymore. "Does *not* look like me!" he said, kicking it away. Of course, the monkey came scurrying right back to him, so he kicked at it again—the monkey jumped out of the way and Stinky fell on his butt. And started wailing like an injured banshee. People were staring at us now, some of them angrily, as they threaded their way around us. We were blocking the access to the exit gate.

Dad got really angry. He scooped up the monkey and thrust it into my arms. "You started this, Charles. You take care of the monkey!" Of course, the monkey didn't want to be carried. Not by me, anyway. Stinky had thoroughly imprinted it, so all it wanted to do was get back to him. It squirmed and whimpered and trembled and kept trying to wriggle out of my arms. "Stop it!" I said firmly, but the monkey ignored me. I tried feeling around for its off switch, but the monkey started giggling as if I was tickling it. Then it started screeching.

The noise got Stinky's attention. He started screaming at me, "That's my monkey! I want it back! Give it back!" Dad tried to calm him down, but Stinky kept squirming and crying and screaming, just like the monkey, and finally he wriggled out of Dad's grasp and came and grabbed the damn thing out of my arms. I couldn't believe it; they really were twins. I stood there, staring at him, wondering why any kid's parents would ever let him survive long enough to reach adulthood. There must be something about parents—some kind of chemical trigger in the brain—that keeps them from strangling their own children.

I started to say something about that, but Dad just glared at me and said, "Why don't you keep your mouth shut for a while, Charles. You've said enough for one day."

Right. Stinky threw a tantrum and it was *my* fault. If I'd have been Dad, I'd have put that damn monkey into the nearest trash can. In pieces.

They pushed on through the gate, leaving me staring after them astonished, wishing I could be an orphan for a while. Anything would be better than this. Maybe I should just divorce them all and the hell with it. The more I thought about it, the more I liked that idea. I could look up the procedures on the net, I'd done it before, but I'd never followed through. Maybe this time I'd stay angry long enough. In the meantime . . . I reshouldered my backpack and followed. Like I always do.

From the train terminal, there's a shuttle-train on a sort of circular track that winds back and forth and in and out of everything all around the Terminus dome. It's free, and you can get on it anywhere and just go around and around all day long. The shuttle goes through at least a dozen hotels and a couple of big shopping centers and several huge museums and an amusement park and over an indoor lake and through a whole bunch of permanent apartments and offices. There are theaters and clubs and parks and restaurants everywhere and I don't know what else. If you can imagine it, it's probably here.

Climbing up the inside of the tent, there are at least fifty stories of balconies and terraces all of them piled up high like a man-made crater wall. Dad said someday it'll be a *hundred* and fifty stories of apartments and offices and stores on the inside. And probably more outside too.

Dad had a book about the cable, and he started pointing out stuff and explaining it to us as we went. Even though I was still angry, some of it was kind of interesting. He said there were even more city levels higher up the Line, some already developed, some awaiting future expansion. In fact, there were public parts of the structure all the way up to six kilometers, because some people *like* living that high; some of the industrial levels went even higher. There were a lot of weather stations too. The meteorologists loved the Line because it gave them a real-time core sample of the atmosphere. And there were all kinds of factories that needed high altitudes for various processes and stuff. Above that, there were observatories and broadcast stations up the entire length of the orbital elevator. So it wasn't all empty cable.

There was no shortage of vertical space, and there probably wouldn't ever be, at least not for a long, long time. Dad said that the industrial development of the cable would eventually prove more important than the transportation aspects, because the beanstalk had effectively tripled or quadrupled Ecuador's usable land area. In fact, they'd be dropping new cables to handle the increased traffic long before they used up all the available vertical space on the existing lines.

Dad said that the Orbital Elevator Corporation was planning to start dropping the first of the next three cables in a few months. Each new cable dropped would create another triangle and another area of interior space. When I asked how that would affect Terminus, Dad had said that Terminus would get even bigger. The area covered by the tent would be expanded—quadrupled, at least—so obviously the ground-level expansion was already planned for too.

But by then, the Kenya cable would be up and running and that would be serious competition, so there wouldn't be as much pressure to grow as fast, although Dad said that the Ecuadorian cable could probably lower their fares and shipping costs by then, because so much of their initial investment would already have been amortized, so they could probably give the Kenyan group a pretty hard time.

Dad said there was also a Singapore–Malaysia investment group preparing a cable of their own, and British Canada was dropping a cable down into the Pacific Ocean, just south of Christmas Island. That didn't make sense to me, but Dad said there were a lot of military and scientific reasons for having a cable of your own.

There was something about the way he said that last part.

"Do you think there's going to be a war?" I asked.

He looked at me with a sad look in his eyes. "I hope not," he said, "but sometimes I think it's already started and we just don't know it yet."

ALL ABOARD

IT WASN'T TOO HARD TO find a ticket lobby. There was this big circular balcony all around the cables. It was as wide as an avenue, it had two levels, and there were check-in counters on both levels. It was high enough above the floor of Terminus that you could look down over the railing and see the big well where the cables disappeared into the Earth. You could see everything, even how the cars were loaded and moved into position for launch. We all wanted to look, but Dad insisted we get our tickets first.

The ticket counters on the lower balcony were only for day-trips up to One-Hour. That was real popular with tourists who wanted to visit the beanstalk and who wanted to go into space but who weren't planning to go all the way up to orbit, which was a much longer trip. There were elevators leaving for One-Hour every five minutes.

One-Hour was open twenty-four hours a day, but we had to go to a different line. Tickets for Geostationary and even farther out, like to the launch stations beyond, were sold on the top level. Those cars launched every fifteen minutes.

Dad had made reservations for a 2:15 elevator, but we

were early. The woman behind the counter had a shiny
brown face, and she kept smiling at Stinky like he was her
own little boy. She suggested that we go straight on up to
One-Hour now and see all the sights up there, and then we
could catch our reserved cabin on the 2:15 car when it
stopped at One-Hour to pick up passengers. That way we
could leave almost immediately without any waiting and
we'd get to see everything up at One-Hour too. Because of
the storm coming in, traffic up the elevator was heavier than
usual, she said, so it was probably a good idea to leave now.
Dad agreed and so did the rest of us, so the woman rewrote
our reservations. She scanned our IDs and then gave each of
us our own boarding cards.

She asked if we wanted to check our luggage, but Dad
said no. We didn't have that much and we'd prefer to keep
it with us. She had a pretty smile and she made us all feel a
lot friendlier—like we were actually going to have fun for a
change. She gave each of us an elevator badge to wear. I
started to shove mine in my pocket, until Weird pointed out
that it was also a life-monitor and a locator chip and a
beeper-communicator. We had to wear our badges at all
times, Weird said.

After that, Dad took us back over to the edge of the balcony to look at how the cables worked. The three cables of
the Line plunged straight down from the very top of the tent
each into its own separate hole in the floor of the station.
They were as big around as buildings. Bigger. Dad said each
one was as thick as a baseball stadium. The bottom of the
Line looked like three huge pillars from God with a big open
space between them—enough for another dozen stadiums.
Probably more.

This wasn't the *real* bottom of the Line, of course. That
was anchored four or five kilometers underground. Above
us, below us, all around us, all the separate filaments of the
cable were peeled off into underground tunnels and threaded
down into the bowels of the earth, where each one was knot-
ted around a couple zillion tons of basalt or whatever. They
couldn't pull loose. Every filament was separately anchored,
some as far as fifty klicks away so there would be a firm

anchor for the Line even if there were a massive earthquake here.

From our vantage point on the balcony, we could see everything. Dad pointed out the details of this and that as happily as if he'd built the Line himself. He explained the purposes of each of the different tracks, talked about what the lights meant, and made sure we noticed all the smaller cables running down the sides of the big ones.

As we watched, an elevator car slid down one of the cables into a reception bay; at the same time another one popped up on the other side of the same cable. On the next cable over, a pair of linked cargo pods came sliding down, direct from orbit; they had a Lunar insignia painted on them. As they slid out of sight, a loaded cargo container rose up to balance them. "Look! That one's going straight to the moon," I said to Stinky. We watched as it rose up and up and up until it finally disappeared through the roof.

That's when it hit me. That we were going up *too*. This wasn't another one of Dad's didn't-happen promises. This was for *real*. And that's when I started to feel very nervous. Especially about the stuff Weird had said. I was beginning to think he might be right. This whole trip—it *wasn't* normal. Not for Dad.

I wished I knew how to ask Dad to reconsider, but I knew whatever I said, he wouldn't change his mind. Certainly not after traveling all this way. And Weird and Stinky were so hyped up about the elevator, they probably wouldn't let him reconsider anyway. I would have waited down here at Terminus for them, but I knew Dad would never agree to that either—and I didn't dare ask.

It wasn't that I didn't want to go. I sort of did. I just didn't want to go *right now*.

"Is that where *we're* going?" Stinky asked, pointing up the elevator.

"Yep," I said, my voice kind of strangled. I took his hand so he wouldn't get lost. Weird looked at me funny, but I turned away before he could say anything, pushing Stinky after Dad and wishing I were big enough to be taken seriously.

Dad herded us down to a platform next to a long queue

of elevator capsules, all moving slowly in line toward the launch bay. Each car was as big around as a house and at least five or six stories tall. There were at least a dozen of them, with a new one popping into the queue every few minutes; every time a car at the front slid into the launch rack, a new one thunked up at the other end.

Weird pointed past the row of cars. On the other side, we could see down into the space where they went through their final service check before being thrust up into the boarding queue. Preloaded cargo pods were slid automatically into the bottom levels of each car—so the capsules were even taller than I thought.

Weird said that balancing the load on the Line was so critical that they had to plan the cargo schedule months in advance. And yes, there was always a little room held out in each pod for last-minute things that needed to be shipped up the elevator. And there were always six empty slots a day for standby cars or for cargo that missed its normal launch slot, which sometimes happened if a car failed its pressure test.

Dad came back and grabbed both our arms then, complaining that we didn't have time for gawking. He had *that* tone in his voice, so Weird and I just traded looks and followed after.

Dad hurried us all the way to the front of the queue, to the front-most car being loaded. The cars were shiny blue metal with silvery trim. Lined up the whole length of the platform, all creeping forward together, they looked like a giant subway train. The edge of the platform was a moving slidewalk, rolling at the same slow speed, so boarding the elevator car was a lot like getting on a car in an amusement park ride, only you stepped in through a triple-layered hatch. The walls of the cars were thicker than I expected, but that's because the whole thing had to be pressurized for space.

Dad entered the car first, then Weird and Stinky. I hesitated a bit—I don't like cramped places and the door to this one was just small enough that you almost had to duck to get through it—but inside it was all comfortable chairs and tables, so I followed. Reluctantly.

An attendant told us to take any seats we wanted. They

were spaced around the room in clusters, like a lounge. We sat down and we waited.

As soon as the car was full, they slammed the door shut with a scary *thunk*—once that door was closed you *couldn't* get out again—and then we waited several forevers while they ran the final set of launch tests.

Weird said they have only five minutes to check the pressure and weight. This is when they pump or drain extra water into the ballast tanks to equalize the weight of the car. Weird said the load engineers have to equalize the strain up and down the entire length of the cable—if you calculated the total weight of tonnage on the line at any given moment it was enormous, so balance was critical.

So was the water. They always needed a lot of fresh water up topside, not just for the various stations on the Line, but for export too. In fact, Weird said, the folks at the top of the Line considered the water more important than the passengers.

If the elevator car failed either the final pressure test or the weight check, Weird said, it would get shunted to a side track, and a standby car sent up in its place. I hoped that would happen to us. But Weird said that hardly ever happens. Most of the time the standby car gets sent up as the last car in a shift. The shifts were four hours long.

There were several attendants aboard to help us stow our backpacks, and they even offered us drinks and snacks. There were video screens everywhere, each one showing the inevitable "for your own safety . . ." instructions. But there's not really a lot to know about the elevator. Either it works or it doesn't. The cars up to One-Hour are equipped with breakaway bolts and parachutes for emergency return, but except for the occasional test launch, none have ever been fired in a real emergency. In case of a pressure drop, each level of the car could be sealed off from all the others, but that was unlikely too, because the cars were triple-hulled. You'd have to hit one with a meteor to put a hole in it. I looked for seat belts, but there weren't any. That surprised me at first, but Weird said we'd never be going fast enough to need them.

One of the levels inside the elevator car had floor-to-ceiling windows, one had waist level-to-ceiling windows for people who need the feeling of a railing, and the third passenger level had only portholes, because some people need to have a wall between themselves and all that height. The rest of the car was reserved for cargo and life support and stuff like that. There was no pilot, but there was a senior attendant. In our car, he looked and acted more like a head waiter than anything else, but Weird told me he was also trained in all kinds of medical and safety procedures, even in law enforcement. Weird is full of stuff like that. He's a lot like Dad that way. It's like being online 24/7.

He said that the cars used to be a lot smaller, but the beanstalk had been designed from the beginning for expansion and as soon as there were enough filaments to support the weight, they started switching over to the larger cars. About twenty years ago, Weird said. And then Dad added that we could probably see some of the older cars on display up at One-Hour.

Our car was filled to capacity—not exactly crowded, but you had to watch where you were stepping. There weren't that many tourists aboard; it was mostly locals. That was because there was a big tropical storm moving inland and a lot of the locals were going up to One-Hour to wait it out. Apparently, it was the safest place to be. There were hotels and restaurants and theaters up at One-Hour, so they were probably going to make a party of it.

At last, our car was in the number one position. Stinky and Weird and I watched as we moved suddenly away from the platform. There was a gentle bump or two, and then the car was locked into the launch tube. We were right next to the cable—it looked like a huge curved wall. I imagined I could hear it *humming*. That's when I started getting *really* scared. I wanted to ask if I could get off, but I didn't want Dad and Stinky and Weird to know how scared I was. So I just grabbed Stinky's hand tighter and said to him, "Any minute now. Don't be afraid."

He looked at me with a funny expression as if he couldn't understand why I would say such a thing. "I'm not scared. It's only an elevator."

Besides, the attendants *couldn't* let me off. Even if they

wanted to. It was already too late. There were so many cars traveling each way on the Line at any given moment that everything had to be tightly scheduled and every launch had to be precisely timed. So once a car was sealed and had passed all of its integrity tests, it was effectively launched. A car had to slide up this track every five minutes, no matter what. I didn't know what would happen if a car missed its launch, but I got the feeling the elevator engineers wouldn't like it.

Coming down, the whole process was reversed. A new car arrived every five minutes. They were strung the entire length of the Line, so each car had to be moved out of the way before the next one arrived. They'd never had a collision, but apparently in the early days of the Line there had been a couple of near misses. Only a few times had they ever had to halt downward traffic to clear the track. Weird said they didn't like to do it not just because it was bad publicity but because every minute of stoppage cost half a million dollars of lost income.

There was a chime then, and everybody else who hadn't yet found a spot at a window came pushing in behind us. Then some music started playing, something dramatic; it took me only a moment to recognize it. *Carmina Burana* by Carl Orff. The first movement. *O Fortuna*. Very theatrical. Very powerful. One of Dad's favorites. I could tell by his smile that he thought it was appropriate music for jumping off a planet.

At first we didn't feel anything, but the cable-wall next to us started sliding down, and then we rose up out of the launch cradle. A moment more, and we were rising up through the core of Terminus Station and my heart did one of those sudden flip-flops like it does at the top of the roller coaster when you realize you're strapped in and it doesn't matter what you want to do anymore because *this* is what you're *going* to do, *whether you want to or not*.

We were on our way. Up.

UP

WE WERE ON THE SECOND level, where the windows started at waist level and angled outward toward the top, so we could lean out and look almost straight down. I swallowed hard and tried not to look, but I couldn't stop myself from seeing anyway.

First we rose up through the service core, then all of the terraces and balconies began dropping away like toys. At least that part was fun to watch, because we could see how everything was laid out inside the tent. It was a whole different view of Beanstalk City and we could see how big the world under the dome really was.

We rose all the way up to the top, and then the view closed in for just a few seconds as the car slid up through the top of the tent. The elevator starts out slow, so it takes almost two minutes to get to the top, but the timing is perfect because that's where the music gets sort of quiet for a bit, anticipating the next part, then it comes back with a big crescendo just as the car rises up out of the roof and into the open air. The music pounds toward a big dramatic punch and you get to see how the whole city around Terminus is spread out like a giant Monopoly board. And then . . . the elevator starts going up even *faster*.

Even though the day was overcast, Terminus City seemed to have a ghostly bright quality. As it spread out below us, everything shone in vivid colors.

Mostly around the tent there were parks and lakes, but we could also see all of the industrial areas too—all the warehouses, and the shipping and receiving areas, and the highways and tracks and canals. And beyond, there was the rest of the city that grew up around the Line: the dorms where a lot of the construction workers and their families lived while it was being built—and still lived today, because most of them had been guaranteed jobs on the Line when it was finished—and farther out, all the office towers and hotels for tourists and visiting business people, and then the rest of the city beyond, where everybody else lives, the ones who provide groundside services for the Line and its constant stream of traffic.

We also saw a lot of Tube-Towns scattered below. The slums. Just like home. They ringed the whole area. The gray day made them look almost as depressing from above as they were close up.

If I leaned out far enough, I could see how the shining cables of the Line speared straight down into the center of everything. Its shadow was like a triple knife cut, slicing west across the landscape. It arrowed out toward the horizon, eventually fading away in the distance.

We kept rising and the effect was like one of those pullback-into-infinity shots that you see on TV all the time. We rose up and up and everything else got smaller and smaller. Pretty soon we could see the dark blue line of the ocean to the west, and more banks of clouds piling up on the horizon, a thick wall of them.

We passed through a small patch of clouds and then a bigger one, and somebody nearby said something about the big storm that was heading in from the Pacific, how we'd probably be able to see the whole thing from One-Hour. Somebody else said if you stood real still you could feel the wind rocking the elevator car, but I tried it and couldn't feel anything. Maybe it was just imagination. It was pretty hard to tell.

Most everybody stood there at the window for at least fifteen minutes, pointing things out to each other while the ground kept dropping away below. It wasn't as bad as I was afraid it would be. At least, not yet. Maybe higher up.

The view of the cable was sort of interesting too. The Line zips past the window like a vertical highway—so fast it's just a big blur. It looks like it's all one smooth surface, but it isn't. A lot of it is studded with solar cells, and every thousand meters there's an outer ring of those high-powered sulfur-incandescent lamps that are brighter than the sun; the ring is *outside* the elevator tracks so the lights don't accidentally shine in. The projectors are there so the Line will be visible from hundreds of miles away. From a distance, all those lights blend together to look like one solid line of brightness. That's why we could see the Line so clearly all the way to Mexico. The lights are partly to warn airplanes and partly to aid people who are aiming their communication dishes and partly as a navigational aid, and partly just for national pride. I mean, if you had a beanstalk in your country, wouldn't you want to show it off?

The other thing about the beanstalk is that there's a lot of space between the three cables. A couple of square kilometers, at least. But it wasn't *empty* space. For one thing, most of the tracks on the parts of the cables facing each other— the insides—were for cargo pods. We saw them zipping up and down past us; the cargo pods weren't normally pressurized for passengers and they traveled a lot faster in both directions, because cargo didn't suffer from motion-sickness.

But in addition to the cargo tracks, there were also these great billowy tubes of transparent mylar; they were inflated chimneys of all different lengths. Their bottoms and tops were at different heights and they looked kind of like a big ghostly organ. Some of them reached as high as the four-kilometer mark. Their purpose, Dad said, was to irrigate the atmosphere via the "chimney effect." Apparently when you have two chimneys of different heights and you get wind blowing across the top, you get air current down one and up the other. This is how prairie dogs cool their burrows. Here, at the beanstalk, the idea was to create a steady flow of air from the upper reaches of the atmosphere down into the lower and back up again. The air flow generated some electricity, but more important, it helped cool the land around the base of the Line. Weird said that the Line produced three degrees of local cooling, which could make a real difference on a hot day at the equator.

But—Dad said, some of Ecuador's neighbors blamed the chimneys for the persistent *El Niño* condition in the Pacific that had been screwing up rain patterns for the past twenty years or so and generating some really nasty storms—like the one growing out in the Pacific right now. But who knew for sure? Weird always said that everything was connected to everything else, but if that was true, then the weather had to be caused by *everything*, didn't it? Nobody knew for sure, and that was part of what everybody was angry about. According to Dad anyway. That's what fat Señor Hidalgo had been talking about on the train—how the Line was destabilizing *everything* in the world. Even where people lived.

That was the real surprise—there are people living on the Line. All the way up to the five-kilometer mark. And someday even higher. Every so often, we'd pass through a platform city, three or four or five levels suspended from all three of the cables—with holes of course for the elevator tracks and the chimneys. We zipped through them too fast to see much detail, but what we did see as they dropped away below us was pretty impressive. They were like vertical villages. The first three were open to the air, and we saw clusters of offices and homes and shopping areas—*real* homes with big windows and yards and even a few swimming pools. There were also public launch balconies for gliders of all kinds.

I wondered what it would be like to live in such a place. You'd have to be *very* rich to live this high. The sky cities were where important corporation people lived as well as some of the people in Ecuador's government.

One of the attendants said that eventually there would be at least a hundred of these platform towns on the Line; there was room for thousands of sky cities, of course; but every platform town required multiple new filaments on the Line, not to mention the installation of an equivalent weight at the other end of the cables to balance it—the attendant said there were already hundreds of water tanks at the far end of the cable, moving up and down all the time to keep the Line in equilibrium—so there was a practical limit to how much could be hung on the Line.

And then the last of the towns disappeared beneath us, and there was nothing for a while except the humming of the cable. By the time we hit ten kilometers, the sky had turned a very deep blue. I'd never seen it that color before. Now the only settlements we were zipping through were scientific or industrial ones, and there weren't too many of those.

The ground below had become mostly featureless; a blanket of clouds covered most everything below us. To the north we could see a few patches of brown and green. To the east, we could see the wall of the Andes stretching north and south. It looked like a crumpled white sheet. I couldn't believe how steep and jagged the mountains were.

Dad said that the original plan had been to drop the cable down onto one of those mountaintops, but when they looked at the problems of anchoring the Line to a mountaintop so high you needed an O-mask to breathe, they had second thoughts. Even if you could build Terminus on the mountaintop, you'd still have to extend the elevators down to the foothills; you'd have to build a second Terminus. It was easier to just extend the bottom end of the cable a couple klicks farther. What you traded off in additional stress and tension on the anchor, you got back in construction savings and maintenance benefits.

By now, the view had gotten to be pretty standard airplane stuff, except that the cables sparkling all the way down until they disappeared into the clouds below made it impossible for me to pretend I was in an airplane anymore. As long as I didn't think about the cables, I was fine, but this view was a little too scary for me.

That's when Stinky said, "Is this all there is to do? Stare out the window?"

So Dad said, "Well, let's see what else there is. Come on, let's go upstairs." So we all trooped up to the top level of the car, which wasn't really much of a level, just a little room with a glass dome over the top so you could look straight up the Line if you wanted to. There wasn't much to see up here either, just the cables of the elevator stretching endlessly up into the dark blue above. For some reason, that was even *more* disturbing. But it was also more boring, so I went back downstairs to the restaurant level, where I bought myself a Coke and tried to avoid looking at any windows.

About the time I began to wonder how often people freaked out on one of these trips and what the attendants would do if I started screaming, Weird came down the stairs and seated himself next to me.

"So?" he said.

"So what?" I answered.

"Now do you believe me? He's gonna do it."

I shrugged. "You can't prove that." And then another thought occurred to me. "Do you want to go back?"

"Do you?" he countered.

"I dunno."

"If we could prove it, we could tell someone. . . ." Weird offered half-heartedly.

"Oh yeah, get Dad arrested. That would go down really good. Mom would like that. A lot. But Dad would never forgive us. Not that it would matter. But we'd probably never get to see him again. The courts would terminate his rights. Is that what you want?"

"No. But it isn't right for him to do this without asking us what *we* want to do."

"Well, what *do* we want to do? You tell me, Douglas."

Now it was his turn to shrug. "I dunno."

"Well, what do we have to go back to? At least, this is . . . *something*."

"Maybe," he admitted. "But I don't like being pushed into it like this. Do you?"

"Maybe we don't know all of what's going on. Mom has been really angry about a whole bunch of stuff she won't talk about. What's that about?"

"Mom is always angry." Douglas said. "That's why Dad gave up on her. Dad was raised different. He doesn't like arguments."

"Well then, he must really love being around us. That's all we ever do."

"Not always. We're not arguing now."

"No. But we're not doing anything else either, are we?" I said one of those words that Dad doesn't like me to use. Just in time for Dad to hear it as he and Stinky came back downstairs.

ONE-HOUR

THE ONE-HOUR PLATFORM IS called that because it takes exactly one hour to get there. It's also the legal limit of the atmosphere, so anyone who visits One-Hour can say that he or she has traveled into space.

One-Hour is also one of the biggest of the platform cities. Seven stories thick, it's suspended from all three cables; it fills the space between them and extends quite a ways out beyond as well. It's a city floating in the sky. If you could stand away from it, you would see that there are towers projecting up from it and more towers hanging down.

And the view from One-Hour is spectacular. You're high enough to see the curvature of the Earth in all directions. You can see as far as Mexico to the north and Peru and Bolivia to the south. To the west, the Pacific Ocean curls away out of sight under a frosting of clouds.

There are balconies and observation posts all around the edges of One-Hour and all over the bottom, so there are places where you can look straight down . . . if you want to.

I didn't want to, but everyone else wanted to see the storm, so we went—except it wasn't a storm anymore. Now it was a hurricane. And it looked ferocious. It was a great whorl of white, so big it covered more than half the globe visible below us. From up here it looked as peaceful as a swirl of whipped cream on top of a big lemon pie, but if you watched long enough, you could see the banks of clouds moving majestically around a common center. The attendants said that the winds were already up to 200 kilometers per hour and expected to rise as high as 250 or maybe even 300 by the time the storm started inland. Somebody else said that the winds might get as high as 350 klicks before the storm hit the coast. They said the eye of the storm was expected to pass very close to the beanstalk. In fact, the storm was the only thing anybody was talking about up here.

The U.N. Weather Authority had tried seeding the storm's western edge in an effort to steer it southward, but this storm had a mind of its own and was still moving east. The Line Authority was beaming microwaves into it too; that wasn't helping either. The news was calling it Hurricane Charles, but I didn't feel honored.

Then Stinky asked the important question: "Can we call Mom now? And tell her where we are?"

"No. Let's wait until we reach Geostationary," Dad said. "Like we agreed."

"But I wanna talk to Mommy *now*." There was something real frantic about the way he said it.

Dad looked uncomfortable. He glanced to both Weird and me as if looking for help—but Weird just said, "It might not be such a bad idea, Dad. Mom might be a little worried about us. We should let her know we're out of the storm."

This made Dad even more annoyed. "I said *no*."

But Stinky had already run to a phone booth, one of the ones with the glass bottoms, so you could see all the way down, and he was already punching for Mom. "I wanna show her my monkey!" He'd already put his phone-home card in the slot, so there was nothing for Dad to do except step sideways out of camera range. Me, I studied the walls, the ceiling, anything but the floor, until the screen finally lit up. First it showed a map of North America, and then it zoomed down in as it tracked her location.

Mom wasn't at home; she was in San Francisco. She answered almost immediately; she looked tired but happier than we'd seen her in a while. Behind her we could see somebody's apartment, and out the window, we could even see what looked like trees or bushes. In the background, I got a quick glimpse of someone—a woman, Mom's age—but I didn't see her clearly.

"Hi, Mom!"

"Bobby! Where are you calling from?" At first her expression was surprised—as if she hadn't expected to see any of us for a while, but then her eyes flicked down as she read the information at the bottom of her display. Her expression darkened immediately. "Put your father on!"

Dad stepped into view then. "Hello, Maggie," he said grimly.

"You're doing it, aren't you!"

"I told you I would. It's the only way to be fair."

"You son of a bitch! The court said no."

"The court said not without your agreement."

"And I said no! So that means the court says no too!"

"Maggie—" Dad was keeping his voice deliberately calm. "I will not let you abuse the children as a way of getting even with me. They're old enough now, they're entitled to make up their own minds." Douglas shot me an *I-told-you-so* look.

"I'm going to stop you, Max—I'll see you in jail, you lying pig!" Abruptly, she remembered that Weird and Stinky and I were there too. She said, "You kids—Bobby, Charles, Douglas—why did you let him do this? You stay where you are! Don't you go *anywhere* with him. I'm calling the police." Behind her, a woman's voice was asking, "Maggie? What's going on—?" And then the screen went blank.

There was silence in the phone booth for a moment. Finally, I said, "So this wasn't such a good idea, was it, Dad?"

"Shut up, Chigger!" said Weird.

"I wanna talk to Mommy!" Stinky wailed.

I realized then that after her hello, she hadn't said a thing to any of us kids, except to order us to stay put. For some reason, that made me feel really angry at her. If she really cared about us as much as she said she did, why was she yelling at us? At least, Dad didn't yell. He just went silent.

He was silent now. He looked uncertain. Actually, he looked old. Beaten up.

"Dad?" asked Weird. "Are you all right?"

"No," he said. "Look. I need you to understand something. All three of you. Your Mom didn't want me to bring you on this trip. So I did it without her permission. Maybe it wasn't the smartest thing to do. But I needed to do this. I really did." Dad dropped to his knees in front of Bobby and me and put his hands on our shoulders. "I've made a lot of promises to you kids, and I haven't been able to keep all of them. Maybe none of them. And I know you resent me for it. You're probably right to do so. I guess I haven't been the best dad in the world. I'm sorry about that. It hurts me something awful to know that I've let you boys down. You mean more to me than anything else in the world. That's why I did it. Just once in my life, I wanted to do something extraordinary for you. And this is it. And I wasn't going to let anybody say no."

He looked so sad and vulnerable—and for a moment, he even looked *old*—that I couldn't help myself. I flung myself into his arms. And so did Bobby. And Douglas. Not because he was right, but because he was Daddy. And he *needed* us. And suddenly it was very scary, the whole thing, and I guess *we* needed him too, and then Stinky started crying. And I have to admit, even I—

Dad pulled back and looked me in the eyes. "Are you all right?" I guess he'd felt me trembling.

"Yeah," I said. "I'm fine. I just don't like her yelling at us all the time. That's all."

"Me neither," said Stinky petulantly.

Dad looked at Weird. "Douglas?"

Weird shrugged noncommittally. "It's just Mom. That's just the way she is."

"Do you want to go back?"

"She's going to call the cops on you."

Dad sighed and nodded. "I hope she doesn't. For your sakes—" he added sadly. "Because then we could both lose custody. And you guys would end up in foster homes. And that wouldn't be good for anyone. That's why." He looked sorry he'd said it, but it was too late to take the words back.

Abruptly, he looked at his watch as if he had an appointment to keep. He straightened up. "So? Are we going to Geostationary? Gotta make up your minds now."

I looked to Weird. He gave me a half-and-half expression, and finally said, "Well, it'd be silly to come all this far and not go all the way."

"Yeah!" I said. Because I really did want to go, no matter what Mom said. And so did Stinky.

We were going up again.

A CHANGE OF PLANS

NO, WE WEREN'T.

At least, not right away.

"What's the matter, Doug?"

"Mom said she was going to call the police." Weird looked genuinely worried.

Dad nodded. "We're seventy-two hundred kilometers away . . . and sixteen klicks up."

"She could phone someone," I suggested.

"She could," Dad agreed. "But it's a question of jurisdiction. She'd have to get the local authorities to agree to detain us. And that would require a judge's order and an international warrant. And that would require—" He looked at his watch and thought for a second. "It won't happen this late on a Saturday. Tell you what, though. Before we start looking around the station, let's check our reservations"—Dad led us over to a customer service desk; the woman who was working there had almost no hair at all—"just in case that storm screws things up."

Dad shouldn't have said that. Stinky looked worried. "Are we going to feel the storm up here, Daddy?"

Before Dad or Weird could answer, the hairless woman said, "Nothing to worry about, young man. The orbital elevator was originally designed to withstand wind forces of more than four hundred and fifty kilometers per hour. Since then, its strength has been upgraded to five hundred and fifty."

"Yes, but what are we going to feel?" I asked.

The woman was annoyingly cheerful. She pointed. "Over there by the information center there's an educational display that will show you exactly what will happen the entire length of the cable. You'll see these big leisurely waves that rise gently up the Line. They're hundreds of kilometers long. We'll get some rocking up here, but the waves will come in such long slow cycles that you won't be able to feel them. If you feel anything at all, it'll be like being on a very large boat on a very gentle ocean. We had a storm four years ago as big as this and it wasn't any problem."

"So there's no danger—?" Dad asked.

"None at all. Only a little inconvenience. But just for safety's sake, everybody is locking down all up and down the Line. It's a standard procedure. Most of the platform towns are already secured. Terminus might take a beating, they did last time, but nothing that couldn't be set right in a few weeks of regular repair duty."

"Will they still be sending up elevators?"

"Only cargo and supply pods. No passengers. It's too uncomfortable. Not the ride, the view. And it takes too long to get above the worst of it. They'll probably be sending up some scientific teams in one of the maintenance pods to look at the inside of the storm, they usually do, and of course the cable engineers like to look at the situation first-hand, but no—we won't be sending up any passengers."

"We were supposed to catch the 2:15 up to Geostationary—" I started to ask.

"Mm," she said, and touched her ear to listen to her communication channel. "Let me check on that for you." She made a face as she listened. "It's likely to be cancelled. Or they might send it up empty. But they're getting some pretty high winds already, so they're more likely to send up a water-pod in that time-slot. Let's see if we can get you onto another car instead." She turned to the workstation at her desk. There was a big vertical display behind her, showing the progress of all of the cars between Terminus and One-Hour. Already the cars lined up at Terminus were colored blue for water-pods instead of pink for passengers.

"The 12:15 will be here in forty-five minutes," she said. "It looks like a full load. 12:30 is full too. A lot of people were trying to get out before the storm hit. They shouldn't have waited so long. All right, let me see if I can do anything earlier. Hm, I can put you on standby for the 12:00, that'll start loading in fifteen minutes. Let me do that right now, but don't get your hopes up . . . and then let's see what else we have. You were lucky you came up when you did. The last car out will probably be the 12:30; it's just launching. I'll try and grab you space on the 12:45 or the 1:00, in case they get out, but don't hold your breath. It looks like they're locking down early. There's no danger, but they don't like to scare the passengers." She frowned.

"Is there anything *sooner?*" Dad asked. "Is there anything open on the car loading now?"

"I don't know. Wait a minute—" She studied her screens, biting her lower lip thoughtfully. "How fast can you run?"

"Huh?"

She picked up her phone. "I've got a cabin open on the 11:00. A no-show. I guess they'll forfeit their deposit. The car is already loading. It's a first class booking, but we'll upgrade you. We don't like sending them up empty—" She explained. "You've got ten minutes left before they seal it for launch. Down this corridor, the gate is at the end. I'll call ahead. They'll be expecting you. Go now! You should be able to make it."

We ran.

It wasn't that far, but halfway there Stinky suddenly started crying and screaming, "Aren't we gonna see One-Hour? You promised! You said we were gonna see One-Hour! I don't wanna go up in anymore elevators! Daddy, you promised! I wanna go on the rides!" Weird tried to shush him, but Stinky was on reverse—the more you shushed him, the louder he got. Then he went limp, refusing to move at all. I'd have walloped him, but then Weird would have walloped me and Dad would have had to break us up and we would have missed the elevator, so I grabbed Stinky's other arm, and Weird and I carried him along, him screaming bloody murder all the time, while Dad ran ahead, shouting and waving our boarding cards.

The elevators up to Geostationary run every fifteen minutes. As each one arrives, it slides off the track and into a loading bay. It has a one-hour layover, during which time it's serviced and loaded for the rest of its journey up to Geo-stationary. Fifteen minutes before launch, it's sealed and weighed and checked for hull integrity again—same like at Terminus. If it doesn't get triple green lights, a standby pod goes up instead; then depending on the seriousness of the problem, it either has to wait until the slack time at the end of the shift, or every other pod on the Line gets delayed fifteen minutes.

We made it—in fact, we made it with five minutes to spare, but Stinky was howling like a banshee, and if there had been an open balcony—not likely at this height—Weird and I would have been happy to toss him over the edge. Well, I would have, but I suspected Weird was starting to think like a grownup and would have probably hesitated on the third swing over the railing.

Anyway, we made it—almost—except right next to the boarding ramp Stinky broke free of both Weird and me and went running back down the ramp, his monkey bouncing along behind him. "Run away, Toto!" He shouted. "Run away!" Weird threw himself after Stinky, catching him in a flying tackle, but the monkey kept going. Of course. Stinky had given it orders. I went chasing after it, careening around people and robots, while behind me Stinky crowed, "He got away! He got away!" I don't know how Stinky had pro-grammed the little monster, but I couldn't get near it—

I stopped where I was, gasping for breath, and looked back to Dad. He pointed and gestured. "Get that damn thing!" I couldn't believe it. I chased the monkey around and around the souvenir booths and the newsstand and the little pizza kiosk, but I couldn't get near it—and the monkey started singing and whistling like a calliope. Only after a moment did I recognize the song and realized that everybody who was watching was laughing like crazy. *Pop Goes The Weasel.* "All around the cobbler's bench, the monkey chased the weasel. . . ."

"Three minutes, Chigger!"

The hell with it. It was Stinky's monkey, not mine. I stopped chasing, took three deep breaths, and then started loping back toward the boarding ramp. If Stinky started screaming about his monkey, it was his own damned fault. And sure enough: "Where's my monkey? I want my monkey—"

"Go get it yourself," I yelled at him. So of course he did. That is, he tried to, but Weird grabbed him in mid-leap and pulled him backward off his feet. He screamed in rage, as loud as he could, and people all over the lobby turned to stare. Then Dad demanded as I came running up to the door, "Where's the goddamned monkey?" And I said, "Screw the goddamned monkey! Stinky programmed it to run away. You want it? You go get it."

For a moment, Dad looked like he was going to hit me— "Go ahead!" I shouted. "Prove Mom right!"

He put his hand down, glaring at me.

"It's not my fault, Dad. He's a goddamned spoiled brat and you shouldn't have bought him the goddamned monkey in the first place. And now that it ran away, the hell with it— he's had his three hundred dollars worth of fun. Let it go for all I care. Isn't it about time he learned about consequences? I never got a goddamned programmable monkey—" I pushed past Dad into the elevator.

Dad looked like he wanted to kill something, but he knew I was right. He also looked like he wanted to go after the monkey, but the attendant said, "I'm sorry, sir. We're closing the door in thirty seconds. You won't have time." So Dad and Weird and screaming-Stinky came grumbling in after me. Dad looked apoplectic. And justifiably so. But I'd just about had it with Stinky shrieking and Stinky running away and me always being expected to chase after him and drag him back. Dad was treating me like a full-time baby-sitter, and instead of paying me, he bawled me out whenever anything went wrong. Well, the hell with that!

And then, just as the triple doors started sliding shut, the

damned monkey came hurtling through it like a hairy tor-
pedo. The launch attendant—he was another guy with no
hair—hit his button and the doors bounced back open; he
gave us a dirty look as the monkey leapt over a couch and
launched itself into Stinky's arms. I ignored him. Dad had
told us they always tried to close the doors a few minutes
early to give themselves a margin of error for launch checks.
Meanwhile, the monkey was clinging desperately to Stinky,
screaming, "Bobby, no run ray! No run ray!" Right then, I
promised myself that as soon as I found a screwdriver, I
would dismantle the damn thing, but Weird spoke up first.
"After he goes to sleep, I'll install override commands, Dad.
This won't happen again."

Dad didn't answer. I turned around to look, and he was
leaning up against the back of a chair, just breathing hard
and looking so pale I thought he was having a heart attack
or something.

Anyway, we were aboard.

FIRST CLASS

OUR CABIN ATTENDANT WAS NAMED Mickey and his hair was so short, he was almost bald. He looked so shiny and clean he could have been a robot. He had one of those perpetual smiles that wouldn't quit, and he acted like he was genuinely glad to see us and he kept trying to make friends with me and Stinky and Weird as if he'd been waiting all his life for this moment. He was so sincere about it I had to hate him. I wouldn't give him a chance to hate me first.

Our cabin was up at the top of the car. This car was bigger than the one we'd caught at Terminus. It was ten stories high and each level was big enough to hold as many as ten cabins. The level we were on, there were only four cabins and they were all big. We had a wall of windows with drapes that were secured at both the top and the bottom, and a big overhead window too, so we could look straight up.

What was weird was the way everything looked. Even Weird said it was weird. Mickey just smiled and explained that this was because the inside of the car was built to rotate around its central axis, so that it could be spun like a top as we approached micro-gravity. Then the outer walls would become the floors, and all the furniture and appliances had to swivel; that's why they were built the way they were. He said they'd spin us up to one-third gee, and it would feel almost normal.

Most people think that space is all free fall, but it isn't really. Weird started to explain how it's really micro-gravity, he should know because he's not really from this planet anyway, but that made Mickey the attendant look at him impressed, and then Weird looked at Mickey surprised that someone had actually noticed him being smart. And then the two of them took turns explaining it to me and Stinky as if either of us actually cared.

Micro-gravity means the pull of gravity is so small it might as well be free fall, it's mostly irrelevant to whatever else is going on. Anyway, right now we were inside a horizontal pie-wedge; later on, as we went up, we would be inside a vertical pie-wedge. I pretended I didn't much care, but I was really wondering what it would be like to have windows in the floor. Mickey explained that there were automatic shutters that would close when they started spinning the car, so we wouldn't have those windows anymore. That was good. I was pretty much over my nervousness about how high we were, as long as I didn't have to look out any more windows, but I'd just as soon not have windows under my feet anywhere.

Mickey showed us where to stash our suitcases and how to unfold the beds and the chairs and how to tell the TV to turn on, all that stuff. He showed us how the bathroom worked too—it was mostly familiar, but the toilet and the sink were on swivels for when the cabin started spinning. The shower was a sealed box, kind of odd-shaped, and instead of an actual sprayer, it had vacuum hoses. Mickey said that the blue hose was for washing and the red one was for shaving.

"Shaving?"

In answer, Mickey just grinned and brushed his hand across the top of his shaven head. "If Douglas doesn't want to explain, there's a program you can watch on space-hygiene. We have the most exclusive cable channels of all." He grinned at his own joke, but I got the feeling he told it to everybody. "And we have a very extensive library."

There was a chime then, and Mickey said, "I've got a launch station to attend to. I'll be back later to sort out the paperwork on the change in your reservations." He bounced out, leaving us in a cabin that was bigger and more comfortable than our living room back home in El Paso.

The TV came to life automatically then. By now, all four of us could do the speech in unison. "Welcome aboard. . . . For your own safety. . . . etc., etc." The usual blather. "Our upstairs restaurant is now open and will remain open until thirty minutes before arrival at Geostationary. There are lounges and snack bars on levels three and seven. It's our pleasure to serve you and we hope you'll enjoy your journey with us."

"Dad?" Weird asked. "Can we go downstairs to the bottom lounge for departure? That's supposed to be the best view."

Stinky didn't want to leave his monkey behind, but Dad insisted and said he wouldn't be allowed to play with it if he fussed any more. "You'll have your toy all day—now it's our turn." Stinky didn't see the fairness of this, but he shut up and followed. We headed down the spiral staircase at the center of the car.

The downstairs lounge was full, but not crowded. The elevator held only a hundred and fifty people per trip, not counting attendants, so there was enough room at the windows for everybody. But the best views were on the sides near the cables. The car was just moving into launch position onto the cable track, so apparently we'd passed all our integrity checks.

Below us, the Earth was bathed in ghostly sunlight. The storm clouds shone so cold and white and bright that it was hard to believe how ferocious the winds must have been underneath them. I was glad we were well out of it. Someone said that the storm was likely to disrupt passenger traffic up the Line for as long as three days. Somebody else said that with all these storms, four in the last ten years, they should encase the bottom couple of miles of the cable so that the cars wouldn't be buffeted by the winds and that traffic wouldn't have to be affected. That sounded like a good idea to me, but when Weird started explaining how it could be done and real quickly, the whole idea got boring.

The last chime sounded, and the car started sliding upward. We hardly felt anything, but out the window the beanstalk started moving downward. This time the music was much more playful: Beethoven's Fourth Symphony, fourth movement. Another one of Dad's favorites. I smiled over at him and he smiled back at me in recognition. The symphony starts out with a joyful surge; then, possessed by its own enthusiasm, it weaves its melody into a powerful surge upward. It's one of Beethoven's happier works, and it sent us cheering up through the levels of One-Hour like a rocket.

Actually, it looked more like One-Hour was falling down the Line while we hung motionless in place. As we watched, it dropped away faster and faster until finally it disappeared into the distance. Within a short time the cables were zipping along again and we were truly alone in space—except we weren't. Long dead Ludwig had given us the perfect music for a journey he could not possibly have imagined, even in his most fevered days. We weren't just leaving One-Hour; we were leaving the Earth behind. Our next stop was (approximately) 22,300 miles above. 35,770 klicks. Compared to that, the distance from Terminus to One-Hour was insignificant.

There was a half-globe of the Earth built into the ceiling of the downstairs lounge. A glowing wire stuck straight out from the equator, representing the whole length of the Orbital Elevator. The wire was three and a half meters long—350 centimeters. Each centimeter represented a hundred miles. One-Hour was so close to the globe it couldn't really be represented in scale; it was just a button at the base of the Line. Geostationary was more than two meters out; 223 centimeters along the wire. The last 127 centimeters was there for balance. "Upline" they called it. There was a marble on the end representing Farpoint—the ballast asteroid tethered at the flyaway end of the cable. It takes a day to get to Geostationary; it takes another six hours to get to Farpoint.

What made the model so interesting was all the little lights creeping up and down the wire, representing all the separate elevator cars. There was even a red one to show where ours was on the beanstalk. We were still at the bottom. After waiting forever for it to move and hardly seeing any movement at all, I went back to the windows.

Now we were passing through the rings of lights again, but this time so fast that it was almost like they were dotted lines on the InterContinental Expressway. We still felt motionless. It was the lights that were falling. They dropped down the cables into the glaring sea of clouds below. I'd seen pictures of it, just about everybody has, but it's a lot different when you're there yourself. You'd think it would get boring really fast, but it doesn't. The Earth is just too beautiful. And besides, up here, you can't hear Mom.

"Anyone hungry?" Dad asked.

I thought about it. We'd had breakfast on the train; we hadn't had time to eat at Terminus; the snacks on the elevator up to One-Hour hadn't been much, and we'd missed most of our stopover. We hadn't eaten since breakfast. Now that Dad asked. . . . "Yeah," I said, almost in unison with Weird and Stinky. So we all took the elevator up to the top.

That's right. The elevator car had an elevator in it. It was inside the spiral staircase, not very big; it only held about eight people, but that was okay—the whole place felt kind of cozy. Everything was designed to save as much space as possible.

The restaurant was on the very top of the elevator car and it had a glass roof, so you could look up and see the stars and the cables reaching up into the sky. It was eerie seeing stars above and daylight below, but you get used to it really fast and then it looks normal. One thing I thought was interesting was that there was a large round solar panel on a swivel above the car to keep us from looking directly at the sun; it was large enough so that the car stayed in its shadow the whole time, but it was also small enough that it worked kind of like an artificial solar eclipse and you could see the sun's corona glowing out around the edges. The waiter said that the elevator was the only place in the world where you could see a perpetual solar eclipse.

Also—Dad thought this was clever—there was a scale near the entrance, so you could weigh yourself. There was one downstairs too, next to the model of the Line. The higher we got, the less you weighed. Micro-gravity. So everybody who was worried about how much they weighed could stand on the scale and see how much they'd lost—except of course they hadn't really lost anything. Weird did fifteen minutes on the difference between weight and mass while we were waiting for our salads.

The food was pretty good. Better than we get back home. All the vegetables were fresh and crisp. Mickey the attendant stopped by our table to see how we were doing and to invite Weird and Stinky and me on a tour of the car later. When Dad remarked on how good the food was, Mickey told him that most of the veggies had come from the farms hanging just above One-Hour. There were more farms higher up. There were a whole bunch of farms out at Farpoint for seeding the farms of the interplanetary ships.

Mickey said once we reached micro-gravity, we'd be seeing large solar installations hanging off the Line; some would be factories, some would be power generators for local installations that needed to be energy self-sufficient—especially the maintenance stations. If there were ever an emergency, the engineers would be stranded unless they had an independent power supply. There were maintenance stations spaced regularly along the whole length of the Line. If for any reason an elevator car were in trouble, a high-speed maintenance pod could jet down to meet them from the next highest station and be there in less than five minutes. I wondered if a counter-balanced pod would be launched at the other end of the elevator. Probably. Everything else was balanced. Weird said that the cable was strong enough to handle little imbalances, but that the engineers were under orders to balance the load as rigorously as they could along the entire length.

It was okay, I didn't need to find out first-hand. I wanted the trip to be interesting—but not *that* interesting.

ELEVATOR MUSIC

THE THING IS, NOTHING HAPPENS on an elevator. It goes up. It comes down. You stand and watch the numbers and nobody talks to anybody. It's the same way on the space elevator, only the numbers are bigger and it takes longer to get to the top. As boring as an elevator ride is, try to imagine one that takes a whole day. It doesn't matter how good the food is or how big the view is—after you've eaten and after you've looked at the view, there's not a whole lot else to do.

Okay, so there's a casino on the bottom level and a game room for the kids and 5000 video and music and game channels and unlimited net access and library functions and . . . so what? We have most of that stuff at home—everything except the casino, which I was too young for anyway. But if I didn't care about all those channels at home, why should I care about them here. It's all just bits and bytes and humming phosphors.

Oh, and there's a swimming pool. Actually, it's part of the water-storage system; the water is for ballast and weight-balancing, and it's needed for the production of food and oxygen all up and down the line, but on its way up it's for swimming too. "Have you ever wanted to go swimming in space?" They say the micro-gravity makes it very interesting. The higher you get, the weirder the water moves—except that after a while, it's almost like free fall and then they close the pool area, to keep people from drowning in globules of runaway H_2O.

Naturally, Stinky wanted to go swimming. I thought about it, but not for very long. I didn't want to be around Stinky anymore. Or Dad. Or Doug. As much fun as swimming in space might be, going with them guaranteed that it wouldn't be much fun at all.

Of course, when I announced my decision, it started another fight. "Come on, Charles—" Dad said. "We need to do more things together."

"We already do lots of stuff together," I said. "We fight. We run away from each other. We throw tantrums. We blame Chigger for Stinky getting water down the wrong pipe. We pose for the cover of *Dysfunctional Family Magazine* . . ."

Dad looked like he wanted to slug me. Good. It just proved my point. "I'm not going," I repeated. "Blame someone else this time."

"Let him be, Dad," Weird said. "It's not your fault if Chigger wants to be a sociopath. You can blame it on Mom." He said it deadpan.

Dad gave Weird an even dirtier look than the one he'd given me, but instead of arguing, he just sagged and gave in. "I'm tired of fighting," he said. "I don't care anymore. You kids are about as much fun as a visit to the proctologist. Come on, Bobby."

"Huh?" I looked to Weird. "What's a poctorologist?"

"It means you're a pain in the ass," Weird said, and followed after.

"You too—" I shouted, but he didn't hear me. Or didn't care.

I found a dark corner where I could be alone and curled up at one end of a couch, plugged into my music. With my eyes closed, with my headphones turned up, I could try again to climb all the way into the sound. Sometimes I almost made it. And sometimes I even got there. And sometimes—

but not very often anymore—I got there and kept going so far into it I couldn't stand it, I had to get up and scream and dance—but ever since Mom and Dad had declared war it was harder and harder to get to the other side, because you can't dance in a battle zone. But even when I did get away from the house, it still didn't work, and if it wasn't the music that wasn't working, then it was me—so now I just wanted to be alone so I could go looking for the music again. Different music. Music that would take me there again.

There was a lot of stuff to listen to—most of it overrated. I clicked through the music, flipping from page to page without interest. As much as I loved all the music Dad had given me, Beethoven and Bach and Brahms and Mozart and Orff and Stravinsky and Mussorgsky and Shostakovich and Mahler and Wagner and all those other dead white Europeans—as much as I loved their music, I didn't want them anymore. That was Dad's music. Not mine. I wanted something that belonged to me, not him; something that I discovered myself.

There was this guy I'd found. Almost by accident. I'd been reading about the history of jazz, and there was this article about him and his influence, how he'd faded from memory and been rediscovered, again and again. The writer had said, "Listen to the music! Turn off the lights and just fall into it. And think about the time and place it came from. This guy Coltrane was so fucking subversive that afterward, nothing else was ever the same!"

I didn't know anything about historical jazz—which is nothing like the stuff they call jazz now—so I listened to something called *A Love Supreme*. And I hated it. I didn't get it at all. But I kept listening because I wanted to know what that guy meant by "so fucking subversive" that I kept listening and listening, even though all I really wanted to do was rip the headphones off and wash my head out. Except I couldn't—because I couldn't stand the thought of not knowing, so I kept playing it over and over and over. I tried reading a couple of the analytical essays, but they didn't help. They distracted. Knowing that the music wasn't about love for a woman, but love for God, was interesting—but it wasn't the music. And knowing that this part of the music was really Coltrane reciting a psalm through the saxophone was interesting—but that wasn't the music either.

So I'd turned it off and listened to something else—*tried* listening to something else. Except nothing else worked anymore. Everything sounded shallow.

And that's when I got it—

—not all of it, but enough.

Jazz isn't music. Jazz is what happens when the music disappears and all that's left is the sound and the emotion connected to it. Jazz is a scream or a rant or a sigh. Or whatever else is inside, trying to get out.

And when you listen to it like that, you don't have to understand it. All you have to do is get it. And in the middle of the night, with my headphones clamped to my head, in the middle of a scorching saxophone riff that had to be about anger and love and frustration and hurt all wrapped into one gritty scream of sound, I got it—that sound was about how somebody felt and right now it was about how I felt. And I got it.

And after that, whenever I wanted to get away from Mom or Dad, but especially whenever I wanted to get away from Mom *and* Dad, I went to the music and the music I went to was John Coltrane, and I'd listen with my hands holding the headphones tight to my ears until I heard the sound that was me, and then I knew I was all right. I wasn't alone. There was someone else who knew. Or who had known. And it was all right for a while. A little while, anyway.

J'MEE

IF I HAD MY WAY, I'd listen to music forever. But sooner or later, usually sooner, somebody wants something, and they're never polite about it. They never say, "Oh, I see Charles is listening to his music, I'll come back later." Instead, they always say, "If you're not doing anything . . ." Excuse me? I *am* doing something. I'm listening to my music. But what they're *really* saying is, "What I want is so much more important than what you want that what you want is irrelevant." And usually, it comes out as "*Chigger, would you take those damn headphones off and listen to me!!*" I don't think I've ever gotten to the end of any music.

And this time, I didn't either—

This time it was a kid. A skinny kid in T-shirt and baggy overshirt, shorts, and scabby knees. I had a weird feeling like someone was watching me and I opened my eyes and there he was, standing right in front of me, staring. My age maybe. But smaller. Brown hair, cut very short. Goofy smile. He tilted his head sideways with a funny sort of expression, but I couldn't hear what he was saying, and even though I didn't want to take off the headphones—I was listening to *The*

Paris Concert—my concentration had already been broken, and wherever I had been I wasn't getting back there tonight, if ever, so I peeled the headphones off my ears and said, "What?"

"I *said*, 'What are you listening to?' " He had a soft girlish voice.

Nobody ever asked *that* before. Nobody ever cared enough. "Why do you want to know?"

"Because you had such a strange look on your face, I wanted to know what program you were running."

"I wasn't running a program. I was listening to music. Have you ever heard of John Coltrane?"

He scratched his head—some people do that when they think, probably because thinking makes their brain itch, but this kid actually went into a momentary trance—then he snapped out of it, frowning. He said, "One of the most influential jazz saxophonists of the nineteen-fifties. Died of liver cancer in 1967. Recorded with Miles Davis and McCoy Tyner and Thelonious Monk. The recordings he made for Impulse are generally regarded as his best, in particular—"

"What are you plugged into?" I interrupted.

"Nothing." He grinned.

"You've got all that in your head?"

He nodded and tapped the space above his right ear. "Built in."

I didn't say anything, I just sorta sucked in my cheeks. Augments are expensive. Whoever this kid was, he was worth a lot of money. Or his family was.

"Is he any good?"

"Who?"

"Coltrane."

"I thought you knew—"

"Not yet, but I will . . . in a little bit." He scratched his head again.

"That won't work."

"Why do you say that?"

"Because it won't. You can't listen to Coltrane. Not like you listen to anybody else. That's why."

"How *do* you listen to Coltrane?"

I shook my head. "It can't be explained. You just gotta

go out there where the music lives and live there with it."

He frowned, puckering up his mouth while he turned my words over in his head. It was a funny expression. I bet his grandma liked to pinch his cheek and say, "Look at this, isn't this such a cute little face, I could eat it up." And I bet he hated it too.

Abruptly, he finished with whatever he was thinking about. He said, "My name's J'mee, what's yours?"

"Chi—Charles."

"How far are you going? We're going to the moon."

"For a vacation?"

"Uh-uh. To live. What about you?"

"Um, we're supposed to be going to Geostationary, but . . . we might go farther."

"The moon?"

I shrugged. "Dad was talking about a brightliner. I don't know if he was serious."

"Your Dad is like mine."

"Huh?"

"Daddy says the Earth is getting too dangerous."

"I don't think it's that bad."

"Where are you from?"

"El Paso. Where are you from?"

J'mee shrugged. "All over."

"Yeah, but where do you call 'home'?"

"The last place was Edmonton. Daddy does a lot of traveling for the company."

"What does your dad do?"

"He's a conductor."

"Really? So's mine!" I was suddenly interested. "What orchestra does your dad work with?"

"No. My dad's an *electrical* conductor. Or sometimes he says he's a 'power broker.' For the Line. Do you know that the Line generates electricity? A lot. It has something to do with poles and potentials and moving through the Earth's magnetic field and generating super-currents. Do you know what super-currents are?"

"Lightning."

"Yeah, that's the short explanation. But super-currents are part of what holds the Line up. You probably don't want to know this, most people don't, but the Line isn't strong enough to hold itself up. Earth's gravity is just a little too high, and the molecular bonds aren't strong enough to withstand the strain. But when you run a supercurrent through superconducting carbon-doped titanium-ceramic alloys you get a superbond, with the current doing most of the work. Daddy says the Line is made of lightning, that's how much power is flowing through it."

"Oh, yeah," I said. "I knew that." Sort of. Lightning, huh? I looked at the huge cables just outside the windows with new respect.

"Don't you think it's scary?" J'mee said.

I shrugged. Yes, it was scary. But I wasn't going to admit it. I looked around the lounge, feeling suddenly uncomfortable. This was the feeling that I'd had down below just before we started up, only worse. I wished J'mee would change the subject.

Instead, he nattered on: "Daddy says, if you could turn the current off, the whole thing would fall down—the Line would come apart in a million little explosions. Doesn't that make you feel gooshy inside? But don't worry. You can't turn the current off. It's automatic. The Line generates it because one end is sticking out in space and the other is connected to the Earth, and even if it weren't covered with windmills and solar skin, it would still generate electricity because of all the different potentials. And that electricity has to be drained off to keep the potentials unbalanced and keep the current flowing.

"That's Daddy's job. To keep the electricity flowing. He sells it to whoever will buy it. And there are lots of people who need it all over the world. He's real good at explaining it; he's got a whole VR program that lets you see exactly how it works. The peak power flow follows the day. In any particular place, the need for power starts just before sunrise and goes up and up all day long. On a hot day, when everybody has all their air conditioners going, the hours around noon are the most profitable, and then the power demand ebbs, peaking again at dinner time and sunset, and then ebbs away, dropping off after ten or eleven and hitting its lowest levels at three or four in the morning. But that's only if you look at one location. If you watch the way the daylight moves around the planet, so do the waves of power demand, and that's what Daddy does. He makes contracts to sell the power to fill in the peak demands all up and down the entire western hemisphere and even across the oceans to parts of Africa and Australia and a lot of the Pacific islands. The Line almost generates too much power. Sometimes Daddy has to give it away. Or even throw it away. The Line has got microwave beaming stations that can send the excess anywhere there's a receiver, but if there's no one who will pay for it, Daddy dumps the extra power into space or sometimes even into the ocean or the atmosphere—wherever someone needs to heat up the air or the water because they want to try to divert an ocean flow or a hurricane or something."

"They didn't do too well with Hurricane Charles," I said. I didn't mean it badly, but apparently J'mee took it that way. He made a face and turned away to look out the window. The hurricane was a vast white sweep below us.

Finally, J'mee said, "I don't know why they didn't stop the hurricane. I know they were going to try. Daddy was talking about beaming power at it all last week. I thought they were. We were in Terminus, and Daddy had meetings all day. He was awfully worried about something. I don't know what." He stared out the window again. "It's hard to believe we'll never go back."

"You're jumping off the planet too?"

"Yeah. You too?"

"Uh-huh," I admitted. It gave me a weird feeling just to say it aloud.

"Why're you going?" J'mee asked.

I shrugged. I really didn't want to talk about it. How could I explain it anyway? I can't even explain jazz. And explaining jazz is easy, compared to explaining life. Except maybe the same principle applies: If you have to have it explained to you, you don't understand it.

Weird says it's possible to tell your whole life story in thirty seconds. That's another one of the weird things he says. But I sort of understood what he meant. You have to leave out the details. The details aren't interesting. It's the interpretation. Like in music. The notes themselves don't mean anything—it's how you put them together—and how you play them.

When I was little, I used to pretend my life was a grand concert. The overture was Mom and Dad meeting. Two conflicting motifs. She was a singer and he was an arranger, so naturally they spent a lot of time together. Making beautiful music. That's enough to overwhelm anyone. They had so much fun making music they got confused, they thought they were in love. Decided to live happily ever after and create a glorious symphony of joy. Or something. . . .

First movement. Melody plus counter-melody equals harmony—a new theme, full of expectation. Whoops, a little too expectant. A pregnant diva? A tremulous minor chord. Does this portend disharmony or resolution? The diva stops singing and stands aside. For just a bit. But the movement has to resolve. Will it be joyous or tragic?

So they get married and have me. This is supposed to be good news. So the second movement opens with a triumphant fanfare. Bridge to a tableau of pastoral beauty. The diva returns to center stage and sings the second movement sweetly toward a promise of greater triumphs still to come. The conductor is glorious and everything sparkles in the afternoon. I like the second movement. I want to go home to it. But it's over too soon. It's just there to provide contrast for the horrors to follow.

Suddenly, the third movement. Unasked, the composer expands the wind section with the worst of all possible untuned wind instruments: a baby. Some people think there's beauty in cacophony, if you know how to do it right. Ives unanswers questions all over the stage. Mom and Dad get the cacophony part right. The diva starts shrieking invective at the conductor, claiming it's his fault the music isn't working. The conductor waggles his baton at the diva warningly; he tries to get the rest of the musicians to play. But suddenly he is dragged kicking and screaming out of the concert hall by the ushers while the diva throws music stands after him. She is hissed by the audience, who start throwing eggs and tomatoes.

Fourth movement. Everybody in the orchestra plays whatever they feel like. If no one listens, they play louder. The diva shrieks a monotonic babble, like something out of a minimalist opera, only not as melodic. The conductor sneaks back into the hall and kidnaps the wind section. The strings light torches, grab a rope, and go charging after.

And that's the nice way to explain it.

Mom had a career. So did Dad. Until they got married. Then Mom didn't have a career and Dad did. And Mom hated him for it. It was no secret. I heard her say it to him enough times, "You still have a career. Why don't you come home and wash a few stinky diapers in the toilet once in a while—then you'll see what I'm so angry about! I'm flushing my best years away! I thought we were going to record together—"

Whatever Dad did, it was wrong. Mom complained that he wasn't earning enough money to support a family, so he went out and worked harder. But when he worked harder, Mom whined that he wasn't spending enough time at home. But that wasn't it. Mom was unhappy because Dad was having a life, and she wasn't. And it never occurred to her that maybe Dad didn't want to spend too much time with her because she wasn't all that much fun anymore. But if she wasn't all that much fun for him, why did he assume she would be any more fun for us?

Weird tells me I've got it all bass-ackwards, that it was more Dad's fault than Mom's, because he kept promising to get her back in front of a microphone, and he never did. It was all broken promises to her. Just like all the broken promises to us. He said that we don't take Dad's promises seriously because we've never seen him keep any—but Mom always believed him because she always *wanted* to believe him. And that's why she's always so angry, because she's frustrated that no one around her keeps their word.

But she takes it out on me. Every time she sees me caught up in my music, she has to interrupt. She rants at me, "You're just like your father. He hides out in music too. It's a waste of time, Charles! And the sooner you learn that, the happier you'll be. It'll never make you a nickel."

So how am I supposed to take her side in that argument? Or any argument? I'd have to give up the only thing I have left.

Mom says that the music is my way of trying to get close to Dad. But she's wrong. The music isn't my way of getting close to Dad or anyone. It's my way of getting away from both of them and going somewhere else. Someplace where things always resolve in the final eight bars.

After the divorce, it was all I had left. Mom didn't have any money. And I guess, neither did Dad because he never sent us enough. So we couldn't take the piano with us. Mom had to sell it. I remember crying when the moving men came to take it away. I had a keyboard, but it wasn't the same. And Mom wouldn't let me continue my lessons anyway. She said it was time for me to get practical—but what she really meant was that it was time for Dad to get practical. And because he wasn't there, she was going to make sure I didn't grow up like him. Which was why I didn't want to go back. I was tired of her punishing me because she couldn't get her hands on Dad.

But I couldn't tell that to J'mee. Or anyone. Because I was embarrassed for both Mom and Dad. And myself for having them as parents.

It was easier to change the subject. "You want to go swimming?" I asked.

I don't know why I'd said that. Only after the words were out of my mouth did I realize what a mistake that would be. I hoped he'd say no.

"Okay—"

"Uh, let's not. I changed my mind."

"Uh-uh. You don't get to change your mind. Come on." J'mee grabbed my hand and pulled me to my feet. For a little guy, he was strong. Wiry. Or just determined. I dunno. He pulled me along and I went along reluctantly.

When we got to the pool, I realized I didn't have any swimming trunks. J'mee said not to worry about it and put his card into the slot of the machine. He punched up two disposable swimsuits and gave one to me. I got the feeling he was used to buying whatever he wanted, whenever he wanted to.

In the changing room, J'mee was a little shy, which was fine with me, because I don't like changing clothes in front of other people either. I followed J'mee into the bathroom;

he went into one stall and I went into another. He must have been very shy about being so small and skinny. He came out still wearing his T-shirt and hugging his arms across his chest.

"You going swimming in your shirt?"

"Yeah. I always do."

I didn't think this was the truth, but everybody is weird in their own way. It's that geek business again—that thing Weird said once—everybody's a geek somehow. I'm a music geek. Weird's a techno-geek. Maybe J'mee was a shy-and-skinny-geek. Or something. I guess the way geeks get along with other geeks is that we pretend not to notice each other's particular geekiness. Or maybe we just don't care. I dunno.

The pool was kind of small and funny-shaped. But that's because it wasn't a pool as much as it was a tank with a door. It didn't have a deep end; it had a deep side and a shallow side. This had to do with the way the room was shaped and how the water would slosh sideways when the elevator car was spun for pseudo-gravity. But there were a bunch of people in it anyway, shouting and laughing, even Dad and Weird and Stinky. J'mee jumped right into the water in the deep side. I like to get in slowly and get used to it, but when J'mee jumped in, so did I. The water was warmer than I'd expected and I shouted with surprise.

"Hey, look who's here," Dad said. "Chigger decided to join us after all."

J'mee looked at me. "Chigger?"

I made a face. "It's a nickname. My grampa used to say I was no bigger than a chigger. And it stuck."

"I won't tell you my nickname," J'mee said, and ducked under water swimming off to the opposite end. I swam after.

We played tag for a while, trying to duck each other, until Weird and Stinky challenged us to a game of horse-and-rider. Stinky rode on Weird's shoulders. J'mee rode on mine. I thought it would be a fair match because Stinky was so small. We got knocked down a few times and so did they—until Stinky started crying (which was inevitable) because he got ducked once too often and got water up his nose, and I was sure Dad was going to yell at me, but instead Dad just came over and got Stinky and told him he had to take a break for a while. He complained about that until Dad told him he could be referee. Dad put him on the sidelines to watch, and I thought the game was over, but then Dad came back and put me on his shoulders and J'mee rode on Weird, and this time the game was a lot more ferocious, with Weird pushing at Dad and me pushing at J'mee—and a couple of times we all fell down together, laughing. And for a while there I even forgot that I was angry.

So, yeah, it wasn't all bad. Once in awhile it was almost nice. And later, when we got out, we stood around for a bit, just laughing and grinning. J'mee hugged his chest again and pretended to shiver even though we were standing under the tanning lamps. I just stretched my arms up and out and leaned as far back as I could, basking under the narrow-spectrum UV rays. J'mee started to do the same, then stopped when he saw me looking at him. "I'm gonna go get dressed," he said abruptly.

"Okay, me too."

We went back to the changing room. This time all the bathroom stalls were filled, so we had to change in front of each other—except that J'mee turned his back to me when he pulled down his shorts and then he pulled on his underwear real fast. And that's when I figured it out. "You don't have any brothers, do you?" I asked.

"Huh? No. How can you tell?"

I shrugged. "Just the way you change clothes. That's all. Lotsa guys are shy."

J'mee didn't answer. He turned away and pulled off his wet T-shirt, then quickly pulled his sweatshirt on.

"Do you have any hair yet?" I asked.

"Huh?"

"You know, down there."

"Uh—"

"Let's see," I said. "I'll show you mine." I yanked down my shorts and turned so he could see. I didn't have a lot of hair, but enough so I didn't look like a baby anymore. J'mee glanced, in spite of himself, probably just to see if I meant it—then he glanced away quickly, face reddening.

"It's okay," I said. "You can look—"

"No thanks," he said, sitting down to pull on his sandals.

"Come on," I teased. "It doesn't bite."

"No!" he shouted, a little too loudly. He grabbed his other shoe and ran out of the changing room like he was suddenly scared of me.

Okay. So that was that. I shrugged and pulled my underwear up and finished getting dressed. When I came out of the pool area, J'mee was gone, and I couldn't find him in any of the lounges.

So I went back to the cabin and listened to my music until Dad and Stinky and Weird came in and interrupted me. Again.

CLOSE SHAVE

STINKY WAS WHINING ABOUT WANTING to play with his new monkey and Weird had gone back to being the techno-geek and Dad was annoyed about something else, I didn't know what. They just came in like a door blown open in a sandstorm and swept around the room for a while before they settled in.

I guess we were all tired. And not just physically. We'd been through a lot, and now it was catching up with us. Dad said that traveling was tiring, and even though most of what we'd been doing was sitting around and watching the scenery slide by, what little there was of it, I could see why he would think so. *Not* having anything to do is a lot more tiring than having everything to do. But I think we were tired of each other. I know I was.

The screen was blinking with a reminder to please watch the important informational video. Weird is datatropic or something. If it's educational, he has to read it or watch it or listen to it, so he punched up the program immediately. I flung myself down on a chair and glowered while Weird watched intently. Eventually, Dad put down his book and watched too. Off in the corner, Stinky happily made up his own code phrases and taught the monkey to do silly things whenever he said them. He had the monkey belching, pretending to fart, giving the finger, mooning and waggling its butt. If he could have taught it to crap on the rug as well, I bet he would have.

The video turned out to be a lot more interesting than it looked at first glance. It was full of funny stories about how to look like a jerk in micro-gravity. They had that red-haired comedian, you know the one, with his hair flaming out in all directions, stumbling through all the different ways to hurt yourself. So it was kind of interesting to watch after all.

There was one part that gave us pause. The guy who was narrating said, "If you're planning to go on to Luna or any other deep-space destination, body shaving is strongly recommended. If you are heading out to any military or scientific destination, it will be *required*."

"Huh?" I asked. "Body shaving?"

The program went on to show how the body flakes off zillions of tiny bits of skin and hair every day. In micro-gravity, this stuff floats around like a nanotech snowstorm. The hair is apparently the worst, cause it can clog up the micromachinery. As a long-term maintenance measure, the Loonies shave themselves and rub stuff on their skin so it doesn't flake so much, and apparently this was now recommended for anyone who was planning to spend any amount of time in space.

Dad said this was part of the economics involved in Elevator Theory. Macro events have micro effects; micro events have macro effects. In space body hair is a luxury. Hair holds dirt and bacteria and smells. When you have hair, your scalp also flakes a lot. And underarm hair and pubic hair gets into everything too. It's nasty.

And if that weren't disgusting enough, the program showed how all that stuff builds up in the recycling equipment and sometimes you get pockets of goop where bacteria can live—so minimizing all those flakes of skin and hair floating around is also good for preventing the spread of infection. The show didn't specifically mention what hapened on the *Miranda*. They didn't have to. The lawsuits still hadn't been settled.

But they also said that without hair on your head or on your body, you don't use up as much water washing. So if you want to have hair, you have to pay for it. Dad said that there's a surcharge at some of the orbital hotels if you don't shave, because it costs more to clean up. More Elevator Theory economics.

Then the program showed the red-haired guy shaving everything—and I mean *everything*—even his head. He looked real sad about losing his hair and even sillier without it, but they let him keep a real short buzz on top, so you could still tell he was the same guy. The short hair looked better on the women, for some reason.

I thought the whole thing was a little extreme, but Dad said that it made sense to him, and the next thing I knew he and Weird were in the bathroom looking at the shaving equipment. Mostly, there was this big vacuum tube that came out of the wall with a kind of clippers in a big mouth at the end. It sucked up all the hair as fast as it clipped. The clipper was really a forest of micro-machines, first you set it for your age and your sex and how close you wanted to be shaved, and then you moved it slowly back and forth across your skin until the light on the end showed green, then you moved on to the next place. You had to do this for the hair on your head and your legs and under your arms and down below if you had anything there yet, which I did, but not really very much and I wasn't sure yet I wanted to lose it.

Weird said we should have gone to a shaving station at Terminus, where we could have gotten the full treatment, including the services of a professional shaver, and it was too bad we hadn't taken the time, but Dad just shrugged it off. "We have twenty-four hours of travel before we reach Geostationary. The equipment here will be sufficient."

Dad also said that the micro-economics of space were already becoming a part of Earth society. A lot of people who never went into space were shaving now, some because they thought it was sexy, but just as many were doing it to cut back on their water consumption. I could understand that. Mom was always complaining about the clean water taxes,

which were almost as much as the water bill in El Paso. Now
that he'd mentioned it, I realized there were a lot of bald
people back home in our Tube-Town. I'd just never noticed
it or thought about it before.

Anyway, after you shaved, you were supposed to take a
special shower. It wasn't a shower like on Earth where the
water jets come out of the wall. Instead, you get a little
sprayer at the end of a hose, which you use for getting yourself wet, then you rub yourself all over with some foamy
stuff, which is supposed to keep your skin from drying and
flaking so much, and then you *shloop* it all off with another
vacuum tube. If you do it right, your skin ends up feeling
all slick and slippery, as soft and smooth as a baby's ass.

Dad went first, then Weird, then me, then Stinky. I thought
we ended up looking like fat brown slugs. *Bald* fat brown
slugs. Mom was going to kill us when we got back. And it
felt kind of weird to be so smooth all over. My clothes felt
a lot rougher too.

There were some nylan space-clothes in one of the closets.
All different sizes, each set a different color. They were real
light and soft, like one of Dad's silk shirts. When you opened
the package you were automatically billed for them, but they
didn't cost that much and Dad said we'd probably all be a
lot more comfortable than if we tried to wear Earth-clothes.
Earth-clothes are for protection from the weather. Space-
clothes are for comfort and cleanliness.

The nylan space-suit is sort of a one-piece jumpsuit that
you step into and zip up the front. It's one of those nano-
zippers that disappears when you zip it. You can't even feel
it. The wrists and the ankles are snug-fitting. So is the collar
around the neck. This is again to keep skin flakes and hairs
from being spread around. There are slipperlike shoes to
wear too. The whole thing is kind of like dressing for a clean-
room. There were also shower caps for people who didn't
want to cut their hair and other caps for people who did, but
the caps were optional; we didn't have to wear them. Stinky
and I both did. Dad and Weird decided not to.

It felt like Halloween and after we were done, we all
looked like Hallo-weenies. After Weird told him he was as
smooth and as cute as a girl, Stinky went dancing around the

room singing, "I'm a girl now, I'm a girl now." I just made a face and looked embarrassed. Was this really necessary? But Dad said we'd get used to it and we'd probably find it a lot more comfortable than trying to keep wearing our Earth-clothes. So we packed them all up in the dirty clothes bag and put them in the closet and forgot about them.

TELEVISION

IT TAKES TWENTY-FOUR HOURS TO get to Geostationary. If you take an express, you can do it in six hours, but they only run express cars two or three times a day, and they're very expensive because they use rocket assists and special tracks. There are also maintenance tracks and balance tracks. The cables are thick enough now so that they can have multiple tracks on each one.

The balance tracks are mostly above One-Hour. They're on the opposite side of the cable from the main tracks, but every so often, you can see the long bulge of a water-pod hanging in place. There are several thousand water-pods on the Line, and they move up and down on their tracks as needed, to counterbalance any big waves in the cable, like the ones caused by Hurricane Charles below.

Most people think the cables are rigid, but they're not. Well, they are if you look only at a small section at a time—like a few thousand meters or so—and gravity helps too. But when you consider that the cable is really thousands of kilometers long—all the way up to Geostationary and then half again as far out beyond for balance—a whole different scale of physics comes into play. Dad says that on that scale, a continent has the consistency of chocolate cake, and the cable is like a piece of spider web, so it will react to certain kinds of very big movements—like a hurricane, for instance. It sets up waves. That's why the water-pods are moved up and down to different places to help damp the waves. I don't really understand all of the mechanics, but it has something to do with breaking the rhythm—or maybe that's *braking* the rhythm. Anyway, it's like not letting all the soldiers march in step across the bridge or it'll collapse.

This was all explained in another program. It didn't matter what time it was, there were always programs about the orbital elevator: about how it was built and when the first cars were dropped down it and when public service began and how many passengers use the cable every day and how many people there are on the cable at any given moment—stuff like that.

There was a whole program just on the elevator cars alone, all the different types, how they work, how they're constructed inside, how they're connected to the tracks. The bigger cars have longer carriages and they stand away from the cable more. They're mounted at the tops and bottoms, so they look like handles with windows in them sliding up and down the Line.

It's all done with magnetic induction. The car never even touches the cable unless it has to stop, in which case there are contact brakes, because the track-riding mechanisms aren't really designed for slowing and stopping; they're designed for moving a thousand miles an hour. You can't just slow an elevator down and hold it in place because magnetics don't work like that, so that's why there are contact brakes; but even contact brakes have to be specially designed, because the cars are moving so fast that to try to stop one, the brakes would generate enough heat to permanently weaken the cable. So stopping a car isn't a simple operation.

If the car is going up, they just turn off the magnetics and let the car coast for a bit until it burns off most of its speed. When it's still going about fifty miles an hour upward, that's when the contact brakes grab hold. But stopping the car when it's going down is a whole other story; they have to reverse the magnetic inductors and slow the car, and that takes whole lot longer to reduce its speed.

Restarting a car is easier going down, but almost impos sible going up, because the magnetic inductors are space too far apart for an easy start. They don't really expect car to stop and start on the cable anyway. Weird said that in th event of a real problem, the Line engineers would rather po the car off and either let it parachute down if it's low enough or catch it somewhere in orbit if it's too high to land.

The most interesting show we saw was a rerun of the *Nov* episode called "Breakaway Revisited" about what woul happen if the cable snapped. First they showed clips from the movie *Breakaway* which supposedly depicted everything that would happen in such an accident. They showed all th best shots, of the cable falling and falling and falling and finally wrapping itself around the Earth, slicing across con tinents, jungles, deserts, oceans, mountains. They extrapo lated all the damage that could occur. It was pretty scary stuff—I was surprised they were even showing it on th cable channels.

The most likely place for the Line to break would be low Earth orbit, around the 1000-kilometer point, because that's where the most and fastest orbital junk is—and the most ionized gas too, which also has a corrosive effect. But the part that fell back to Earth would be relatively short and thin. And it would fall almost vertically. A break at the 1000-kilometer point would result in the broken end arriving at ground level about eight minutes later, at a speed of nearly 4 km/sec, about 25 km west of Terminus Station—the foot-hills of the Andes.

A break higher up, though, would be much more serious. If the beanstalk snapped at Geostationary, the upper half would fly away into space, but the lower half would be 40,000 kilometers long. It would wrap itself around the planet—*all the way around the planet!*

It would be like detonating nuclear weapons along every inch of the equator. The destruction could be as bad as the asteroid that killed the dinosaurs. When you calculate mass and impact, you're talking about an object 40,000 kilometers long, circling the Earth and hitting the ground with the equiv-lent force of twenty times its own weight in TNT. It's an extinction-level event.

We would lose millions of lives, first from the immediate destruction around the equator and vicinity, then millions more from all the after-effects. Slumbering volcanoes might be shaken back to life. Earthquakes would very likely be triggered along fault lines. Uncontrollable firestorms would be started across the Amazon and the heart of Africa. A gigantic wall of ash would climb into the atmosphere—at least as bad as anything caused by an asteroid impact—and all that soot in the air would create a nuclear autumn and probably a decade-long disruption of the seasons, maybe longer. The impact of the cable across the Atlantic and Pacific oceans would cause immediate tsunamis on every coastline, and noticeable heating of tropical water temperatures as well—enough to trigger super-hurricanes. After that, the *real* disaster would begin: the inevitable extinction of many species; the disruption of rainfall, migration patterns on land and sea, and crop-growing seasons; long-term famines.

Oh, and one other thing. If one Line failed in a big way, enough to wrap around the Earth, it would very likely knock down all the others with it—the one in Africa, and the one at Christmas Island. And each of those failures would have equally disastrous effects.

Of smaller import, but equally significant to human beings, would be the near-total collapse of the global economy.

The Line represents such an enormous part of the wealth of the planet that its destruction and the destruction of property on land and in space would essentially bankrupt every insurance company in the world. The loss of capital would also bankrupt every investment company. The interconnectedness of everything would pull down everything.

The failure of the beanstalk would also maroon many people in space with no safe way to return, simply because there wouldn't be the spacecraft available. Without regular supplies, the folks in the asteroids, the Lagrange colonies, and other bases would run out of food, water, and air. Only Luna and Mars were anywhere near self-sufficiency. The death toll in space would be proportionally more severe than the death

toll on the ground. Three out of every five. As many as si
million people.

But then the show started examining all of the movie'
premises and took each one apart to show that for all of th
events in the movie to actually happen, the cable would hav
had to have been designed to fail. They showed how the
individual fibers of the cable were manufactured out of su
perlong molecules, how they were braided, strengthened
linked, and energized by superpowerful currents—so tha
even if a terrorist were to succeed in planting a strong enoug!
bomb on an elevator car, it still wouldn't destroy the bean
stalk. All three cables were now cross-linked every hundred
klicks, and those linkages were designed to provide enoug!
support so that a broken cable would stay in place until a
repair crew could arrive to secure it. In fact, any single one
of the cables was thick enough and strong enough to hold
the other two in place if a break occurred. They showed tha
even if all three cables were broken at different places, the
beanstalk would still survive long enough to be repaired. The
only way a terrorist could destroy it, he'd have to snap all
three cables at the same place, which just wasn't possible
because the cables were held far enough apart from each
other to put them well out of each other's blast radius. Even
a piece of orbiting space junk colliding with the Line could
only take out one cable, not all three, because they were
spaced farther apart than the size of any known piece of junk.
Anything short of a nuclear device would be insufficient to
snap the Line.

Part of the show talked about some of the proposals to
add self-destruct mechanisms to the beanstalk. One guy
wanted to mine the entire length of each cable with binary
explosives, so if the cable snapped, the whole thing would
be blown to bits and all the bits would vaporize on the way
down through the atmosphere, so nobody on the ground
would get hurt. But the analysis of that plan showed that it
was not only too expensive, but even if you could do it, and
even if all the cables snapped, it still wouldn't work. The
resultant meteor showers would do almost as much damage
as a falling cable, and the radius of destruction would be far
wider. And besides, there was more chance of one of those

self-destruct units failing and blasting the Line apart than there was of a terrorist snapping all three cables at once. So much for that idea.

But if the Line was in serious danger, you could snap it at One-Hour, the low-Earth orbital boundary about 200 klicks up, and let everything above that fly into space, and then you'd only have to worry about less than 200 kilometers of Line hitting the ground.

Most of that stuff burns up on the way down, of course, the stuff that has to fall the farthest—so we only have to worry about the bottommost lengths of Line, the stuff that doesn't have time to burn up. And remember, it's all Line-cable, the strongest material ever manufactured, so you can't depend on it all vaporizing. You're much more likely to get a rain of hot, flaming chunks. Which is why you want to keep the area west of the Line clear. At least a hundred klicks. Then once you've reduced the global scale of the disaster to a domain of a couple hundred klicks, you can start to argue that Line failure is a tolerable risk, especially if the Line is on a western coastline, so that a failure drops most of the debris into the ocean. But even so, you're still dealing with a lot of mass hitting the planet, with significant consequences. And of course, regardless of what happens to the planet, the financial cost of a Line failure would remain the same: global economic meltdown.

But then the program showed how the Line is regularly maintained, how new filaments are being added to the existing cables at the rate of twelve per year. Every month, each cable gets a new filament started. Although filaments aren't supposed to wear out, their projected life is about eighty years per wire, so the idea is that each filament will be replaced every forty years. The show didn't say how they were going to remove the old filaments, but I assumed there was some way to do it. But even if they stopped the regular maintenance, they figured that the beanstalk could stand untended for thousands of years. Maybe more. By then, who knew what advances in technology we might have?

It was all supposed to be very reassuring—but it wasn't. Not really. It was as comforting as a flight attendant saying, "In the unlikely event of a water-landing . . ."

After we got tired of watching programs about the construction of the beanstalk, Weird started scanning through the entertainment and news channels. There were hundreds. Eventually, he found a station from home. That's when things suddenly got *very* interesting.

"Hey, Dad, look—" Douglas said. It was hard not to look. One whole wall was a screen. And it had Stinky's picture on it. And mine. And Weird. And Dad. Uh-oh . . .

The announcer was saying, ". . . believed to be somewhere on the orbital elevator. With the exception of the phone call received earlier today, the Dingillian children have not been heard from since their father took them last week for a regularly scheduled vacation. Line officials refused to comment, saying that to do so would violate their passengers' privacy, but TNN's own travel desk has determined that Max Dingillian had made reservations for four on the 2:15 elevator to Geostationary. That car was never launched due to the high wind conditions of Hurricane Charles, and Ecuador Security is now investigating the possibility that Dingillian and his sons are still somewhere at Terminus. Margaret Dingillian is seeking an International Court Order requiring the Line Authority to consider this a security situation and detain Max Dingillian. More on this developing story as it breaks. . . . In other news, the hotly contested Baby Cooper lawsuit took another legal blow this week when it was revealed that one of the company's lawyers had failed to—" Weird switched the television off and looked at Dad. We all did.

FAMILY MEETING

DAD SAT DOWN, LOOKING KIND of weak. He began to do that thing he does when he's winding himself up to make one of his speeches. He flustered.

And the more he flustered, the more I knew this wasn't going to be good. And I was already feeling all *squooshy* inside. I didn't know which was more mixed up, my stomach or my head. And Dad's performance wasn't helping. Finally, I turned to Weird and said, "You better ask him."

Dad said, "Ask me what?"

Weird cleared his throat and managed to stumble over a whole paragraph. "Well—it's about you and us and Mom. Chigger and I were talking—and well, I mean—you *are* kidnapping us, aren't you, Dad?"

Dad nodded his head as if he had been expecting this conversation for a while. He sighed. "You know that your Mom and I aren't on very good terms. I'm sorry about that. I wish it were different."

"Mom always maintained that the divorce was your fault."

"I asked for the divorce, yes, but I think you should know why. I found your mother in bed with someone else—"

"That woman we saw on the phone?" Weird asked.

Dad shrugged. "I don't know if she's the same one or not. It doesn't matter. Your mom asked me to forgive her. And I—I just couldn't. I felt betrayed. Yes, your mother and I had problems. I thought we were working them out. I was honestly trying, but things weren't happening. I wasn't getting the work or the money—"

"Dad," I said, exasperated. "You and mom have explained this to death. I don't know about Douglas and Bobby, but I don't care *whose* fault it is."

"Well, I do," he said. "Because I've had a lot of time to think about this. I'm paying a terrible price, because I don't get to be with the three people I love most in the world—you kids."

"Yeah, Dad, and what about the price we're paying?" I said. "Every year when we go on vacation, you always spend the first three days trying to make up for everything. Except it can't be made up."

He nodded his agreement. "Charles, I think you're the one who's been hurt the most by all this, and I wish I knew what to do for you to make it all right. It isn't easy being the middle kid. You're always getting overlooked and taken for granted, and I don't blame you for feeling the way you do."

"Yeah, Dad, yeah," said Weird. "And we've all heard that speech too. Tell us what's going on now." I was mad at Weird for interrupting. I had thought for a moment that Dad was finally going to say something that would make a difference. But maybe not, because he just let Weird change the subject without even noticing how unfinished I still felt.

"I've been thinking about this for years," Dad said. "Leaving Earth. It's something I've always dreamt of—going out into space and never coming back. But I was never sure where I should go. There were too many possibilities, and I could only have one of them. And then one day, I realized that not choosing meant I wasn't having *any*. So I made a choice. And then I started thinking—if I leave, I'll never see you boys again. And if you hated me for not being there when you were growing up, you'd hate me all the more for abandoning you. And I just couldn't stand that thought. So—"

He stopped to take a breath and figure out how to say the next part.

Weird filled the silence. "So you decided to just grab us and take us with you?"

"No." Dad shook his head. "No. that's not it at all. I do have tickets for you, but they're refundable. I'm taking you only as far as you want to go. I'm trying to give you two things here, Douglas: the trip I've always promised you, and the choice you never had before on how you want your life to turn out."

Dad turned back to me. "You said something once, Charles, that has stayed in my head like a ball bearing bouncing around the inside of an empty steel drum. You said that it was your family too, and nobody ever asked you what you wanted. Well, this is me asking you. All of you."

"Do we have to decide now?"

Dad shook his head. "No. There's time enough when we get to Geostationary. You can go back down if you want. Or you can come on out to the launch point with me. From here on in, whether you come with me or not is all your own decision. But at the very least, you're going to have an out-of-this-world vacation."

"But everybody will be looking for us—"

Dad pointed to the now-blank wall. "They're looking for the people in that picture. They won't be looking for us the way we look now, will they?"

Weird went thoughtful at that. Then he started frowning. Then he looked at Dad with that faraway squint he gets when he sees something that no one else has seen yet. "How much of this did you plan in advance, Dad?"

Dad looked embarrassed. "What do you mean, Douglas?"

"We drove across the border and we didn't buy our train tickets until Mazatlán, and you paid cash. You only bought tickets as far as Acapulco. It was only after we were on the train that you upgraded them to Beanstalk City. You didn't want Mom to be able to find us by your credit card purchases, did you?"

Dad scratched his ear while he tried to figure out some polite way to say it. He couldn't. "Yes, you're right, Douglas. I didn't want your mother to know where we were going."

"And the reservations at Terminus? You knew we could catch an earlier car up to One-Hour too?"

"I didn't plan the hurricane—" he started to say.

"No, you didn't. That one was lucky. But wasn't it convenient that there was an empty first-class cabin on the 11:00 car? Wasn't it also convenient that we checked in at the reservation desk just in time to catch it? And wasn't it also convenient that you kept looking at your watch all over One-Hour? Did you make this reservation in another name so it would be waiting for us? You did it first class too, didn't you? So they'd be less likely to give it away."

"You're very observant, Douglas. You'd make a good detective." Dad sighed and admitted it. "I wanted you to have the chance. That's all. The chance your Mom didn't want you to have. I asked her—I said I wanted you to come with me up the Line, and then I'd send you all back home again. She said no. She was sure that I was going to try to steal you. But all I wanted was to give you one great memory of your Dad, and the trip I always promised you. And then she threatened to go to court and I realized just how angry she was and that she was going to try to hurt me any way she could. Even if it meant hurting you too. That's when I started thinking that if jumping off the planet was a chance for me to have a better life than is possible on Earth, well, then maybe it might be a chance for you kids too. But I promise you, Douglas, I won't take you anywhere against your will. I just want to spend some time with you before I go. Is that too much to ask?"

"Why didn't you tell us this before?" I asked.

"If I had, would you have believed me? Would you have come?"

I thought about that. He was right. I wouldn't have believed him. Would I have come? That was a harder question. Not believing him, I don't know what I would have done. In reply, I shrugged.

Stinky had been silent the whole time. I wasn't sure how much of this he understood, but he'd been listening carefully and suddenly he piped up, "Aren't we going home? I wanna go home!"

Dad and Douglas and I exchanged looks. Dad scooped up

Stinky and held him on his lap. "Hey, kiddo. You're going to go home real soon, if that's what you want. But Daddy's going away for a long time, and I wanted us to have some time together before I say good-bye, that's all."

"Where are you going?"

"Very far away. So far away that you can't even imagine it."

"Why?" demanded Stinky. "Don't you love us anymore?"

"I love you more than anything, sweetheart."

"Can't you take us with you?"

"Well, that's what we're talking about now. Whether or not you want to go."

"But I don't want to go. I want to go home."

"Okay. You can do that, if that's what you want."

"But I want you to come too."

"I can't do that."

"But why are you going away?"

"Because it's something I have to do."

The frustration on Bobby's face was evident. He began to cry. "*But why . . . ?* It isn't fair!"

"I'm not sure I understand it all either, kiddo. This is just the way it is." Dad hugged Bobby close, probably because he didn't have anything else to say.

Douglas gave Dad a weird look then—one of those looks that got him his nickname. He shook his head over some personal annoyance that maybe only the two of them understood and headed for the door.

"Where are you going, Doug?"

"Nowhere. Out."

Yeah. Like where *could* he go? And then he was gone anyway.

I wanted to follow him, but I felt I should stay with Dad for a bit. There was something else going on that I still didn't understand. Whatever it was, Douglas hadn't said, so I felt just like Bobby: it wasn't fair and I didn't know why.

MORE UP

AT FIRST, DAD WAS A little worried about Doug leaving the cabin. He was afraid that someone might recognize him from the pictures—or any of us—but we'd cut off all our hair and Dad and Douglas were wearing their space hats and Stinky and I were both buzz-cut, so we didn't look very much like the pictures on TV anymore. And then we also realized that it was unlikely that anyone else on this elevator car had even seen that same broadcast. Doug had been watching an El Paso news feed. All the other news was talking about Hurricane Charles and the damage it was doing all across Ecuador. Nobody was going to be looking for us; they were all too busy with much more serious problems.

And even if somebody did recognize us, what could they do? We hadn't broken any laws. And even if we had, who was going to arrest us? The elevator attendants? We couldn't run away anyway.

Of course, once we got to Geostationary, they could have the police waiting for us, but Dad didn't think that was likely. Geostationary wasn't signatory to the SuperNational Treaty and there wasn't any extradition from space. This was because the Loonies weren't willing to agree to it and Geostationary usually sided with Luna more than Earth. According to Weird, anyway.

But there were private security agents available for hire at Geostationary, and if Mom really wanted to make trouble for us, she could hire a couple of those guys to meet us. But what could they do? Could they force us to go back to Earth? Dad wasn't sure what might happen in that case.

Just to be safe, Dad said I should probably stay in the cabin anyway. So I glowered and sulked and tried on different angry faces. And then I got bored. And when I get bored, I get nasty. And when I get nasty, I get disgusting. Just to see how disgusting I can be.

It didn't take long. Dad got so disgusted watching me fart and belch and flick my boogers at the TV screen that he finally said, "Okay, Charles. You win. I can't stand it anymore." He muttered something about teaching hygiene to chimpanzees. Then he said I could go out and walk around again, but only if I promised to keep out of trouble.

It was probably the boogers that did it. Boogers always work. Adults can't stand boogers. They can't even stand the word "booger." Booger booger booger. I didn't even like it when Stinky flicked his boogers, so it was probably a lot worse for Dad when I did it. But it worked.

I went down to the bottom of the car and up to the top, with stops everywhere in-between, looking for a place where something interesting—anything—was happening.

Nothing was happening. Nothing. And more nothing on top of that. The only thing to do was wander around—which I was already pretty good at. Mom called it my "restless lion" prowl. She said all I needed was a dead antelope leg to drag around. Ha ha. That's a grownup joke, only funny to grownups, annoying to those carrying the burden of genetic progress. But at least there was more room to drag my antelope haunch in the whole elevator car than there was in the cabin. Up and down and all around. The only thing weird was that I didn't see Weird anywhere, but I wasn't really looking for him anyway, so I didn't think about it. He'd probably found a terminal somewhere and was redesigning someone's government or something.

So this was what I'd flicked all those boogers for. The big discovery: there isn't anything to do on an elevator. All elevators are the same. You watch the numbers. That's it.

It doesn't matter how pretty the numbers are presented, they're still numbers. You go down to the bottom level and look at the lights on the wire to see if the red one has gotten any farther out and it looks exactly the same. It's impossible to tell. So then, you go up to the top and get something to eat. And after that, you go down to the lounge and watch TV. But you can do that in your cabin, and at least in your cabin, you can choose what you want to watch. So you get up and walk around some more. You go upstairs, you go downstairs.

If you want, the attendants will take you on a tour of how everything works, only it's all the stuff you've already seen, and there isn't that much of it anyway, so out of total boredom, you go back and look out the windows again.

If you go up to the top level, you can see . . . the Line and the stars. The cable zips past at a thousand miles per hour, 1600 klicks. It's going so fast, you can't see any details on it at all, it's just a long shining bar of light that stretches up and away into nothing, like a big pointer into the night.

And everything else is stars—godzillions of them. Like God's dandruff on night's black velvet, or something like that. The higher you get, the darker the sky gets and the more stars there are to see. The top observation area is kept mostly unlit, except for tiny guide lights in the carpet, so your view isn't hampered by any glare. Up this high, the stars don't twinkle, so they look *different*.

Downstairs, the Line points straight down at the Earth; but it doesn't go all the way down, it just disappears into the distance again, so it looks like the elevator is hanging above the world, while this long bar of light drops away beneath you.

And every time you go downstairs to look, the Terminator Line has crept a little farther west across the world. And each time there's a little more world to see as more of it creeps up over the curving horizon. One half of the world glows with reflected sunlight. The other half is dark, speckled with little city lights.

But directly below us, the bright swirl of the hurricane covered everything like a big white eye glaring up at us. The hurricane was really pounding Terminus now. All the news reports were bad. The airport would be out of service for days, and they'd probably have to do a lot of track and highway repair too before anyone could get in or out.

It's supposed to be exciting, a trip up the elevator. But it isn't. Instead, time seems suspended. Everything looks motionless.

I was standing on the longest tightrope ever. A suspension bridge between a rock and a planet. Caught in the middle, between Mom and Dad, Weird and Stinky. Not a child, not an adult, but something in-between.

And all alone. More alone than ever.

DISTANCES

I WAS HEADING BACK TO THE CABIN when I bumped—literally—into J'mee running down the staircase. At first he didn't recognize me, because my head was shaved, but I grabbed his arm and said, "J'mee, hey! It's me, Charles! Where are you going?"

"Uh, nowhere—"

"Then why are you going so fast?"

J'mee looked annoyed. His face clouded. "That wasn't very nice, what you did." He pushed past me down to the lounge. I followed after.

"I'm sorry. Can we be friends again?"

"No. You're not a nice boy."

"Neither are you."

That stopped him. "Huh—?"

"You're not a boy."

"Huh? I'm not—" J'mee started to protest, saw it was useless, and gave it up as a bad effort. "I thought I fooled you."

"You almost did."

"How'd you figure it out?" she demanded.

"The way you changed clothes."

"You shouldn't be looking at other boys."

"You shouldn't be pretending to be one."

She turned away for a minute, staring out the window at the distant edge of sunset. Then she turned back abruptly "So why are you and your brothers and your dad running away?"

"Huh—? We're not running away. We're on vacation."

"Don't be stupid, Charles." She tapped her head. "Every time I meet someone, I do a net-search. My dad taught me where to look for all the really good stuff. It's the only way to be safe." She went blank for a moment. "You don't have to worry. They think you're still at One-Hour. They don't think you got out in time."

"Thanks, " I said. I didn't mean it. I didn't like her knowing so much about us.

"Your mom and dad are really screwed up, aren't they?" she said.

Well, yeah, they were, but I didn't want to say so. Not to her. Because they were still my mom and dad. "They're not that bad," I said. "Everybody has problems."

"Everybody has babies," she said. "Daddy says tube-town people have too many babies. That's why everybody has problems."

"Well, if no one had babies, then what?"

"Then maybe we wouldn't have so many people on the planet and things wouldn't be falling apart," she said. "Your mom didn't want to have babies. She wanted your dad to have them. She said that in an interview once. Want to hear more?"

"No," I said. I thought about telling her that she shouldn't be poking around in other people's privacy. It wasn't nice. But I didn't think it would stop her. So I didn't say anything.

"So why are you and your family running away?" I asked.

"We're not running away. We're just . . . moving." And then she added, "Daddy says it's not safe to be rich on Earth anymore. That's why we're moving someplace safe."

"So why do you have to pretend to be a boy?"

"Because it's a secret that we're leaving Earth."

"That's running away."

"No, it isn't."

"Fine. Have it your own way." That was how I usually ended arguments at home. "Why didn't you shave *all* your hair off?"

"I didn't want to. It looks . . . cheap."

"Didn't you see the show about shaving and microparticles and disease?"

"Oh, that. Yeah. Daddy says that's for other people. Not us."

"Oh." There wasn't anything else to say to that. At least nothing polite. I knew what my ethics teacher would have said to that. People who negotiate loopholes for themselves are criminals in training.

He said that most people see rules as some kind of burden that someone else makes them carry—like Mom or Dad—but the rules are really agreements that we make with each other on how to behave so we can all get along. And when we don't follow the rules, it's like breaking a promise to everybody at once. Break enough rules and nobody will trust you anymore.

But . . . he also said that there are people who have so much money that they can buy themselves exceptions from the rules. And that's dangerous, because if you get into the habit of always buying exceptions for yourself, you end up in a bubble with a wall of money between you and everyone else. You won't know how to connect to anyone and they won't know how to reach you. And all the folks around you will be more loyal to your money than to you.

That was what my teacher said, but I don't think anybody really believed him. Or cared. I think most of us would have liked to have had the chance to prove that we could handle the burden of money, that we would be different. I know I would. Yeah. Given the choice—living in a bubble of money or scrambling for credits in the Tube-Town—we knew what to choose. Poor and self-respecting is a highly overrated thrill.

But when J'mee said this—"Rules are for other people"— it made me see how big the difference between us really was. It made me queasy. Because all of a sudden I realized just how naked I really was.

So I just rubbed my head and said, "It's still a good disguise."

"No, it isn't," she said.

"Fine. Have it your way."

"Running away isn't fair to your mom, you know?"

"What do you know about it? You don't even have a mom!"

"I know about moms."

"You don't know my mom."

"I know she's the one who works the hardest. Your dad doesn't do anything."

"Yes, he does!" I knew she was right, but I wasn't going to let her be the expert on my family. Besides, if she was right . . . then we were wrong to be going up the Line. And even though the Line scared the yell out of me, I didn't want to go back either. Not after coming this far.

"I know that you're really hurting her."

"You don't know anything. You don't live with us."

She tapped her head. "I bet I know more about you and your family than you do."

"Oh, yeah—?"

"Yeah." She went blank for a moment, then came back and said, "Your mom and dad are divorced. Your dad filed for bankruptcy six weeks ago. Then he applied for an off-world emigration permit for himself and you and your brothers. His debts were paid off by a private debting company, conditional against a bid he has on file for indentured-service with the Sierra Colony." She went blank and came back again. "Your older brother applied to UCLA under a rechanneling contract, but it wasn't accepted. Your little brother takes medicine to keep him from wetting his bed, but it doesn't always work. And you—" She stopped.

"Go ahead—" I could feel my anger rising at this invasion of privacy, but I still had to hear what she knew.

"Your school record has a note in it that says that you're antisocial and you need emotional therapy." She looked at me with a smug superior expression. "Lots of flow-through kids need help." And then she added, "It's normal for poor kids." Like that excused it.

I stared at her, astonished. I'd never met any kid so . . .

spoiled. It was as if an enormous gulf had just opened up between us that could never be bridged again. I could feel my face getting redder and redder—and she just smiled at me like an arsenic-flavored princess.

I couldn't think of anything to say, so I just blurted, "You're a goddamned nasty little bitch." Then I left as quickly as I could.

THE ELEVATOR CLUB

WHEN I GOT BACK TO the cabin, all I wanted to do was think about the stuff that J'mee had said, but Stinky insisted on showing me all the tricks he'd taught his monkey. Stupid things—like crotch-grabbing and booger-flicking and pretending to fart and vomit and all the other stuff that little kids think is funny. I guess if I'd been in the mood, I might have thought it was funny, but I wasn't in the mood and I thought it was stupid and annoying. And when I said so, Stinky just looked up at me and said, "You sound like a grownup," which was probably the nastiest thing of all he could have said. If this was what it was like to be a grownup, permanently angry, perhaps I should just open a window and jump out now.

Instead, I turned on the television.

Maybe I didn't really want to think about it at all. What J'mee had said was worse than nasty. It was true.

I flung myself into a chair and flipped through the channels, looking at the views from all the different observatories all up and down the Line, but not really seeing any of them. There were also telescopes mounted in the bottom of the car that you could control yourself to look at anything you wanted, so I was playing with the view from one of those for a while, looking straight down the cable. At full magnification, I could see the next car, 250 miles below, very clearly. It was racing up toward us at incredible speed, but never gaining.

The views of the Earth were also pretty spectacular. We were high enough now that I could see El Paso from the air. I tried to spot our tube-town, only it was off toward the side, not quite around the curve of the planet, but far enough to make the angle tricky, and I couldn't be sure which one it was anyway. They all looked alike from here, and the atmosphere made everything fuzzy and twinkly, even with digital correction. I did spot the meteor crater again. That was easier. You tell the telescope what to look for and it just slides across the landscape to the target. From here, the Barringer crater looked like a big dimple in the ground. It was even farther away than El Paso and even farther around the curvature of the Earth, but it was big enough to be clear despite any atmospheric interference.

Finally, Dad looked up from the papers he was working on and said, "All right, Chigger, what is it?"

"Nothing," I said.

"No, it *is* not nothing. The way you're clicking through channels—"

"I hate being poor," I said.

"We're not poor."

"Then why did you file for bankruptcy?"

He was silent for a beat. "How did you find that out?"

"It doesn't matter. I found out."

"Your mother, right?"

I didn't want to tell him about J'mee and everything she'd said—he'd probably just get mad at me, even though I hadn't done anything. J'mee was wrong about us anyway. I didn't need help. I was fine. If people would just leave me alone. Once we got to Geosynchronous, this whole adventure would be over anyway and we'd all go home—except Dad, so it didn't matter, did it? And I really didn't need to have another one of those "sympathetic conversations"—not now, not ever, and certainly not with Dad. So instead I just said what

I was feeling. "Screw the moon. This is another one of your good ideas that didn't happen."

"Chigger—"

"Dad, why couldn't you just take us to Disneyland and leave us alone? I don't want any more of your good intentions—"

The argument was just getting warmed up when Weird walked in, looking weirder than usual. Even for Weird. He looked flushed and upset and scared, but he also looked excited about something—kind of like the time he got off the roller coaster and discovered he'd crapped his pants. He looked at both of us, then retreated hastily to the bathroom without saying a word.

Dad looked at me—looked at the bathroom—then looked back at me. "We'll talk about this later." He went and knocked softly on the bathroom door. "Douglas? Are you all right?"

The reply came back muffled. "Yes. No."

"Do you want to talk about it, Douglas?"

The bathroom door opened and Douglas stepped back into the cabin. He looked from Dad to me, then back to Dad again, decided it didn't matter, gulped, and nodded. He couldn't even talk. He managed to blurt, "I just joined the Elevator Club."

Elevator Club—?! Huh? I wondered who the unlucky girl was.

Stinky was already demanding—"What's the Elevator Club? I wanna join too!"

I stared at Douglas in amazement—suddenly realizing that my big brother had crossed a line, and even though he was still my big brother, he was finally and irrevocably a grownup too. He finally had the secret handshake. Bobby and I were still children. I turned to Bobby and said very calmly, "You have to be eighteen to join. It's like a driver's license. I can't join either."

Dad gave me a surprised and appreciative glance. "Thank you, Charles," he said. He patted Douglas on the shoulder. "You want to talk privately?" Douglas nodded and Dad steered him back into the bathroom and shut the door behind them. I thought I heard Douglas stifle a sob, but I couldn't be sure.

After they were gone, Stinky looked at me. "Well, what kind of a club is it—?"

"It's a secret. You have to be eighteen."

"Well, what do they do that's so secret?"

"That's the secret."

"But that's not fair!"

I shrugged. "You're finally starting to get it, Bobby. Nothing is fair. Grownups make the rules—and they make them for grownups, not for kids. And that's the way things are."

"When I'm a grownup, I'm not gonna be like that."

"Oh, yes you will. So will I."

"No, I won't—"

"Yeah, you will, and I'll tell you why: because when you're a grownup, you'll have waited all your life for your chance to make your own rules, and you aren't going to give it up when you get it. Nobody does."

"It's still not fair."

"Yes, it is," I said, and all of a sudden, I could see Dad and Douglas's point of view a lot clearer than I could see Bobby's. I wondered if that grownup thing was starting to happen to me. It's that thing that Dad is always talking about. Personal responsibility. Was this what it felt like? I said a bad word.

"Umm," said Bobby. "I'm gonna tell."

"Go ahead. I don't care. Maybe I'll even tell Dad myself."

Dad and Douglas were in the bathroom for a long time, and when they came out, neither of them looked like anything had been settled—but they were smiling, so at least I knew they were talking to each other again, and that was something.

But it still didn't solve anything.

DINNER

SEÑOR DINGILLIAN?"

Dad turned around to see who had called his name. We all did. At first, none of us recognized him—he was as shaven as we were—but then Dad said, "*Señor* Hidalgo, how are you?" and I recognized him as the fat man from the train. He strode over and pumped Dad's hand enthusiastically, as if they were old friends. "You have become quite famous, no?"

Dad looked worried, but *Señor* Hidalgo reassured him quickly. "Oh, please, sir, have no worries. I don't think anyone else knows who you are. I only found out by accident myself. And even if anyone else on the car is aware of your . . . ah, circumstance, I wouldn't fear. Here, come sit with me—" He indicated a booth in the corner.

Dad tried to beg off, but *Señor* Hidalgo insisted, and he had a firm grip on Dad's arm. "*Señor* Hidalgo—"

"*Doctor* Hidalgo," he corrected. "Doctor of Political Science."

"Since when is politics a science?" Weird asked.

Hidalgo laughed. "I've often wondered the same thing myself. Here, you sit next to me, *muchacho*. Roberto, correct? No? Bobby, *sí*. And you are Charles, yes? And of course, this handsome young man, so tall and skinny, must be Douglas. You have fine sons, *Señor* Dingillian. I know of your work, of course. You didn't know you were world famous, did you? But the set of recordings you did of ancient Inca music was quite wonderful. I always meant to write you and tell you, but I never found the time. Tell me, do you still work with the Columbia Jazz Quartet? *The Coltrane Suite* remains one of my favorite recordings. Let me buy you dinner. I want to talk with you, if you don't mind."

Huh—? I wanted to ask Dad about that last part, but there wasn't time. Dad shrugged off Señor Doctor Hidalgo's inquiries with noncommittal answers, but I could see him mentally counting his pennies. Despite the wad of cash he was carrying, he had to be worried about expenses. He accepted with a nod and dropped into a chair, but not before turning to the rest of us and cautioning us not to eat like pigs, we were guests.

"Don't be silly, *Señor* Dingillian. You are my guests. Order anything you like. I'm not paying for it anyway. I will charge it to, let me see . . ." He pawed through a fistful of credit cards. "Ah, here we are. These people owe me many favors. And I owe them nothing. They shall pay for your dinner tonight." In explanation, he added, "I have many sponsors. Politics costs money—especially when you are on the side of the poor. The rich can buy as many politicians as they want; the poor have only the leftovers and the cast-offs." He laughed, as if this were funny. "Nevertheless, do let me recommend the ceviche. Or the conch. The fish farms are quite good on the Line. Don't look so surprised, young Charles. Do you think that all that water just sits and waits. No, the Line engineers put it to work. Everything works— or it gets tossed over the side. No, no, that's a joke, don't mind me. I have been sampling the excellent wines. No, the Line does not produce its own wine yet, but the vineyards have been designed, and someday they will be built, have no fear. Have you ever had fresh lobster? I'll bet you haven't. Let me recommend the lobster as an entree. Someone has to eat it, son—the more those arthropods travel, the more expensive they get; so eat it now while my sponsors can still afford it. And you, Douglas——?"

After a while, Dad finally interrupted. "Your courtesy is welcome, Dr. Hidalgo, but you barely know us. I can't help but wonder——"

"Forgive an old man his vanities——"

"You're not that old," Dad said.

"Old enough to be working on my second bottle of Tabasco," Hidalgo said. "You don't believe me? Cut me in half and count the rings. I'm old enough to have seen *Lucy* first-run——"

Weird shook his head. "Now I know you're teasing us, Dr. Hidalgo. Lucy was born before the First American Civil War."

"Ahh, the *first* Lucy—I was thinking of the second one. And you're thinking of the Second American Civil War. But yes, you're right, I'm not quite that old, but almost. Nevertheless, please accept my hospitality. I have no one else to share my table—now, let's have a look at this menu and see if they have an old-fashioned chocolate soda for Roberto here. You do like chocolate, don't you? I'm sure you do not get very much of the real thing. It's quite expensive, you know. Trust me, the chocolate sodas here are very very good."

Dad was curious about Dr. Hidalgo's intentions, and some of his impatience was starting to show, but the old man just kept chattering away about inconsequential things, refusing to let politics—or anything else—interfere with a good dinner. And it was a good dinner. There were things on the menu I couldn't even pronounce, but the *Señor* Doctor ordered them anyway, and when the waiter put the plates in front of us, they looked and smelled delicious, and tasted even better than that. So for a while I didn't care what Dr. Hidalgo wanted. I was too busy eating. And Dad too, finally gave in to the inevitable and ordered himself a steak so thick you could have insulated a wall with it.

For dessert, the waiter rolled a big cart up to the table, covered with cakes and puddings and things even Dad didn't recognize. I'd never seen so many different kinds of fruits in one place before in my life. And chocolate! I mean, *real* chocolate! Stinky's eyes went as wide as saucers, and I guess mine did too, and I think for the first time, I began to realize just how much we didn't know—*and* how poor we really were.

I didn't know what to pick, and even Stinky and Weird were overawed, because everything looked too good to eat. Weird actually smiled at me. It made him look almost human. All three of us—four, counting Dad—stared at all the desserts so long that Doctor Hidalgo just started pointing and ordering. "Apparently, the boys cannot make up their minds, and neither can I. So we'll have it all. Just the best. We'll start with some of those fat red strawberries in cream and definitely the fresh grapes on a bed of thick rice pudding—and a big slice of the Chocolate Death, *por favor*, we shall all share that. Bring extra forks. And, oh my, the spiced peaches and mangoes also look very good tonight, and so do the raspberries and kiwis; is that coconut sprinkled on top? *Bueno! Un poquito más*, don't be stingy. And some of that delicious pineapple trifle as well, please. We'll have a taste of everything. Oh, and two cups of your most dangerous Kona espresso."

"Doctor Hidalgo—" Dad began slowly, "I appreciate your generosity, almost as much as my boys do, I'm sure, but it makes me very uncomfortable—as if you're trying to get to me through my sons."

Hidalgo wiped his mouth with his napkin. "Ahh, *Señor* Dingillian, a thousand apologies. Sometimes my generosity overwhelms people. I am used to giving. Sometimes I forget that other people are not used to receiving. I meant no offense. I only wanted to share some time with you—a man so committed to his sons that he will risk his freedom for them. I think I understand your situation, sir. And I think I might be able to help you. Conversely, you might be of some use to my people too."

Dad shook his head. "I'd prefer not to get involved, sir. Fame is a terrible mistress. She takes a great deal and gives very little in return."

"Ahh, very true, very true. Nevertheless, you are already famous. Twice over, indeed. And it is the foolish man who doesn't use every opportunity he has. Fame can be useful, sir. If you don't take charge of your own—how shall I say it?—your own 'reputation' in the media, I am sure that your wife, or her lawyers, will certainly take charge of it for you. It is a matter of publicity, and in your situation, you are probably going to need some useful friends, *comprende?*"

Dad sighed. "Doctor Hidalgo—"

"Please, call me Bolivar. Or Bollie. We have broken bread together." He waved at the table. "A great deal of it, indeed."

"Doctor Hidalgo—" Dad tried again. "I'm grateful for your hospitality, but—"

"You have not heard me out, *Señor* Dingillian. Please—you have enjoyed my hospitality, you owe me a bit of your time, don't you think? *Por favor?*" Dad looked unconvinced. "Are you in a hurry? Do you have someplace to go, something better to do . . . ?"

Dad sat back down again. "All right," he said. "I'll listen. But I want you to understand something first. I'm *not* kidnapping my children. I'm giving them the choice that their mother tried to deny them."

"Yes, I'm certain that's what it looks like to you, and I'm not so big a fool as I seem, that I would try to argue that with you. And that is not the discussion I want to have with you anyway."

"Oh?"

"Do you like money, *Señor* Dingillian? *Sí? Bueno.* Everyone does. Money is like gravity. When you have enough of it, it draws more money to it, increasing its gravity even more. When you have too much money—*is* there such a thing as *too much* money? The SuperNationals don't think so—but when you have too much money in one place, it stretches the fabric of the universe like a great black hole, sinking deeper and deeper into itself. Nothing escapes, not even light. If a black hole is an astrophysicist's nightmare, then a SuperNational corporation is an economist's nightmare. The money flows into it, nothing comes back. We don't even know where the money has gone. It leaves no trace of its passage, *nothing comes back*—not even light. Did the money pass through Atlantis or Oceania? Did it leave the planet? Where did it go? Who knows?" Hidalgo sat back in his chair comfortably; he held up a hand for patience, while he stifled a belch. Even with the napkin in front of his face, it was impressive. Stinky and I looked at each other and giggled.

"A *nine!*" whispered Stinky.

"Nine point five," I whispered back.

Dad glared. We both shut up.

Hidalgo glanced around the table. "Would any of you like anything more? No? You do not eat enough, *Roberto y Carlito*. You will never grow as big as me unless you practice your eating. But getting back to my point, *Señor* Dingillian, money is neither good nor evil—but it can be dangerous. Because money does what money wants. Money goes where money wants to go. And money doesn't care who it rolls over. It just wants to collect itself—like I said, like gravity. You should respect money; you should never get in its way. Unless you have a big enough bucket. Do you?"

Dad started to answer, but Hidalgo patted his hand and stopped him. "Never mind. I have no right to ask that question. But the answer is the same for everyone: 'Not as big as I'd like.' But if the bucket is big enough to take care of your children, then you are truly a wealthy man." He looked around at us. "Clearly, you have done well with your young men. I am envious. You should be proud of them." Hidalgo wiped his mouth again and conveniently looked at his watch.

"Oh, *Madre de Dios*, look at the time. I have a very important conference call that I must be a part of. *Muy importante*. It starts in five minutes. I must rush. Thank you so much for your company tonight, all of you—you have been very kind to an old man, listening to me prattle on like a teacher in search of a classroom. No, no, sit down, finish your desserts. Do not leave the table until all of these plates are clean—" He shook hands all around. "I shall see you again before we reach our destination, I'm sure of it. *Señor* Dingillian, we still have much to talk about. Let us connect with each other tomorrow. For breakfast, perhaps? Or lunch? Please. Your company has been most gracious. *Au revoir*."

Douglas giggled. *"Au revoir—?"*

Dad smiled. "Perhaps he forgot he was supposed to be Spanish." He glanced at his own watch. "That certainly was a convenient departure on his part. Just when he was getting to the punch line."

"Do you think he timed it that way?" Douglas asked.

"I think *Señor* Doctor Hidalgo is way too good a snake-oil salesman to leave anything to chance. Yes, I think he timed it that way."

"Snake oil?" Stinky asked.

"It's what you buy when your snake gets squeaky," I said, wondering what it really meant. Mostly, it meant another trip to the dictionary.

"Right," said Dad, heaving himself up from the table with a grunt. "And right now, it's time to get our squeakiest snake into bed—"

DECISIONS

LATER, AFTER STINKY HAD FINALLY fallen asleep, the three of us sat around and talked about Doctor Hidalgo and what he might want. Dad had no idea, but he was sure that the old man wanted something. "No one spends five thousand on dinner without expecting at least a good-night kiss." We all laughed at that. Even I understood the joke.

"Hey, it was good food, and the conversation was interesting—if a little one-sided," Dad concluded.

"I bet he could be a great baritone, if he wanted," Douglas said. "I've never seen anyone go that long without taking a breath."

"I didn't know there were so many different kinds of dessert," I said.

"Yeah, well—don't get used to it," Douglas sounded like a grownup. He turned to Dad. "Are you going to tell him?"

Dad looked suddenly serious. But he didn't look old anymore. He looked *relaxed*. Sort of. He nodded and turned to me. "It's like this, Charles. Douglas isn't going back to Earth."

"Huh? What?" I looked to Douglas, dismayed.

"I'm going with Dad. To the moon," he said. "And beyond."

I shook my head. "Yeah—? And what about Mom? What if she has the cops looking for us at Geosynchronous?"

Dad shook his head. "Earthside jurisdiction doesn't apply. As indentured colonists, we're the property of the corporation. If I haven't broken any starside laws, they can't touch me. I checked it out before we left, Charles. As long as we have a valid contract, we're safe."

It sounded too easy, but maybe—I didn't know. There was too much happening for me to figure out. "I don't get it. I thought you said this was a stupid idea."

"Yeah, but staying is stupider. For me, anyway."

"Why?" I demanded.

"It's about my scholarship," Douglas said. "I'm not going to get it."

"I know."

"How do you know?"

"Same way I know about the cops. A kid with a wire and a big mouth."

"Do you know why?" He took a deep breath. "They don't give you the scholarship if you don't need rechanneling."

"Oh," I said. And then, *"Oh!"*

"It was Mickey," Douglas said.

Mickey? The elevator attendant?! For a moment, I didn't know what to feel. Angry. Or jealous. Or hurt. Or curious. Or just disgusted. While I hadn't been looking, Douglas really had turned into a grownup.

I didn't know what to say, so I said something I'd never said to him before. At least not like this. "I'm sorry, Douglas."

He reached over and put his hand on mine. "There's nothing to be sorry about, Chigger. This is how things turned out."

"I know, but—you wanted to go to UCLA."

"There are good schools in the outbeyond."

"Yeah, but you said it would be slavery—" I shut up. I had the feeling that I didn't know what I was talking about anymore.

"It's an economic decision. You sell what you have. If

you don't have anything to sell, you sell who you are. It's only seven years, Chigger. And then I'll be a free man on a new world." He sounded resigned. As if he hadn't finished convincing himself. "And it's not like the old kind of slavery. It's not—not really."

He sounded more like a grownup than I'd ever heard him sound before. I didn't like it very much. It made me feel abandoned, sort of. More alone than before—like someone had taken away my security. Again.

Now, Dad spoke up. "You know what the joke is, Charles? I'd asked Douglas to come with me to the outbeyond, because I wanted him to have the chance at a life *without* rechannelling. Now—it turns out that it doesn't matter. But it's still a good choice, Charles—I think it's one that will work out all right for him in the long run."

"Yeah," I said, "I sort of see the joke. And I sort of understand. But what about me and Stinky? What happens to us?"

"I really wish you wouldn't call your brother that," Dad said, but that wasn't what he really wanted to say. He tried to run his hand through his hair, he only ended up brushing his near-naked scalp. He looked annoyed, sighed, and started again. "You see, Charles, here's the thing—I was pretty sure that Douglas wasn't going to want to come with me. He'd made that clear back in Mexico. So I'd been counting on him to take you and Bobby back to Earth. That is, if you didn't want to come any farther with me. Now that he's decided to go on, that puts the responsibility on you. Do you want to go back? Or do you want to come with us?"

"But what about Sti—Bobby?"

"First we need to know what *you* want to do."

"If I go back, I'll be living with Mom again, won't I?"

"Your mother is a good woman," Dad said, but he didn't sound like he believed it.

"Oh, yeah," I said. "She's good enough for me to live with, but not good enough for you."

"Point taken," Dad said.

"And if I go with you—"

"When I put my name in the registry, I also put your name in, as a possible. And Douglas and Bobby too. So far, we have one bid from the Sierra Corporation. That's not too bad. But I haven't accepted it yet; I'm waiting to see who else bids. Then we'll pick the best. I'm more valuable if I bring sons, but it'll be your choice to come with me."

"What if nobody else bids?"

"Then we go with Sierra. I'll accept the bid before we disembark."

"What if we don't like the Sierra contract?"

"I took out an insurance policy against that. We're guaranteed a suitable bid or our passage home."

"Oh," I said.

"So you don't have to let that influence your decision."

"But it does," I said. "This really is a Magical Mystery Tour, isn't it?" Just like you said—we're not going to know where we're going until we get there."

"So you're coming?"

I shrugged. "What's to go back to?"

"You know that I'm breaking the law if I try to take you against your will."

"You've already broken the law, Dad."

He nodded. "Consider it a measure of how much I love you."

DECISIONS POSTPONED

WHEN YOU'RE A KID, YOU just keep on going like you're going to be a kid forever. And every time someone calls you young man or young adult or talks about grownup responsibilities, you just blink and wonder what they're talking about. How can a kid make that kind of decision? But that's what Dad was asking me to do now.

Would the grownup I was going to become feel that I had done the right thing? Or would he hate me for condemning him to whatever bad consequences came of this decision? What was I supposed to choose here?

Weird tried to help. In his clumsy way. He punched up some programs on the TV to give me an idea of what the options were.

One program was about the different colonies. What it was like to live and work there. None of the colonies really looked like a fun place to live—they were either too hot or too cold. The sky was the wrong color on all of them. And none of the colony planets had any life at all, except what you brought with you and grew in your own indoor farms.

What was true about all of them was that it took a lot of work just to stay alive. *Hard* work.

On the other hand, none of the colonies had seventeen billion people all competing for the same jobs and the same houses and the same mouthfuls of food. The per capita comparisons were astonishing. Dad said that on Earth the chances of becoming a millionaire were one in seventeen million. On any of the colonies, right now, the chances were one in twenty. All you had to do was survive.

"Why don't they use robots?" I asked.

"They do," Dad said. "But robots can't do it all. They need people to do the hard part—make decisions and babies. In that order."

"But Douglas can't make babies—"

"Yes, I can," said Douglas. "It's the how that's different."

I shook my head. I didn't want to argue about that stuff.

"Look, kiddo," Dad said. "The human race has eaten the Earth. We're walking an ecological tightrope. A crop failure here, a plague there, a war somewhere else—and every time the system collapses a little bit more, we patch it up somehow and keep on going for a little bit longer. We add a few more mechanisms around the edges to help keep it from collapsing quite the same way the next time, but the basic inequilibrium just keeps on going. The whole thing is staggering like a drunken sailor—sooner or later he's going to fall down. It's not a question of *if;* it's a question of *when.* There are sixteen billion people too many on the planet and there's no telling how long that condition can be sustained. But whether it's sustained or whether it collapses, either way, most of those people aren't going to have the kind of freedom in their lives that you can have out in the colonies. The freedom to design your own possibilities."

"We have freedom—" I started to say.

"No." Dad shook his head. "We don't have freedom. The only freedom you have is inside your head, and there's not too much of that left anymore. We *can't* have freedom the way Earth is presently constituted. If freedom is the ability to swing your fist, there are seventeen billion places on Earth where your freedom stops. In order to keep all of those people alive, we've sacrificed all kinds of individual liberties—

including the right to be who you want to be. The more people you have, the more accommodations you have to make to society. But good grief, Charles! What do you think my argument with Douglas was all about? It wasn't about what he would be—it was about the fact that he was being *pushed* into it. And someday, you're going to be pushed in that same direction. And Bobby too. That's when I started thinking about getting you boys offworld somehow. Someplace where you wouldn't have to make any concessions or accommodations to anyone else."

"What about loyalty to the community and the other stuff like that?"

"All that stuff they teach you in school?" He snorted. "They *have* to teach you that, Charles—their job is to make you fit in. But loyalty to the community means one thing when the community is seventeen thousand people and quite another thing when it's seventeen billion. The global community is too vast, Chigger. It's out of control. Who do you think goes out to the stars? People who are satisfied with the way things are? Or people who are so dissatisfied with the constraints on their lives that they're willing to put up with colossal hardship so they can have a chance at something better?"

For the first time in a long time, Dad sounded like he cared about something. But I still wasn't sure.

I think Dad could see it on my face, because he stopped himself and said, "Think about this another way. Where do you think you'll be in five years? In ten years? In fifteen years? What is it you want to do most? More than anything else in the world—this world or any other? What do *you* want, Charles?"

"I don't know—" I started to say, but then I saw the look in his eyes, the desperate look that I hadn't seen since the day he'd moved out of the house and tried to say good-bye to us kids. I hadn't said to him then what I'd wanted to say ever since. I almost said it now. But I swallowed hard and looked away. My throat was starting to hurt. Kids don't know how to think about these things or make these kinds of choices. Why do grownups push us into these conversations? Finally, I just blurted, "I just want to be someplace where people treat each other nice. Whatever that's like."

"That's a good wish, Chigger." He put his hand on my shoulder. "I want the same thing too. Especially for you. Because you're the only son I've got who loves the music as much as I do."

I turned around and stared at him. I never knew he'd noticed.

"I see you with the earphones pressed to your head. I notice what you're listening to. I'd love to talk to you about the music, the way we used to. But there's this wall between us now. Just know that I love you, Charles. I want you to have the best life you can. Please don't hate me so much. I'm trying so hard—"

That did it. The tears flooded up into my eyes and I fell into his arms, sobbing. And I finally said it, after all these years: "Daddy, please don't leave me. I'll be good. Please don't leave me again!"

He held me for a long time, and finally he whispered into my ear, "I want to be here for you, son. I really do. Just please give me a chance."

I wanted to say yes to that. I really did. But I couldn't. Not yet. First I had to know that this time wasn't like all the other times.

INTROSPECTION

IT WASN'T JUST A CHOICE between Earth and the stars, because that's a no-brainer. That part was easy. The hard part was that Dad was asking us to choose between him and Mom.

Mom wasn't bad. She was just angry all the time. And if we went back, things wouldn't be much different—just more of the same, probably worse. Like that time I stayed out in the hills too late. I was afraid to go home because I knew I'd get yelled at for not coming home, but I didn't want to get yelled at, so I stayed where I was, but I knew I'd have to go home sometime, and the later I stayed the worse the inevitable yelling would be. So I only stayed out until hunger and cold outweighed my fear. This time, though, the yelling would go on forever. I could hear Mom already. It'd be like that phone call, only I wouldn't be able to switch her off.

One thing I knew: me and Weird and Stinky, we were a family, no matter what. We had to stay together. Except that Weird wasn't going to go back, and Bobby couldn't go back by himself—so it was sort of up to me to decide what was right for both of us.

And if I went back without either Bobby or Douglas, or

without both of them, what would Mom say? She'd probably blame me. She'd bawl me out three times over, once for me and once each for Bobby and Douglas. And I'd probably have to listen to all the stuff she wanted to tell Dad as well, except he wouldn't be there to listen, so I'd have to stand in for him too.

And I really didn't want to listen to any more of her angry rants about Dad—or anyone. I was getting awfully tired of all the ranting, no matter who it came from. And that was sort of what clinched it for me. I could think of all the reasons why I shouldn't go with Dad, but I couldn't think of any reasons why I should go back to Mom.

But even if I could sort everything else out, there was still the fact that in my own way I *did* love Mom, and if I was never going to see her again I was going to miss her badly. This was going to hurt. A lot. And probably in ways that I still hadn't realized yet. There were a lot of good things about Mom: the way she made spaghetti and the way she laughed when one of us kids said something really funny and the way she said "attaboy" when one of us did something good. Dad was right, Mom wasn't a bad person, and we shouldn't think of her that way—even if it would make leaving easier. Because we'd probably end up feeling a lot worse in the long run.

I guess what I really wanted was just to be able to say good-bye to her. And have her say it was all right for me to go. Except I knew she would never say that. So I couldn't say good-bye to her, could I? And that was the part that really hurt. Because I would be trading the part of me that was incomplete about Dad leaving for a new part that would be incomplete about *me* leaving.

And that brought me back to that same old thing again, the one that *always* bothered me—how do grownups deal with this stuff? From the evidence, not very well.

Grownups are supposed to be able to think things out so that they can always do the right thing. But the more I thought about this, the harder it all became.

Maybe nobody ever really grew up at all. Only their bodies. But inside, they were all still as spoiled and whiny as Stinky.

What I wanted to do was get on my bike and ride out to the hills to one of my thinking places, where I could just sit and look at stuff and listen to my music and watch the sun edging toward the western hills. That's the other problem with elevators. You can't get out and take a walk when you need to.

So I went downstairs and stood on the scale again to see how much I weighed now. Not as much as before. Less than thirty kilos already.

While I was standing on the scale, staring at the numbers, not really seeing them, Mickey came by and saw me. "You okay, Charles?" he asked.

"Yeah," I grunted, not really wanting to talk to him. I didn't know how to treat him anymore.

"Something the matter?"

"Yeah. You. Why'd you have to go and . . . you know, with my brother?"

Mickey squatted down to look me in the eye. "That's between him and me, kiddo."

"Well, maybe you think so. But I think it's really screwed up my family."

"It has, huh?"

"Yeah."

He gave me a sad thoughtful look. "And your family wasn't screwed up at all before . . . ?"

The way he said it, I had to smile. "Well, only a little," I admitted. And then I added, "But now it's worse. My mom has called the cops on us."

"Yeah, I know." To my surprised look, he said, "Do you think I don't care what happens to you guys?"

"Are they going to stop us?"

"Not if you have a valid contract, they can't. Did your Dad accept the Sierra bid yet?"

"He's waiting to see if anything better comes in."

"You'd better tell him to accept it quickly. He's not likely to get anything better. And if he doesn't get a signed paper by the time we hit topside, well . . . it might be a problem."

"What kind of problem?"

"I'm not . . . really sure." Mickey looked troubled. "Y'know, I should make a call and see. I know some people—"

"Would you?" I must have asked a little too quickly.

He looked at me. "I can't make any promises."

"I know—but it's awfully important to my dad. And Douglas."

"Are you thinking about going to the outbeyond with them?"

"I don't know. Maybe. Have you ever been outbeyond?"

"Not yet—but I've been thinking about it. There's a couple of places I'd like to see."

"What do you know about the colonies?"

He shrugged. "Same as you. Whatever there is to know. Some are good. Some aren't. Sierra is supposed to be good. You could do worse."

I studied his face. "So, do you think I should go?"

"Mmm." He considered it. "It has to be *your* decision, Charles. But yes, since you ask me, I think it would be good for you. For all of you." Abruptly, he glanced at his watch. "Listen, it's getting late, and I've got rounds to make. You'd better get back. We're going to start spinning the cabin soon. You tell your dad what I said, about Sierra, okay?"

"Okay. And thanks, Mickey."

"You're welcome, Charles."

MORNING

WHEN WE WOKE UP IN the morning, the gravity was completely sideways. Except it wasn't gravity—it was centrifugal force. We were so high, the pull of the Earth was insignificant. Sometime during the night, they had spun the car on its vertical axis, enough to give the feeling of one-third gravity. We all wanted to see how high we could jump, but after Stinky bumped his head, Dad told us to stop, so we did—at least while he was watching. Instead we practiced walking back and forth for a while. It felt funny to be that light.

Of course, there was a video about it. You couldn't pour a cup of coffee because it would take forever to pour. And if you took a shower, the water would splatter and bounce every which way, and the shower would take an hour to drain. That sounded like fun, but the video showed that it would also be very hard to dry off, and possibly dangerous. You could drown.

And even if you weren't trying to pour a cup of coffee or take a shower, it would still be dangerous—not being used to micro-gravity, you could bounce off the walls or the ceiling every time you took a step. And trying to get upstairs or downstairs would be a nightmare. People would get hurt.

The door we had come in by was now on the ceiling—"How're we going to get out?" wailed Stinky. Weird went to one of the side walls and opened a circular hatch. Last night it was locked, because it would have opened onto a vertical shaft; but now it was a horizontal corridor so we could walk the length of the car—except Dad wanted us to stay in the cabin. He had an unhappy expression and I wanted to ask him if he'd accepted the Sierra bid, but before I could, the door chimed and Mickey arrived with our breakfast trays.

He didn't say much; he just laid out everything on the table and then left quietly. He looked grim. Dad eyed him warily. Douglas looked like he wanted to say something. I was hoping someone would say something—but nobody did. Mickey was as carefully noncommittal as if the room was bugged. Only Stinky, who didn't know better, was in an insufferably cheerful mood, asking questions about everything. I would have happily strangled him. I'd been thinking about strangling him all my life. This morning seemed like a good opportunity, especially when he asked Mickey about how the room had turned sideways overnight. So of course Mickey took the time to answer him. Finally, though, he said, "I have other people to take care of. Maybe you should ask your big brother. He knows a lot about how the elevator works too."

Mickey left and we all just looked at each other. Then we sat down and ate without really tasting—which was just as well. The food had apparently gone tasteless.

Hurricane Charles was all over the news. The winds were still too high for the cleanup and the rescue crews to go in, and there had been a lot more damage at Terminus than they'd expected. They were already calling this the hurricane of the century. They expected Line traffic to be disrupted for weeks. There wasn't even going to be enough room to stash all the cargo that was still arriving downside, let alone the passengers returning to Earth. And this would certainly cripple the relief efforts in Africa and Asia. I was glad we weren't dropping back down into that mess. The pictures were awful.

While we were watching, the door chimed—at first we thought it might be Mickey, but it was *Señor* Doctor Hidalgo. The fat man. The nine point five. He looked flushed and impatient. "*Señor* Dingillian, I apologize for interrupting your morning, but I must speak with you. I had hoped to see you at breakfast, but that did not happen. The attendant told me that you were keeping to your cabin—good morning, *muchachos. Buenos días.* Please, may I come in?"

Dad let him in and offered him a seat. "Would you like some tea, coffee? Something to drink? We have a bar."

"No, no—*muchas gracias*, anyway. I appreciate the thought. But you cannot afford to feed me or give me drinks in the style to which I have become accustomed. Even I cannot afford the style to which I have become accustomed. Never mind that—we must talk frankly. Can you send the boys out?"

"Out where——?"

"Yes, there is that. I cannot ask them to wait in the bathroom, can I? Very well then, I shall have to speak candidly in front of your sons. May I?" He pushed Stinky's monkey out of the way and sat down on the couch. He sank down into it, although he didn't sink as far as he would have the night before. Even in micro-gravity, he was still heavy. Dad sat down in the chair opposite him. I noticed he didn't sit too close.

"Please forgive my bluntness, *Señor* Dingillian. There isn't much time—I had hoped to be more circumspect, more gentle. I hope you will forgive me, this is not the way I normally handle affairs of this significance, but things are happening—things that mostly do not concern you—but unfortunately you have inadvertently become part of a larger equation. Events are moving in several different directions at once and I have no idea how all the different crises will resolve, if they will resolve at all. It would take far too long to explain—but the point is, sir, the people I work for know that you are carrying something of some importance. These people would be willing to pay you very handsomely—much more than your present employers—for the package. Two times, three times as much. Plus whatever other protections you need. Perhaps even, a guaranteed colony berth . . . ?"

Douglas and I exchanged looks. I grabbed Stinky—and the monkey—and dragged them both toward the bathroom. "Come on, monster, I've got this neat trick we can teach the monkey. You're going to love this one—it'll make all the girls scream."

"No!" screamed Stinky. "I wanna stay with Daddy!"

"Charles—" Dad held up his hand. "I appreciate your intentions. It's all right. I'd just as soon have you stay." Dad stood up. "Thank you for coming by, Doctor Hidalgo. I appreciate all your courtesies." He offered his hand—whether to shake Dr. Hidalgo's hand or help him out of the couch, I wasn't sure. Dr. Hidalgo took the hint and levered himself up to his feet.

"I am very sorry you feel that way—I had hoped we could negotiate."

"There's nothing to negotiate. I don't know who you're working for, and I don't much care. I'm not carrying anything. And I'm offended at your offer. I'm not the kind of person who sells property that is not his to sell."

Hidalgo sighed. "Yes, I see. Of course. In that case, I must tell you—please do not take this the wrong way, I am not threatening, but I mean this in the sincerest sense—I am seriously worried about what will happen next. I told you about the money. Money does what it wants. Money buys whatever it has to. I am afraid that the money will try to stop you, may even try to hurt you or your sons. They told me that if you would not sell it—whatever it is, you know, they know, I don't know what it is—but if you will not sell it, they will have to try other ways to prevent its delivery, and I do not want to see you hurt, or the boys. Please reconsider—I will be available to you, wherever you are. If there is anything that I can do to help you, I would consider it an honor and a privilege to be of service—"

Dad was standing at the door, holding it open for Dr. Hidalgo. I sort of felt sorry for him, for both of them. I'd never seen Dad looking so grim. I know it hurt him to behave rudely toward anyone.

"We have nothing else to talk about, Doctor Hidalgo. Thank you for your courtesy and your concern. Now please go."

Dr. Hidalgo looked like he wanted to say something more, his mouth opened and closed a couple of times, but no words came out. He looked very upset, like he was going to have to go tell someone some very bad news. He shook his head and sighed and shook his head again and finally pushed himself through the hatch. Dad sealed it behind him.

"Okay, Dad," said Douglas. "If you're not carrying it, where is it hidden?"

"I don't know what you're talking about, Douglas. I'm not carrying anything."

"Uh-huh. Right. And our Christmas presents weren't hidden in the closet behind your file cabinets either."

Dad looked startled. "How did you—" He shook his head, exasperated. "Never mind. Just drop the subject, okay, Douglas?"

"He threatened us, Dad."

"I'm not deaf, Douglas. And I'm not stupid."

"Neither are we, Dad. What's going on?"

Dad turned to Douglas and took both his hands in his own. "If I ask you to trust me, will you?"

Douglas gave him that sideways look he does so well— the one that translates out to, "Excuse me? Did you really just say that?"

"Douglas, please—?"

"The money for the trip, right? That's where it came from."

"I can't talk about this. And you mustn't either."

"Uh-huh. Right. It's our lives too—and we're not allowed to know. You did it to us again, you son of a bitch, didn't you?" Douglas pulled his hands free and started toward the door, but he pulled free too hard and both he and Dad bounced in different directions, which would have been funny if it hadn't been so scary at the same time.

"I'm trying to protect you—goddammit!!"

"I don't want your protection!! I want the truth." And Douglas was out the door—I thought about following him, but didn't. Stinky had suddenly decided he wanted me to show him the new monkey trick after all.

Anyway, after that, everything was back to normal. Totally screwed up.

A BID FOR FREEDOM

THE EARTH STARTS LOOKING A lot smaller as you approach Geostationary. Not farther away—just smaller. It's an optical illusion, because the eye and the brain don't handle infinity very well, especially the brain, so beyond a certain distance, everything is just *far*. Geostationary point is 22,300 miles high. 36,800 klicks. That's a distance nearly equal to the circumference of the planet. It's almost three times the diameter. We were rising to a point almost three Earth-diameters above Ecuador.

From One-Hour, the Earth was a wall that filled half the sky. Now it was just a big blue marble that was so bright it was hard to look at. The Line still pointed down at it. We still hung above it. It was just much smaller than before. For the first time, I was beginning to feel as if we'd jumped off the planet . . . and were falling away into endless space. That squeezy uncomfortable feeling kept coming back, now more than ever.

But at least from here the hurricane looked a lot smaller. And a lot less dangerous. I couldn't tell, but it looked like it was starting to break up against the Andes. It had lost a lot of its circular shape. After a while Stinky got bored and we went back to our cabin. Dad was trying to raise the El Paso station again, but it was temporarily out of service due to the hurricane. Then he started channel-strafing and found out that all the groundside channels were shut down. Which seemed weird, because they could have been rerouted a dozen different ways, but that was what the channel board said. *Temporarily out of service.* And that didn't make sense at all, because they'd already told us that the hurricane couldn't disrupt Line communications.

Later, Mickey came back for the breakfast cart and asked Dad for our boarding passes. Douglas came back with him, looking grim, but not as angry as when he'd left. Mickey said there was some paperwork to take care of before we arrived. He handed Dad some forms to fill out and told us to be sure to watch the departure instructions on TV. He acted like everything was perfectly normal. So did Dad. So did Douglas. I couldn't believe it. But then again, what *else* were we supposed to do? Have another fight? No thanks, we didn't need any more practice.

So we watched the departure instructions. I suppose it would have been very interesting if we'd cared to pay attention. It was that red-haired comedian again. This time they were showing how to navigate through micro-gravity and customs and get down to the spinning sections of Geostationary, or to our connections outward. There was also a whole section on how to find your way from one part of Geostationary to another. The station was big, and getting a lot bigger every year as they kept adding more and more disks to it. And then, the show segued directly to shots of our arrival—views from the top of the car, as well as from Geostationary's underside cameras.

Arriving at Geostationary, they played, *On the Beautiful Blue Danube*, by Richard Strauss. We watched it on the screen in our cabin. They timed it perfectly. The car had been slowing down for the past thirty minutes, so it worked out that just as the huge disks of Geostationary came into view above us, the music surged and built joyously, coming to its final climax just as we locked into place. And then the inevitable voice, in six languages: "Welcome to Geostationary. For your own safety . . . blah blah blah."

I'd expected that we would get out almost immediately, but no—the car has to be brought aboard the disk, moved around, locked into place, washed, and anchored, before passengers can disembark. The whole process takes forty-five minutes. But during that time, the attendants come by with more cards that have to be filled out for customs and whatever other last-minute instructions are needed.

When Mickey came by again, we were already packed and waiting. There wasn't much to pack anyway. We'd left most of it behind. We looked like refugees—like those people in Montreal.

Mickey hardly glanced at me; he spoke mostly to Dad and Douglas. "We have a problem," he said grimly. "Station Security knows you're here. Somebody alerted them. Somebody on this car—"

"Hidalgo?" Douglas asked. He looked to Dad, angrier than ever.

Dad shrugged. "Give him credit, he works fast—"

"No, it wasn't Hidalgo." Mickey said. "That's not his style. This was an anonymous tip. Very childish. Do you have any other enemies?"

Urk—I suddenly realized who had done it. And why. We were in big trouble now. I opened my mouth to apologize—this was all my fault.

"Never mind. Worry about it later," said Mickey. "Right now, there are officers outside waiting to take you into custody and send you back down the Line."

"They can do that?"

"You know they can. Until you set foot aboard the station and pass through customs, you're not under starside jurisdiction. You're legally still on Earth and they can yank you back down with a subpoena. In about fifteen minutes, dirtside marshals will be coming aboard to serve your ex-wife's papers." And before Dad could ask how he knew so much, Mickey explained, "Douglas told me everything. Tell me—did you accept your Sierra bid?"

Dad looked unhappy. "I tried to. I sent in my acceptance last night. When I checked my e-mail this morning, it came back refused. The bid had already been withdrawn. My wife's lawyer filed some kind of a claim and Sierra backed out. They have all kinds of protection clauses in their boilerplate."

"What?" said Douglas, anger rising. "Are you saying we have no place to go? You knew that—and you turned Hidalgo down? I can't believe this!"

Dad looked resolute. "Douglas, I can't sell him what I don't have! And even if I did have it—whatever it is—I still couldn't sell it to him. I don't care if you believe me or not—"

"We could have had a sponsor!"

"We could have opened a window and jumped out!" Dad snapped right back.

"Stop it, both of you!" said Mickey quickly. "There are other sponsors. Better ones." He glanced to me and nodded. "I made a phone call." To Dad and Doug: "I can get you into the custody of an agent who places people. All I have to do is get you legally on the station. It's a different jurisdiction—different bidding rules, a lot easier. But you'll have to go right now."

"Will it work?" I asked. I was desperate. I'd screwed up *really* badly this time.

"I learned this trick at my mother's knee," said Mickey. He picked up my backpack and shoved it into my arms. He turned to Dad. "Your agent is waiting, Mr. Dingillian. We're running out of time. Are you coming?" Mickey glanced at his watch. "They'll be opening the forward hatches in six minutes."

Dad looked to Douglas, to me, to Stinky.

"Can we trust him?" Dad asked Douglas.

Douglas nodded, tight-lipped. So did I.

Mickey said, "Look, I'm trying to make up for some of the trouble I've caused—" He looked to me when he said that last.

"All right," said Dad, reluctantly. "Let's go. Charles, get your backpack on. Bobby, don't forget your monkey."

GEOSTATIONARY

WHEN A CAR DOCKS AT Geostationary, first it slides up through a service tube so tight there's only a few centimeters of clearance. The service tube takes it up through a series of three or four air locks, and then finally up to the docking chamber where the carriage of the car slides sideways off the line and onto a special delivery track that curves around like a *cesta*—that curved basket thing that jai alai players wear on their hands. The car moves out and around on this delivery track and onto a stationary holding frame, just inside the disk hub—it looks like a curved wall, sliding slowly past. All the cars are docked here while they're unloaded, serviced, and reloaded. They look like cans lined up in a rack, while the whole station rotates around.

Mickey said that we had to stop thinking of Earth as down. *Up* and *down* are the same as *in* toward the hub and *out* toward the rim. The only two other directions inside the disks of the station are dirtside and starside—and those are sideways directions.

Mickey led us down the corridor toward the service hatch. There are hatches at both ends of the car. Passengers use the top or *forward* hatch. Crew and cargo use the bottom or *aft* hatch. So while the marshals were coming in through the front, we were already leaving through the rear. There was a service attendant waiting there. He frowned when he saw us, but Mickey said to him, "Thanks, Joe. I really appreciate this."

He shook his head in disapproval. "I wasn't here," he said. "I was taking a leak."

"And we never saw you."

Joe grunted and stepped away from his service panel. He disappeared back down the corridor.

"In through here," Mickey pointed.

"Is this a real hatch?" Stinky demanded. "It doesn't look like it."

"It's a service hatch. Most people *never* get to see this, Bobby. This is where supplies and cargo come aboard and waste is removed—all through this hatch."

"Are we going out in a Dumpster?" I asked.

"Nothing that dramatic. Watch that light. As soon as it goes green, I punch this button and that door opens. There'll be a woman standing there holding a document. As soon as your dad signs it, you'll be under the full legal protection of Partridge Colonial Enterprises."

Dad turned to Mickey. "There's supposed to be a three-day grace period, isn't there, during which time I can back out of the deal?"

Mickey grinned. "Yep, there is. But by that time, you can be on your way to Luna, so—" He laughed. There was no need for him to finish the sentence.

The green light went on and Mickey hit the button. All three doors of the hatch whooshed open and two big men stepped in immediately, scaring us with the hard way they looked and the quick way they came rushing right in, because at first we thought they were security agents, or maybe worse—some of those people that Dr. Hidalgo had hinted about—but they weren't. They were just service technicians. They brushed past us and went straight up the corridor as if we weren't there.

A stocky older woman carrying a big business bag came in immediately after. Her dark hair was even shorter than theirs. "Don't worry about those fellows," she explained. "They didn't see anything either. I'm your lawyer. My name is Olivia. You're Max Dingillian? Pleased to meet you. Sign here, here, and here." She pulled a camera out of her purse.

"You kids, up against the wall. I need your pictures." Snap, snap, snap. Dad too; one more snap. "Raise your right hand. Do you solemnly swear that the information provided in these documents is true to the best of your knowledge, so help you? Thank you. Congratulations, you are now clients of Partridge Enterprises. Would you thumbprint this, please? Right here. And here. Thank you. You kids too, please?" She folded the papers and stuffed them into her purse, then turned to Mickey, wrapped him into her big arms, and gave him a hug that I thought would crush him. "How're you doing, sweetie?"

"I'm fine, Mom. How's business?"

"Lousy. That dirtside son-of-a-bitch is playing games again. I've had it with him. I'm filing a complaint with the Board of Ethics. I'm going to have that scumbag's balls for a paperweight, just as soon as we find them—"

Mickey grinned at Dad. "Mom's the best. She eats human flesh. Raw, if she's really hungry. She can strip a full-grown cow to the bone in seven minutes."

"I can believe it."

Olivia turned back to us, all business again. "All right, you slaves—don't take that personally, it's a joke—let's get you out of here. This way, quickly. Bring your bags. You, the little one—Bobby, is that your name? Is that your monkey? You'd better carry him for now. Or why don't you let me carry him, okay? Let's go. I'll see you later, Mickey. Don't be late for dinner." She shoved the monkey into her bag and we all followed her.

Leaving the car is a tricky process. There are transfer pods at each end of the elevator; they spin to match the rotation of the cylinder, and you get aboard. Then the pod disengages from the car and stops spinning—and the passengers feel weightless. The pod points itself so that its "floor" is outward, which means soon it'll be downward. It connects itself to a track on the rotating inner wall of the hub and then slides outward. It feels "downward." The farther "out" it goes from the hub, the heavier you feel. It's centrifugal force. The same thing that holds the Line up—only the Earth is the hub for the Line.

The departure video had shown us that there would be seats in the transfer pod for ten people at a time, only we were in a cargo pod which was set up differently, and there were no seats in it at all, only handholds set into the wall.

Olivia directed us to hold on tight, then hit the Go panel. Nothing happened first; then we felt like we were getting lighter and lighter. "The pod-drum has disengaged from the cabin. It's slowing down now. As the spinning slows, we lose pseudo-gravity. Bobby, don't try floating. You could hurt yourself. Just hold on, please." For a moment, we were weightless, or close enough that the difference was insignificant. It kind of felt like we were falling, but not quite. After a moment that sensation went away and we weren't falling at all, we just kept feeling like it. Stinky started giggling. I felt like I was going to puke.

Something outside thumped softly and Olivia said, "The transfer pod is now moving off the drum. And another one is taking its place." She hesitated a moment, as if she were listening to the feeling of the room. "Now the pod is lowering down toward the main levels of the disk. Outward is down, just like in the cabin of the elevator car. Feel that?"

That was pseudo-gravity starting to come back. Olivia said, "You'll have the feeling of weight in just another few seconds. Main level gives you one-half your normal weight, just a little more than on the elevator car." Even as she said it, we were already sinking down to the floor.

"Is this really going to work?" Dad asked, indicating Olivia's papers. "I mean, doesn't Earth have some authority up here?"

"Very little," Olivia said blandly. She patted her bag. "This goes to a much higher court. Literally."

The door popped open and we were staring at a hallway long enough that we could see how it curved up in the distance. "We're here," said Olivia. "Come on, I'll walk you through customs. Got your IDs and passports? Now, listen— you're going to be stopped by security agents. You've got to let me do the talking. Don't say *anything*. Nothing at all.

They'll be recording everything." She looked to me, Douglas, and Bobby. "Look determined, okay? Like this is what you want. This *is* what you want, isn't it?"

Dad nodded. He looked to us kids. Douglas nodded. So did I. Stinky said, "I'm going with Chigger," which surprised me. I didn't know what to say in response, so I just took his hand.

"Okay, let's go," said Olivia. She took the newly-signed papers out of her purse and brandished them in front of her like a weapon. We put on our most determined expressions and followed in her wake.

"Do you get a lot of business this way?" Dad asked innocently.

"Not usually," she replied. "But once in a while my son brings home a stray puppy. Don't worry about my fee. I get a finder's commission from the colonies. We'll talk about that later. Here we are—"

HOWARD

THERE THEY ARE—" **THE UGLY** little man saw us first and came advancing like an attack Chihuahua. He wore a wrinkled suit; it looked like he'd gotten it from his older brother and still hadn't grown into it. Two security guards came following after with bored expressions. A fourth man came running with a multi-lens vid-cam aimed at us. I said the word again.

Olivia saw them at the same time they saw us. She put on her biggest smile and said, "Howard, how nice to see you again. I understand we're getting an ambulance up here for you to chase."

"Don't be nasty, Olivia. I have a court order—" He held up an official-looking document. I guessed it was a subpoena.

"Fold it and stuff it, Counselor. I have an agency contract." She held up a paper of her own. Our contract.

For a moment, the two of them faced each other like they were about to start a sword fight—only with folded documents instead of swords.

"It's not valid—"

"Don't be stupider than usual, Howard. Of course, it's

valid. How many of these have you examined already? Would you like to examine this one too?" She shoved it under his nose.

Howard, whoever he was, slapped the paper away angrily. Olivia just shoved it right back under his nose. "You lay one hand on any of these clients, and I'll have you headed dirtside without benefit of an elevator. I'll have you tied up in so much paper, the only way out for you will be a good flush." She smiled and became even sweeter and gentler than before. "You know I have you beaten. Don't prolong your agony."

"I'm filing a complaint with Judge Griffith. You had unfair and unauthorized access."

"My clients requested that I meet them as soon as possible precisely to guarantee their rights of residence. That's all the authorization I needed. You know that. I violated no statutes—"

"Oh, don't give me that. Your son does this all the time, letting you aboard in violation of the Singapore Convention—"

"Don't say another word, you little turd, or I'll have you up on a slander charge as well. Legal representatives have the right to meet their clients before they disembark, precisely to guarantee their rights of representation; you know the precedent as well as I. You lost that one too, as I recall. Why don't you try another line of work, Howard? You're really not very good at this."

A crowd was starting to form. I guess we were good theater. Olivia turned her attention to the guards, incidentally making sure that she was facing enough toward the man with the vid-cam that he would have a good angle on her. "Do you fellows understand the issues involved here? My clients are under the protection of Partridge Colonial Enterprises. Whatever claims any groundside agency has against any of these individuals must come through me. I will receive service of summons forthwith—" She plucked the subpoena from Howard's hand and stuffed it in her purse. "But please be aware that under the terms of the Singapore Convention, custody of my clients may not be transferred without a hearing before Judge Griffith. You may not arrest, detain, or otherwise hinder the movements of these four people. Do you understand?"

Apparently they'd heard the speech before, because they looked bored as she went through the recitation. "Right. We know the drill." One of the guys didn't look happy, but the other said, "Are you going to be at Lemrel's party Saturday, Olivia?"

"Of course, wouldn't miss it for the world. See you there." She stuffed her papers back in her purse and started to push forward.

"Hold it, Olivia. Not so fast. There are minors involved this time!" Howard stepped in front of her. He motioned to the guy with the camera. "Get in here close for this, will you?" He stepped up in front of us and said, "Which one of you is Charles?"

Olivia nodded to me and I held up my hand politely.

"Thank you, Charles." He stepped in closer. He had bad breath. "Now, I want to ask you a question, and I want you to think very carefully before you answer. And I want you to know that you don't have to answer for anyone except yourself. Are you going with your father of your own free will?"

I looked to Olivia, as if to ask her if I should answer. She held up a hand to stop me from speaking. "I take exception to this, Counselor."

"Nevertheless, Counselor—" Howard said right back— "for the purposes of this case, the court has seen fit to require evidence that the children are not being held against their will." He handed her another folded paper. She unfolded it and looked through it quickly. She nodded. "Well, I'll be damned. You got one right, Howard. This is all in order." She handed the paper back. "All right, Charles, you may answer the nice man."

"What was the question again?"

"Are you going with your father of your own free will, or are you being forced? You don't have to go with him if you don't want to. That's why these agents are here. To protect you."

"Oh," I said. "I think I'd rather stay with my Dad."

Howard frowned. He looked to Stinky. "You must be Douglas—"

"No, I'm Bobby. That's Douglas."

"Ah, thank you." Howard turned to Weird. "Douglas—are you accompanying your male parent of your own free will?" Douglas didn't like being pressured, but he nodded slowly. Howard leaned in toward him. "What was that? I need you to say it aloud. For the camera."

"Yes," he said loudly. "I'm going with my father of my own free will. And you need a better mouthwash." The crowd laughed.

Howard ignored it and turned to Bobby. "And you, young man—are you going with your father too, or do you want to go home to your mommy? You know she misses you *very* much."

"Watch it, Howard—" Olivia said warningly.

"I'm going with Chigger and my monkey," Bobby said. "Wherever Chigger goes, I go."

"The monkey?" Howard looked momentarily confused.

Stinky went pawing through Olivia's bag. He pulled out his monkey and put it down on the ground. "Show this man a 'farkleberry.' " He pointed toward Howard. The monkey immediately did a funny little dance in a circle, ending up in front of Howard, where he turned his back, yanked down his pants, and made a horrendous farting noise. The crowd roared. Some of them even applauded. Olivia guffawed like a horse.

Howard was not amused. But instead of losing his temper, he turned to Olivia and waggled his finger in her face. "Judge Griffith's, first thing tomorrow morning. The child did *not* indicate a preference for the male parent. We're calling in Social Services for a Protective Custody Interview. Nine A.M. It's already on the docket."

"As you wish, Counselor," Olivia said calmly. She pointed us toward the Customs officer. "Pick up your monkey, Bobby. I don't want it getting any fleas from the lawyer. See you in court, Howard."

PLANS

OLIVIA TOOK US DIRECTLY TO her offices which were on Disk Three. You count the disks from the bottom up, so it was two disks above Disk One, which contained the arrival terminal and customs, plus hotels and shops and the upside offices of downside companies. We didn't get to see much, though. Dad told her about Dr. Hidalgo's last conversation with us, so she took us straight to the "subway" and popped us all into a tube.

Relative to Earth, we were going "up," but relative to the disks of Geostationary, we were going "across." Eventually, all of the different disks would be linked to become a giant cylinder—like the L5 colony under construction. There would be three subways running along the outermost, or bottommost level. Even though the floors of the cylinder hadn't been started yet, and wouldn't be for several years, the subways were already in place because it simplified the process of moving from one disk to the next. We went "across," but it felt like "forward."

Olivia's offices were also her apartment. She didn't have a great view. Disks One and Two blocked the view of Earth, and Disks Four through Seven blocked the view of deep space. But she had a wall display that showed all the views anyone could want of anything. It wasn't a *real* window, but we'd never had a real window back home either.

"Okay," she said, sitting down at her console. "Power up, Betsy. Momma's got work to do. First things first, kiddos. Do you want Italian or bleu cheese on your salad? You kids, what do you want on your pizza? Let's get the important decisions made first—then we have a lot of paperwork to review. I'm afraid your case has just gotten a little more complicated." She surveyed all of us on our likes and dislikes for dinner, finished punching the order in, then turned back to us expectantly.

"Is there a problem?" Dad asked. He looked worried.

"Yes and no. Your ticket's one-way, isn't it?"

"Yes. Mine is. The boys' aren't."

"Good. Then there's no problem. As long as you're not coming back anytime in the next seven years. Statute of limitations."

"Huh?"

"Let me look over your resumes, your insurance, your tickets, all your paperwork. The problem is I'm going to have to void our contract. Or rather, you are."

"I don't understand."

"You're going to have to fire me for unsatisfactory representation. I'm going to have to advise you against that."

"But then they'll arrest us."

"That's why you can't fire me just yet—not until you get back on the outbound elevator." She hesitated. "No, I have a better idea. Don't fire me. I'll quit. If you get on the outbound elevator, I'll have no choice but to refuse to represent you anymore. Yes, I like that. It'll prove I have some integrity, and the result will be the same. And Howard will be *really* pissed at me. Judge Griffith will have a good laugh. She doesn't like Howard anyway. But I don't know how she feels about *this* case. We'd better cover our asses with a lot of paper tonight." She patted her ample butt. "And that's going to take a *lot* of paper.

"Now, hmm. How're we going to get you out to Disk Seven? Howard will have his goons posted by now."

"What about Dr. Hidalgo?" Douglas asked.

"He's not a problem. Not yet. Whoever's behind him, it's going to take them some time to organize. And I think Dr. Hidalgo would rather negotiate. That's his style—I've seen him in action. Next time around, he's going to offer you ten times what you were paid. If you refuse, then we'll have to worry about your life expectancy." Still talking, she pulled her chair up to the computer and started typing. I'd never seen a woman like her before. I wondered if she had a fuel cell inside or if she was just pocket-fusion powered?

"Max, there's a bottle of scotch in the cupboard. Pour two. Three if Douglas wants one. Juice for the kids. On that rack over there, I've got some of your recordings. Autograph the Copland set for me, will you? It's part of my fee. That was a beautiful job you did on the third. Always one of my favorites."

"Fourth movement?" I asked.

"How'd you guess?" She grinned back at me. "What music did you get on the way up? Anything interesting?"

"*Carmina Burana*, Beethoven's Fourth, and *The Blue Danube*."

Olivia made a face. "Yeah, the usual. I wish they'd be more imaginative. Oh, well." She bent back to her keyboard again.

Dad smiled at me and mouthed the words, "Everybody's a critic."

Olivia was still talking. I'd never heard anyone use so many words per minute in my life. "The real question, Max, how do I get you a Colonial Sponsor so you don't have to go through this again on Luna? And how do I secure that contract so it sticks, even if I don't?"

"What? I thought you already had a contract for us—"

"I do and I don't. I'm a finder. I can find a placement for just about anybody. My finder's fee is based on your value to the colony. I could justify the value of a serial killer, if I had to. In fact, I think I did once. I'd have to check my files. A fellow named Maizlish. Left a trail of dead bodies wherever he went. He got up here somehow, and there was no jurisdiction or authority to send him back, so I found him a contract. Testing vaccines on Gotham. Very appropriate.

Cost him plenty. I think he died of something awful. I certainly hope so—"

Dad was getting just a little upset. What was this woman getting us into? "How can you talk about getting bids on my services when I couldn't even get noticed? I got only one response and it was for basic value only. No perquisites."

"That's because you came in cold. You need an agent. An agent secures your performance in return for a finder's fee. Clients with agents get better bookings."

"I know that," said Dad. "I know how agents work—that's why I hate getting caught between lawyers and agents. I don't know who to hate more."

Olivia ignored it. She'd probably heard it all before. I certainly had, enough times that I could set it to music. She studied her display. "You have a very interesting set of skills, Max. There are a lot of worlds that are desperate to start developing their own arts and culture. The ideal booking for you would be a place where you could train your own orchestra. You'd probably have to do some teaching too, but that wouldn't hurt you either. I think I know of a couple planets that fit that description." She frowned and slapped the side of her monitor. "Come on, Betsy—get your fat ass in gear." Apparently Betsy didn't, because Olivia swiveled in her chair to face Dad. "Y'know—it's risky, but I could put you on the outbound without a firm bid. That way I could get you out of here—wait, let me check." She swiveled back. "Betsy, how soon would Max and his children have to leave to catch the earliest possible lunar launch?"

The computer answered quietly, "The midnight car is the earliest one with open bookings. Should I make a reservation?"

"Yes. Use the Goodman account. If it's not overdrawn again. Two rooms for six people. Cancel two of the people just before boarding and sell the other four tickets to the Dingillians." To us, she said, "That should confuse Howard. He'll be watching for any booking for four, especially in your name." She turned back to her keyboard. "If I can get you out of here and on the way to Luna, that gives me two days to find you a placement." Abruptly, she pushed herself back from the keyboard in frustration. "No, this is the wrong way to do it. Too much work. Betsy, get me Georgia."

Almost immediately, there was a chime and a woman's voice answered, "Olivia, how are you?"

"The pizza's on it's way, Georgia—where the hell are you?"

"Pizza? Tonight? I thought we were getting together on—" The voice stopped, then came back laughing. "Oh, that's a good one, Olivia. Very good. You almost caught me. What do you need?"

"I need you for dinner. I have some people I want you to meet."

"The Dingillians, right? Howard was just here."

"I want you to interview the kids, sweetie. This is a beautiful family. They don't need a Protective Services evaluation."

"I'd rather do this through channels, Counselor."

"Georgia, so would I, but these people have already had one bid withdrawn because of this publicity. And there aren't going to be any more bids for them until this is resolved, we both know that. This is a delaying tactic by Howard—"

"Acting on behalf of the mother—" Georgia put in.

"Nevertheless, it's a delaying tactic designed to keep my client from his freedom to emigrate."

"Downside sees it as a custody battle."

"Yes, that's true. And starside sees it as a freedom-to-emigrate issue."

"Either way," the unseen Georgia said, "it comes back to the rights of the child."

"Precisely," said Olivia. "That's why I think you should meet the children. Tonight if possible. Not in a court of law. You need to see these kids as people, not specimens."

Georgia sighed. There was a pause. Then she asked, "What's on the pizza?"

"Your favorite. Mushrooms, onions, tomatoes."

"No Martian anchovies?"

"Have you seen the price of Martian anchovies lately? Next year, when Mars gets a lot closer, we'll talk anchovies. Can you be here in fifteen?"

"The distance has nothing to do with the price. You're just

a cheapskate. And I'll be there in ten. Open a bottle of Lambrusco and give it a chance to breathe."

"Yes, Your Honor."

"This call is adjourned." Judge Griffith clicked off with a sound like a gavel coming down.

PIZZA

THE PIZZA ARRIVED THEN, FILLING the apartment with thick rich tomatoey smells. I didn't know pizza could smell so good. At home, pizza is an industrial product, little squares rolling out of a machine. But this one was round and Olivia said it was handmade. I couldn't imagine that.

Before Olivia could finish laying out plates on the table, a laughing woman in a wheelchair came rolling in. Judge Griffith. "I hereby declare this dinner officially in session," she boomed. And rolled right up to the table to put a small vase of flowers in the center. "From my own garden, Olivia. You always liked the blue roses, didn't you?"

Her chair had a built-in swivel, she wheeled around to face us. We were both staring at her open-mouthed. "You must be Charles and Bobby. Douglas? Pleased to meet you. Max Dingillian? Wish I could say the same. You sure stirred up a fine kettle of worms. Made a lot of extra work for all of us—but as my old sainted gramma used to say, 'the best reason for stirring up a kettle of worms is to make sure the sauce gets evenly distributed.' Bobby, you must show me that trick you made your monkey do for Howard. And all the other tricks too. My goodness, I haven't laughed so hard since the day the Thomas case blew up in his face." She looked around, blinking. "Where's Mickey?"

"Late as usual," Olivia said. "He inherited that from his father. No matter, we can start without him. Come on, everybody to the table—did you kids wash your hands? No? Well, hop to it. The pizza's getting cold. More wine, Your Honor?"

"How can I have more when I haven't had any yet?" Judge Griffith held out her glass impatiently.

Were all lawyers and judges like this?

"Excuse me?" Dad said, when we were finally all seated and Olivia was passing out thick slabs of fresh hot pizza. "But am I the only one who sees a possible conflict of interest here? The lawyer and the judge and the defendants all having dinner together?"

Olivia and Georgia exchanged glances. And laughed.

Georgia said, "If this were a trial, yes, there would be a conflict of interest. But you're not defendants. Not yet. Tomorrow's hearing is investigatory, not evidential. My coming here is to obtain background information on the case, at the request of your attorney. And just in case you haven't noticed—" Georgia pointed toward two of the corners of the room where cameras were mounted "—your kindly old Auntie Olivia is recording everything. For her protection, and for yours. When did you start the files, dear?"

"When you rolled in, Your Honor. All of the discussions we had before you arrived are in separate files, private-coded. These recordings are being made with grade-three authentication."

"Good." Georgia patted Olivia's hand. "That's why you're such a good lawyer. You don't leave anything to chance." To Dad, she continued, "The point is, if I'm to make a ruling about what's best for your children, I need to see them in a less formal situation, and in relationship with you—not all scrubbed and polished for a court appearance, but in a more relaxed family setting. There are precedents for home interviews and home studies. This is upside law, not downside. We do things differently up here. You may have noticed that already. We don't have time to spend a year or two on a legal matter that should be resolvable in a couple of days.

Nobody benefits from that. Justice delayed is justice denied. And pizza delayed is asphalt. So eat before that piece cools off in your hand."

Dad took a bite. Thoughtfully. Then another. He looked uncomfortable and he kept looking back and forth between the two women at the table. We'd just met the both of them and suddenly our lives were in their hands. How had we stumbled into this? Was this going to turn into an even bigger mess?

Olivia noticed first. "Max," she said, almost conversationally, "do you have community standards classes in your town? Seminars?"

"Sure, doesn't everybody?"

"What's the stated purpose?" The way she asked, there was obviously more to her question than curiosity.

"To establish stability for the entire community. The most good for the most people."

Olivia looked to Georgia. "Sounds good to me—for dirtside. How about you, Your Honor?"

Georgia shrugged and spoke around a mouthful of salad. "Yeah, sounds good for dirtside."

I was starting to get the feeling that "dirtside" was a nasty word. A rude way of talking about people who lived on the ground.

"Well, it is good," Dad said. "There are seventeen billion people on the planet. You can't have everyone running around freely making up their own rules and setting their own standards. The, uh—the social contract and all that. The common good requires that people have a common context."

"That sounds pretty common to me," Olivia nodded.

"Yep," agreed the Judge. "Me too."

Dad finally got it. He narrowed his eyes. "Is there something wrong with the idea of the common good?"

"Nope," Olivia said innocently. "If you don't mind being common."

Judge Griffith leaned forward then to explain. "Max, downside, you can talk about things being common, because for most people, that's exactly how they are. Common. Ordinary. But up here—" She waved her hand to indicate not just the room but everything beyond it. Geostationary. The

Line. The moon. "Up here—*nothing* is ordinary. Everything is *extraordinary*.

"People don't come up here looking for more of the ordinary, they come up here because they want to get away from the ordinary. That's what space represents, the chance at an *extra*ordinary life.

"Most people on Earth *never* get a chance to feel what it's like to be extraordinary. The best they get are pictures of other people being extraordinary. And once in a while, some lucky schmuck gets an extraordinary experience and it transforms the quality of his life from that moment onward. Because once you've had one extraordinary experience you know that once isn't enough. You want your whole life to be like that. So people come up here, Max, looking not just for an extraordinary experience, but, for what they wanted all along—extraordinary lives."

Still talking to Dad, the judge pointed to us kids. "You knew that when you kidnapped them—sorry to be so blunt about it, Max, but let's be honest. You knew what you were doing, and you'd do it again if you had to. You saw a chance and you grabbed it, and you grabbed your kids so they could have the same chance too. And the fact is, there isn't a parent on Earth who doesn't secretly envy your bravado—even while at the same time hating you for it. You've grabbed a piece of something." She waved at the space around her. "This is a lifeline for the human race—a way out of the trap."

Dad shook his head. "The last report I saw said that there are still three million babies being born every day, something like that. The Line would take eight months to boost that many people into space. No, the beanstalk isn't a way out—it's a luxury."

"No, it isn't," said Olivia abruptly. "It's a lifeboat. And there weren't enough lifeboats on the *Titanic* either."

That made for a moment of uncomfortable silence, until Judge Griffith rescued the conversation. "The point is," she said, "we're trying to get as many kids into the lifeboats as possible. And world-builders. And people who know how to make a difference. We might lose the Earth, yes—it sure looks like it this week—but we're not going to lose the game."

Dad made a face. I could almost understand why.

"Yes, I know that downsiders hate it when an upsider talks like that, but the nasty truth is that what's consuming the Earth is everybody's insistence on grinding everybody else down. There's no energy left for anything else. That's why you bailed—"

Dad conceded the argument with a shrug.

Olivia interrupted then. "Your Honor, if I may—?"

Judge Griffith waved her hand. "Go ahead, Counselor."

Olivia leaned toward Dad. "The job of the Presiding Judge of the Superior Court for the Geostationary Jurisdiction as authorized by the Singapore Treaty and confirmed by the local representatives of the Corporate Signatories to the Colonial Agreement is to rule on conflicts between upside and downside law. The unspoken part of that job is to guarantee and protect the interests of upsiders against spurious downside claims." She glanced over to the judge. "Right?"

Judge Griffith waved her wineglass in vague agreement. "We get a lot of interesting actions filed up here. Everybody downside thinks everybody upside is rich." She stopped talking just long enough to push another bite of pizza into her mouth. Still chewing, she held up a hand to indicate that she hadn't finished her thought yet. She mopped her mouth with one of Olivia's ample cloth napkins and held her glass out for more wine. "I shouldn't, but the counselor has an excellent wine cellar—thirty-six thousand kilometers that way." She gestured off to her side. "Or am I turned around? No, I was right. It's that way. Earthside and starside, Charles. Remember that. Keep the Earth to your left and you're facing spinward. Here, I'll give you an interesting little puzzle to consider. If I take away from you the words *right* and *left*, how else can you speak about your right and left side?"

"My heart's on the left," I answered immediately. And then added quickly, "Your Honor."

"You can call me Georgia. We're not in session here. And that's the B answer. Your heart is actually in the center, leaning left. Now, try for the A answer. How would you explain *left* and *right* to a Martian? Someone who doesn't have the same language you do. What physical criteria can you use? Think about it for awhile." She turned back to

Olivia, leaving me puzzling over the riddle. If there was another answer, it wasn't obvious.

After her glass was refilled a second time, Georgia turned back to Dad. "I'm well aware that if I grant your wife's claim tomorrow, I'm establishing a precedent for future downsider claims against upsiders. So even though what's at issue for you is only your future, what's at issue for the rest of us up here is a lot larger. This is one of those really annoying cases that calls into question the whole matter of jurisdiction.

"You see, if I vacate Howard's request for an investigatory hearing, that will be viewed downside as a larger refusal to hear any downside claims, which will lead us ultimately toward a hearing in the World Court. Not this case, of course—you'll be long gone by then—but eventually, the jurisdictional matters are going to have to be resolved. Sooner or later, we're going to get a really nasty test case. I just want to make sure that this isn't it, because if this one ends up in the World Court, it'll be ruled against us. And regardless of the outcome of this case, I don't want that precedent over my head. So the best hope for the upside is to delay those kinds of confrontations for as long as possible to give the colonial signatories a chance to build up a counterweight authority.

"Even though we're well into orbital space, we're still *attached* to the Earth. Therefore Earth assumes that Earth should have authority over the entire length of the beanstalk. Upsiders feel that, as a matter of course, the beanstalk should be viewed entirely as a space-borne agency, because once someone's up the beanstalk they're under beanstalk control, and the bulk of the beanstalk is in space. At the moment, the dividing line is One-Hour, with Earth maintaining authority over One-Hour and everything below, and Geostationary maintaining authority over everything above.

"But none of that is your concern. It's mine." To Olivia she said, "I assume you've got Betsy scouring for useful precedents?"

Olivia nodded. "Have been all afternoon."

Georgia stuffed the last bite of pizza into her mouth and chewed thoughtfully. "Well, you're going to have to show me some damn good reasons for disregarding Maggie Dingillian's claim. No matter what. Now, I'll interview the kids. Douglas? You have a question?"

He pointed to the cameras. "How much of what you just said was for them?"

She laughed. "All of it, sweetheart. These recordings may never need to be shown, but just in case—I have to make the speech. I know who elected me and I know why."

MICKEY

MICKEY SHOWED UP THEN, LOOKING very unhappy. Without a smile, he didn't look like the same person.

"I told you not to be late," said Olivia. "Your pizza's cold."

"I'm not hungry—"

She put her hand on his forehead to see if he had a temperature. "What's the matter?"

He sat down at the table and picked up a piece of pizza anyway. "I got terminated."

Olivia sat down opposite him, immediately all business. "On what grounds?"

"No grounds." He nodded in the direction of Dad. Or Douglas. "Getting involved." He looked embarrassed.

"Do you want me to file something?" She looked to Judge Griffith. "Georgia?"

"It's a little premature, Olivia. Let's hear what the boy has to say."

"I'm not a boy, Aunt Georgia. I'm twenty-two."

"Mickey, I'm your god-mom. I used to change your diapers, for God's sake. Now just tell us what happened."

Mickey shrugged. "The kids were in trouble. I helped them. Kelly found out and reported me to the supervisor."

"Kelly? Is that the ugly one or the nasty one?" Olivia asked.

"Mom—your feelings are showing."

Olivia ignored it. "Anyway, they can't fire you for that."

"They didn't."

"Eh? What were the grounds for termination?"

Mickey looked embarrassed. "Having sex . . . with a passenger."

Silence in the room for a moment. Olivia looked around, saw that Douglas looked particularly embarrassed, pretended she didn't notice, then looked back to Mickey as if she wanted to say a whole lot of things to him, but didn't dare.

"It's not Mickey's fault," Douglas blurted abruptly. "I asked him. He didn't ask me. And he said no the first two times I asked."

"Thank you for that, Douglas—but it still doesn't change Mickey's responsibility in the matter. How old are you, Doug?"

"I'll be eighteen next month."

"Close enough. No problem there. It's consenting adults," said Olivia.

"Line policy," countered Georgia. "They have a case. Tell me, did you do it on your own time?"

Mickey nodded.

"Well . . . at least they can't get him for neglecting the customers," Georgia said, then laughed at her own inadvertent joke.

Olivia turned to Mickey now. She lowered her voice. "Just tell me one thing—"

Mickey already knew the question, even before she asked it. "Yes, Mom. He *is* special."

Olivia gave Douglas a warm smile, then turned back to Mickey. "That's all I wanted to know." She patted his shoulder. "Just so long as *you're* sure." She made me wish our mom were as understanding. Mickey hung his head in his hands and started to cry softly. Olivia pulled her chair closer and put her arm around his shoulders. "Hey, hey—it's all right. Momma's here. Come on, kiddo. I'm right here. Just let it out—"

Mickey looked up, red-eyed. "But it's not fair, Mom. Kelly's got her legs up in the air for anything with a tongue. One year, for her birthday, we got her a German shepherd and a jar of peanut butter."

Olivia reached around behind herself and grabbed a yellow legal pad. "Did you tell Smeagle that? Not the part about the German shepherd, the other part."

"Yes, I did."

"And what did he say?"

"The two cases are different. He said if they fired everyone with a loose zipper, there wouldn't be anyone working the Line. It's when we let our feelings influence our professionalism—blah blah blah. I'm pretty sure there's more to it than that—"

"There always is," said Olivia, scribbling furiously. "But we've got grounds. Unfair discrimination. Do you want me to file?"

Mickey shook his head. "I don't know. We've gotta talk, Mom. Things are getting really bad downside. You haven't seen the traffic we're getting. I don't know if I want to keep doing this anyway."

"Mickey, please—you're too valuable where you are."

"Mom—? Please? You said I could say 'when.' Well, I think I'm finally saying *when*."

Olivia nodded reluctantly and put the pad aside. "Okay. Whatever you want, sweetie—but let me file anyway. Let them pay for your silence. And the money will be useful. We'll talk about this later, I promise." She patted his hand.

Georgia interrupted then. "Tell me about the traffic, Mickey. What's going on?"

"We're getting too many rich emigrants. Whole carloads. Groups. They all know each other, and they're very tight-lipped about where they're going. It's that thing Mom's always talking about—a massive evacuation of rodents. Well, I think it's happening."

Georgia nodded. "We've noticed the traffic through here. We have some idea where they're all headed. It's legal. And you could probably find a lot of other reasons to explain the increase—like having three extra brightliners available, the new catapult, the shift in immigration policies, the changes in the transportation laws—"

"—and the population clock has just hit half-past midnight! Aunt Georgia, this isn't eco-theory anymore. The plagues in Africa are worse than the news is reporting. And they've already leapt across to India and Pakistan and China. A lot of people believe we're looking at the first stages of a genuine population crash—enough people to create a real panic."

Georgia rubbed her cheek thoughtfully. "I'm not willing to rule on it yet, Mickey. I'm still hearing evidence."

"Aunt Georgia, this is really one time I wish you weren't so rigorous—because by the time you have compelling evidence, it'll be too late! The people we have coming up the Line now are the kind of folks who have access to information that the rest of us aren't getting yet."

"Mickey, I know you. I know you're not an alarmist—and I trust your instincts about a lot of things, especially about people. But . . ."

"But—I know. Okay, here's one more for you. Last month, we had a family come up, you know what was in their luggage? Industrial memory. Nothing else. Forty bars of it. Probably three or four billion dollars worth. They had to pay a surcharge for the extra weight; they didn't even flinch at the cost. Georgia, they had enough raw memory for a small government. Or even a corporation. Whose data were they carrying offworld? And why? And *where?*"

"There's nothing illegal about transporting memory."

"No, there isn't. But on this big a scale? Doesn't it make you a little bit suspicious? What if it were bars of gold?"

"It wouldn't be worth as much—"

"That's right. And this is the fourth time this year we've had a passenger like that. At least that I know about. I'm only on one car. There are ninety-five other cars a day between dirtside and here. If what I've seen is one percent, then what would it mean if there were three hundred and eighty more passengers like that?" Mickey spread his hands wide. "I'm just telling you what I've seen, Your Honor. You be the judge."

Georgia smiled. Obviously, it was an old joke. She said, "I already am."

Mickey turned to his mom. "You know that booking we've been talking about? I think it's time to use it."

Olivia's face clouded. She said, "Shh, we'll talk about it later."

INTERVIEWS

JUDGE GRIFFITH LOOKED AT HER watch. "Your mother's right. That's a subject for later, Mickey. Right now, we've got a more immediate matter to attend to. The Dingillian kids." She wheeled her chair over to where Douglas and Bobby and I were sitting. "Okay, Munchkins, let's talk. Douglas, I saw Howard's tape. You're certain you want to go with your dad, right?"

Douglas nodded.

"Why?"

"Not enough money for school. And I can't get a scholarship on Earth. Not even the rechannelling scholarship. This looks like a better idea."

"No money for school, but enough money for a beanstalk ticket. Right. I'll get back to that in a bit, with your dad. But right now, answer this: what if there were enough money for you to go to—where was it?—UCLA? Would you still want to go with your dad, or would you want to go back to Earth?"

Douglas frowned. "If you'd asked me that last week, I'd have probably said I'd just as soon like to stay on Earth. But that was before we came up here. I dunno. Maybe Dad has the right idea." He started to rub his head, then stopped. That's supposed to be rude in space. Like picking your nose and flicking the boogers. He shrugged instead. "I've learned a lot in the past couple days." He looked at Dad and smiled slightly. "I think . . . if I have to decide tonight, then I'll stay with Dad."

"You *think?*" Georgia asked. "This is the rest of your life we're talking about."

"I know—you want certainty. Everybody always wants certainty. And you want me to say I'm sure about this—but who's ever sure of anything? Based on everything I've seen and heard, this is what looks best to me. I hope I'm not wrong."

"For a young man as confused as you are, you're very eloquent about your confusion." Georgia laughed. "Listen, you're close enough to adulthood that I can separate your case out anyway. You can do whatever you want and I don't need to know why. Just be aware that the decisions you make here today are going to stick with you for a long, long time." She turned to me. "Charles, let's talk."

"Okay," I said.

"Have you ever thought about divorcing your parents?"

"Huh—?"

"Just a thought. Never mind."

"Why do you ask?"

Georgia smiled. "You heard what I said to Douglas. You're a little too young for me to grant you the same legal responsibility—although I wish I could. If you were to ask me for a separation of authority from your family, that would be different. But in this case, under these circumstances, it would be difficult to grant. Especially if you then decided to go back to your mother or go on with your father. Then it would only be a slick legal maneuver to step around the intent of the law, and the judiciary board frowns on tricks like that. Not that we don't do them—we just don't like being obvious. But believe it or not, son, some of us actually try to be fair; not just fair in terms of the law, but fair in terms of the people whose lives we're ruling on. I'm looking for that place that's fair to you—and legal as well."

"I want to stay with my dad," I said.

"Why?"

"Because—well, I know this might not make sense to you, but my dad lets me listen to my music. He doesn't interrupt. He *understands*."

"It makes perfect sense to me, Charles. What's your favorite music?"

I thought about John Coltrane. No. That was still my private thing. So instead, I said, "The Copland Third. Fourth movement." Dad looked at me, surprised. But I think he understood why, because he smiled.

"What about your mom?"

"I still love her—I guess. When she's not fussing or nagging or screaming, she can be a pretty funny lady. But . . . she hasn't been very nice to be around for a long time. I'd like to say good-bye to her, but I'm afraid to. Last time, all she did was scream."

"Ah, I see," said Georgia. "What if you knew how much your mom was hurting today and how much she was going to miss you and how much you were going to miss her? Would that affect your decision?"

I swallowed. Hard. I hadn't thought about it that way. Not really. Tears started to come up in my eyes. "If I do this, I'm never going to see her again, am I?"

"No, you won't."

"But if I go back to Earth, I'll never see Dad again either, will I?"

"That's right."

"So you're asking me to choose between one parent and another, aren't you? For the rest of my life."

"Yes, I am. I know it's a tough decision. But this is a lot more decision than you had last time this battle was fought, isn't it?"

"Last time wasn't for keeps."

"I guess not," Georgia said. "Nevertheless, this is the decision you have to make. So what's it going to be, Charles? Do you know?"

I wiped my nose, my eyes. I tried to imagine what life would be with Dad, wherever we were going. I couldn't, because I didn't know where we were going. I did know what life would be like if we went back. If *I* went back. . . .

If I went back, I'd be going without Douglas. And maybe without Stinky too. And even though I always used to joke about wanting to be an only child—or even an orphan—now that I had the chance to decide who I wanted to live with, it was suddenly a much bigger decision than I'd realized. This was like running away from home. Only worse. Because we could never go back again. This was a one-time deal.

"Charles?"

"I don't want to leave my mom," I whispered. "But I don't want to lose my dad either. I don't know."

Georgia sighed. She turned to Olivia. "I've heard enough."

"You haven't talked to the little one."

"Do you think that's going to be any better?"

"No. I guess not."

Georgia patted me on the shoulder. "You did well, Charles. You told the truth. You made my job a little harder, but that's okay. We'll try to find a way to sort this out."

"Listen, wait—" I said. "If I could just *talk* to my Mom. Just to say good-bye. Just to tell her that . . . well, you know . . . that I love her and not to hate me, please. That would . . . I think that would make it all right. Maybe. Because I do want to go with my dad."

"I understand," Georgia said. She patted me on the shoulder one more time, then wheeled her way over to Olivia. "I'm not going to vacate the order. Howard has a case. At least enough for a hearing. You'd better be well-prepared tomorrow, Counselor. Thanks for the pizza."

"Wait a minute, Judge—" Olivia scooted her own chair in front of Georgia's, effectively blocking her access to the door. "You've heard Mickey's testimony about conditions downside. You can't send these children back down into that."

"Are you invoking the Evacuation Act?" Georgia asked.

"I think I'm going to have to."

"It's never been applied to a whole planet. No matter how I rule, it'll be certain to come up for review."

"Georgia, you said that you have to rule on this case based on what's best for the children. That overrides both the mother's claim *and* the father's. Remember the father has a viable custody action too. I'm asking for both of those to be set aside on the grounds that the Earth no longer represents a safe environment for these children, and that the custody cases are therefore irrelevant until such time as *both* parents are available to this court to present their claims. In the meantime, I'm arguing for assignment of custody to the only parent who is available."

Georgia frowned in thought. "If I even entertain that theory in court, you know it'll go right up the ladder of appeals, Counselor. And that's not a direction I want to go. And even if I were to find for the children under such grounds, I'd still have to compel residence until such time as the appeals played out. Do *you* really want to pursue that course?"

Olivia came right back at her. "Georgia, these are children, for God's sake! Do you want to send them back down? You heard what Mickey said. Maybe he's wrong—and maybe he isn't. But what if he isn't? What if the whole thing is finally coming apart?"

"And what if you were on the *other* side of this case, Counselor? What would you be arguing?"

"I'd still be arguing for the children."

Georgia gave her a skeptical look. "Olivia, you and I are like sisters. We have argued about everything that two human beings can possibly argue about. We're both passionate about justice. And we're both passionate about finding the laws that will guarantee it. And sometimes we both get passionate about finding ways around the laws. I don't even have a problem about that either, when what we're in search of is justice. But I do have a problem with this case. A big problem. Where's the justice in this one? I don't see it yet. And we're not going to find it in precedents or emergency acts or anything else. I'm terribly afraid that this is one of those cases where there will be no justice for anybody and everybody is going to end up hurting. We're already quite a way down that slippery slope, and I'm not going to sleep very well tonight, and I don't think you are either. Now, if you'll please—?"

Olivia stood up and pulled her chair out of the way. Georgia wheeled backward and swiveled toward the door. "Mickey, give me a hug. Nice meeting you, Douglas, Charles, Bobby—under different circumstances, I might say

the same thing to you too, Max. See you in court tomorrow."
She wheeled out and the room was painfully silent.

Nobody looked at me, but it was my fault. What I'd said
to Georgia hadn't been good enough. I'd screwed up everything. Again.

PLANS

OLIVIA SAID A WORD. THE word. The word that Dad keeps telling me not to use, and I keep using anyway. "All right," she said. "Let's try something else." She went back to her console, while Mickey began clearing the table. Douglas got up to help him and the two of them exchanged sad smiles.

Stinky had fallen asleep on the couch. The monkey was beside him—picking its nose, pretending to examine imaginary boogers, and then flicking them at me. Ha ha.

I told it to stop, and it did. Stinky still hadn't noticed that I'd installed myself as the primary authority in the monkey's consciousness. It wouldn't do anything that I wouldn't allow. If only it was that easy to control Stinky. Maybe that was the problem; parents think kids are just little programmable robots.

After a while, Dad got up and walked over to Olivia's desk. "Now what?"

She looked at him, almost startled, as if she'd forgotten we were all here. Then she snapped back to reality and said, "Okay, we go back to Plan A. We get your ass off this station as fast as we can. You'll have to fire me—sign that—and then you can hire Mickey as your agent instead. The placement will be on his license and he'll collect the fee. I'll be out of it. Here's his authorization, only don't date it until tomorrow. Otherwise, you'll be putting him in violation of the law when you leave the station."

Dad looked at me. And Stinky. "What about the kids?"

Olivia shrugged. "They're your kids. You know them better than I. Will they be all right with it? Probably not. They're going to have a lot of anger to work out—just like before—only this time *you'll* get the brunt of it."

Dad didn't answer that. He just nodded in acceptance of the truth. Finally, he said, "I suppose I should tell you that I really appreciate what you're doing for me, but—"

"I'm not doing it for you," Olivia snapped. She looked up from her keyboard. "I'm doing it for the children."

She stood up to look Dad straight in the eye. "I hate cases like this. I hate family kidnappings. Even when they're justified. And this one isn't. This one is about you being selfish enough to think you know better than everybody else. The fact that I agree with some of your conclusions about the Earth and about what's best for your kids still doesn't mitigate the appalling selfishness of your actions. So even though I'm your attorney—until you fire me—and I'll fight like a pit bull for you because Mickey asked me to, please do not make the assumption that I am doing this for you, or even because I agree with you. And certainly do not assume that I even like you. I don't. I'm doing it because I'm your lawyer and it's my job to represent you. It's also supposed to be my job to keep you out of trouble, not get you in deeper, and I'm doing a lousy job of that too, thank you very much. I just don't want to see your kids thrown back down the Line. That's the only thing you're right about. There is no future left down there. Everyone knows it's all coming apart." She glanced up. "Mickey? How long will it take you to pack?"

"Huh?"

"You said you wanted out. Well I've got six reservations on the midnight elevator, and Betsy is holding reservations on the next lunar shuttle. Make up your mind, right now—"

"Uh—" Mickey looked to Douglas. Douglas didn't look like Douglas anymore. He nodded shyly. Mickey turned back to his mother. "I'll go."

"Good. Then that'll settle the Dingillian placement too. I'll file it right now." She looked to Dad. "You're a lot luckier than you know. You'd better spend some serious time thanking Douglas *and* Mickey." She dropped back down onto her chair and rolled up to her keyboard. She started typing immediately, and whispering instructions to Betsy as well.

"Where are we going?" Douglas asked Mickey.

"Wait a minute! Wait a minute—!" said Dad. "It's my turn now."

Olivia stopped and looked at him. "Is there a problem?"

"I think I'm going into overload," said Dad. "With everything that's been happening—and it's all been happening very fast—I want to get straight on a few things."

Olivia looked at her watch. "Fifteen minutes."

"This is getting out of control."

"What is?"

"Everything. I violated the terms of a custody agreement in Texas. Now you want to put me in violation of a court-ordered hearing at Geostationary. And what's going to happen on Luna? I'm leaving a trail of angry lawyers behind me."

"Why should you care? You're not coming back."

"This is not the example that I want to set for my children. We don't run from our problems."

Olivia raised an eyebrow at Dad. She gave him *the* look. Definitely a 10. "Excuse me? You should have thought of that forty-five-thousand kilometers ago, back in Texas, when you violated the first custody agreement."

"I saw what she was doing to the boys. I had to get them out of there. And when Douglas told me about—well, I just didn't want anyone messing with his brain. So yeah, maybe I had a lot of good justifications—she was grinding us all down."

Olivia looked at her watch impatiently. "And your point is . . . ?"

"My point is, all I wanted was a way to sidestep this mess, not make it worse. You said you were going to set all that Earth stuff aside. This is a higher court and all that? Remember? Now you're going to have us running from one more jurisdiction—and how far does the reach of this one extend?"

"Far enough. That's why you need a placement fast. And a strong corporate sponsor. Only it may be even worse than you think." Abruptly Olivia turned to her son. "Mickey? What's the rest of it? The stuff you didn't tell Aunt Georgia."

Mickey looked unhappy. "In front of the . . ."

"In front of the . . . yes. Christ, this is a mess. Let's not make it any worse. What's the part that panicked you so badly?"

Mickey looked very unhappy, but he stepped over to his mother and spoke quietly to her. "We had a meeting downside, yesterday morning. Elevator Security. They wanted to brief us about our responsibilities should the, uh . . . cable have to be shut down. Someone asked if they were thinking about it and they said that the corporation was currently examining all of its options if civil unrest should break out. The first step would be to restrict all passenger travel except to corporate passengers, which it looks like they're already doing—"

"Rats leaving the ship?"

"And their lawyers—sorry, Mom. The second step will be to restrict all dirtside access entirely. Nothing at all will move between Terminus and One-Hour. The, uh . . . the third step would be—more drastic."

"What's more drastic than shutting down traffic?"

"Breaking the cables at Terminus and letting the beanstalk pull itself off the planet altogether—"

"What?!!" Olivia came out of her chair so fast, it went flying backward and ricocheted off the wall. "You can't be serious—no, *they* can't be serious."

"Yes, they are, Mom." Mickey's voice was deadly quiet. "The Line has been self-sustaining for nearly a decade. There's enough farms up and down the Line, there's enough supplies stashed in the various pods, if we had to break free, we could. The corporation is prepared to pull anchor and hang free for as long as it takes, and not reestablish a ground base until Earth's governments can guarantee Line security."

"It'll never work!"

"It's already happening, Mom! They're using the hurricane as a first-stage drill. They're already moving the balance-pods down the Line. They have this thing all planned out. I'm telling you, they briefed us on it—on what we would have to do in every eventuality. And the briefing officers looked scared, as if they knew more than they were saying. If we go to stage two, every elevator attendant automatically becomes a member of the Line Security force. There are stun-guns on every car now, and they're going to start advanced stun-gun training immediately. You don't make plans that detailed and you don't brief that many people as a readiness exercise or a thought experiment. It was scary, Mom. Some of the women were in tears. The briefing officers made it sound like it was going to happen any day now and we had to be prepared."

"Why didn't you tell this to Georgia?"

"Mom! Think about it. Georgia has to know already!"

"Don't be silly—" But she stopped herself and turned to her keyboard.

"What are you doing?"

Olivia shook her head. "You don't need to know the details." She typed in a last command, then whirled to the wall behind her. She slid a panel sideways and unclipped three memory cards from their stations. She put one in her business bag, handed one to Mickey, and the third one to Dad. "Stash that in your luggage. Don't worry what it is. It's not illegal, and it's encoded. Your courier fee equals my legal fees. We're even." To Mickey, she said, "Get packed and get out of here. If I'm not at the station tonight, go without me. Can you get aboard through the cargo access?"

Mickey scratched his ear. I didn't feel so bad about rubbing my head so much. He said, "If Alexei's on duty, we can board in a cargo bin—"

"Eh?" She raised her eyebrow.

"Mom, an empty cargo bin can be very useful for . . . you know."

"No, I don't know. And I don't think I want to hear any more. Go get your bag."

"Excuse me?" said Dad. "What's going on?" He waved his hand to indicate he meant *the whole thing*.

"Nothing, I hope," said Olivia. "But I'm too old to be taking these kinds of chances." She stopped long enough to look at Dad. "You picked a *lousy* time. You're trying to leave town in the middle of a corporate war. And this could be particularly bad news for you, because Security is going to lock down the entire Line. Even if we get you on a car, it's going to be tricky. It depends on how screwed up things get. Mickey—are you packed?"

Mickey came back out of the other room, carrying a silvery briefcase-purse thing over his shoulder. He looked like he was on his way to the gym or the skating rink; he was all scrubbed and shiny again. I could see why Douglas liked him so much. Even though I still didn't.

MONKEY BUSINESS

ALL RIGHT," MICKEY SAID. "YOU'RE going to have to do exactly as I say. There isn't going to be time to explain everything. Is that all your luggage? Just those backpacks?" He made a face. "That's still too much. It's a giveaway to anyone watching. You'll have to leave them here. Mom, can you repack them and have them sent on as yours? Or do you think that's too risky?"

Olivia studied our carryalls with a thoughtful expression. She shrugged. "I think we're all better off traveling as light as possible."

"All right, I'll trust your judgment. I don't think we're being watched—yet—but let's not take chances." Mickey turned back to us. "Take only what you would carry if you were sightseeing. If you can't put it in your pocket, don't bring it. Douglas, here, take this shopping bag. Anything that you really need, that you can't fit in your pocket and you can't replace, put it in here, so it looks like you've been souvenir-buying. Mr. Dingillian, that memory card that Mom gave you, toss it in here too. This is all the luggage you've got. Anything else you need, you'll pick up later. Doug, you'd better carry Bobby. No, leave the monkey—we'll get him a new one."

"Uh-uh, no way—" I said. "You've never seen a Stinky tantrum. *I'll* carry the monkey. I'll pretend its mine." I was already opening it up to switch off all of Stinky's programs. "Hey," I said. "Give me that memory bar. There's room in here for one more. The monkey's a perfect place to hide . . ." I stopped in mid-sentence and looked at Dad. He'd gone white as a scream. ". . . stuff," I finished lamely. I looked to Doug. He'd gotten it too—at the exact same time. We both looked to Dad. He saw the expressions on our faces and he knew that we knew. And we knew that he knew that . . .

Douglas recovered first—neither Mickey nor Olivia had noticed, or if they had, they were better actors than we were. They were talking about Olivia's connections; she'd be traveling separately. Doug tossed me the memory card and I shoved it into the last socket and closed up the monkey again, and we both pretended to busy ourselves with other stuff for awhile. Dad too. But for a few seconds, it was very uncomfortable.

Then Mickey said, "Well, what are we waiting for? Is everyone ready? Let's go—"

ICE CREAM

WE FOLLOWED MICKEY UP A level to a promenade and shopping level; he delivered a running commentary as we walked, pointing things out and explaining them as if we were nothing more than ordinary tourists and he was merely a hired guide. ". . . You can't see it from here, but it's something you're definitely going to find interesting—the launch bays on Disk Seven. Let's say Brazil wants to launch a communication satellite. They send it up the Line, we push it out the airlock, right? Not quite, but almost. We're geosynchronous, so the satellite still has to get itself into position over its target site. A little burn speeds it up or slows it down, putting it in a lower or higher orbit, depending on which way it wants to go, east or west—call it geosynchronous with deliberate drift. Sometimes it takes awhile for a satellite to work its way around, a week or a month, whatever, but when it finally gets there, it fires its boosters to slow down or speed up, whatever, and put itself back into a geosynchronous position. *Voila!* There you have it. It's possible to put a satellite into almost any orbit you wish from the Line. But we don't do as many launches from here as we used to, when the Line was first built, because the lower stations have the advantage of being able to impart a lot of thrust almost for free—because they're not geosynchronous, you understand? So the launch facilities are now used mostly for direct-docking of shuttles. We get four a day. It's very impressive. Perhaps we'll have time to see one come in tomorrow, *after the hearing*." Mickey made sure to say this last part loud enough so that the fat lady behind us could hear, the one in the bright red-and-yellow flowery dress. She didn't appear to notice.

Douglas looked to Mickey curiously. Mickey smiled guilelessly. "Come on, let's get some ice cream."

Almost on cue, Stinky woke up, rubbing his eyes and looking around. "I didn't get dessert—" he started to whine. Douglas lowered him to his feet; he wobbled for a second, then hung onto Doug's arm, looking confused and unhappy.

"We know you missed dessert," Mickey said. "That's where we're going. See, we're already here—and you have a treat in store . . . hot fudge sundaes, banana splits, chocolate sodas, trust me on this. This is going to be the best part of your trip. I know, the desserts you had on the elevator were good, but most of them are too rich and too sweet to be really enjoyed. You practically have to wear protective gear.

"No, this is ice cream made the traditional way, without overdoing it—and in case you're wondering, Charles, it's all made right here at Geostationary, up on Disk Two. That's where most of the farms are right now, although we'll be opening up new farm levels when Disk Four is finished. Have you seen pictures of the farms? It's not the same, you've got to see them in person. No, we don't have any cows, Bobby—what we have is even better; we do it the Udder Way. Get it? The *udder* way? Never mind. But we've got the best genetically tailored udders anywhere. You'll see in a minute. You're about to have ice cream that's literally *out of this world*. That's another joke."

"He's tired," Douglas explained.

"And those weren't very good jokes," I added. Douglas frowned at me.

Dad spoke up then. He'd been very quiet ever since Doug and I had realized the truth about the monkey. "Excuse me, Mickey—*why are we stopping for ice cream?*"

Mickey pretended he didn't hear. He was studying the menu. After a minute, he looked across the table at Dad. "I think you should have the banana split. Bananas get more expensive the farther out you go. This might be your last chance to enjoy a banana split." The waiter arrived then, and Mickey looked around the table. "Okay, are we all decided?"

We ordered two hot fudge banana splits and four spoons, and a chocolate soda for Stinky. While we waited, I shifted uncomfortably in my seat. Now was as good a time as any to tell them. "Um, Dad—if I tell you something, will you promise not to get mad at me?"

Dad looked over at me quizzically. "What is it, Charles?"

"Um—I know who tipped off Station Security." Mickey and Doug both looked up at that, but I pushed on anyway. "It was J'mee."

"The boy in the swimming pool?"

"He was really a girl. In disguise. They're sneaking off-planet too. Like everybody else, I guess. She's got an implant. She looked us up. And—well, she said a lot of bad stuff about us . . ."

"Like what?"

"Like about Douglas . . . and Bobby . . . and you. . . ."

"Is that how you found out about . . . ?"

"Yeah, it wasn't Mom." I pushed on with the rest of it. "And she said stuff about me too. About all those reports from school. What the counselors said. And she was pretty rude about it, so I—well, I called her a goddamned nasty bitch."

"Jeez," said Douglas. "You're lucky she didn't file an abusive language complaint."

Mickey shook his head. "Hard to prove. 'He-said, she-said.' And her access to private records taints the case." He added, "Besides, she had a better way to get revenge. No one knew where you were; they all thought you were caught at Terminus or hiding out at One-Hour. She tipped off the marshals. Now we know why—" *Charles' big mouth.*

He didn't say the last part. He didn't have to. Everyone was looking at me. Waiting.

"I'm sorry," I said. It didn't feel like it was enough.

Dad's face was unreadable, like he was having another

one of those private arguments that only he could hear. Mickey had wisely fallen silent. Douglas shook his head and shrugged and did his performance of geek retrieving files about social skills. Finally, he reached over and patted my hand. "It's okay, Chigger. It was your turn to screw up. Everybody else did, why not you?"

"Is that supposed to make me feel better?"

"Nah. I'm just reminding you that you're a Dingillian. You're as normal as the rest of us."

"You wanna get a bigger shovel? You can dig faster."

Douglas spread his hands. "Look at it this way, Chig. From here on out, it has to get better."

"Why?"

"Because it can't get any worse."

I nodded. I heard what he said. But it wasn't enough. The waiter brought our ice cream then and even after he passed out spoons, I didn't say anything. Douglas had said all the right things, but Dad hadn't said anything at all. If Dad had said it, if Dad had said anything at all, I would have felt a lot better about my mistake. The knot that had been churning in my stomach since we'd left Terminus was bigger than ever now.

"Chigger—" That was Dad. I looked up. "Eat your ice cream." I suppose he meant well. It didn't help. It was too little, too late. It still felt like a ticking bomb and it was just a matter of time before everything went boom.

We ate in silence. There was no sound except the clink of spoons against glasses and Stinky making bubbles at the bottom of his chocolate soda. Finally I said, sort of in an effort to change the mood, "This is good ice cream, Mickey. And so is the hot fudge. Thank you."

"You're welcome, Charles. I'm glad you like it." He looked up then, "Ahh, Alexei—*dos vidanya*." He pulled out a chair for the newest arrival, a tall, skinny, geeky-looking guy, all arms and legs. He looked like a spider. He gangled. He wore a Russian-looking turtleneck, shorts, and sandals— except for the shirt, it was pretty standard station wear. To the rest of us, Mickey said, "Alexei is a native Loonie, down here for college and muscles. How go the exercises, Alexei?"

Alexei grinned and made a muscle. There wasn't much to

show, but he seemed proud of it. "I shall be a muscleman when I return home. The girls will flock around me at the beach." He grinned and laughed. "I must remember not to be too rough with them, like some of the Earth boys are." I didn't know if he was kidding or not. Everybody said that native Loonies were all tall, skinny, and weak—but the way he was joking, I got the feeling that wasn't completely true, because he was making fun of it. But I just stared at him; so did Douglas and Stinky. We'd never met a *real* Loonie before.

Mickey must have seen the expressions on our faces, because he made full introductions then. Alexei stood up and bowed to each of us, then offered his hand for a handshake. He shook hands with each of us, grabbing our hands in both of his own to do it. He seemed almost too polite, too effusive to be real. "Alexei's family is from Georgia—"

"The Russian Georgia," Alexei explained, "not the American one. Y'awl." He laughed at his own joke, no one else did. I got the feeling he told it a lot. "I was born in Gagarin Dome. My mother wanted to name me Yuri, my father wanted to call me Neil. So they compromised, and I am Alexei."

"Alexei?"

"Alexei Krislov, Captain of the Allied Worlds Starcruiser *Private Enterprise*—from the video series, you have heard of it, *da*? About an interstellar space trader? He was the only cosmonaut both my parents liked—a fictitious one. Personally"—he leaned forward with a conspiratorial air—"I think they watch too much television." Suddenly he was all business. He swiveled to face Mickey and said casually, "So? You said you had packages?"

Mickey nodded toward us. "Four. Five, if you count me."

Alexei glanced at us again, his face darkening. "I don't know, *Mikhail*. I'm not equipped for a job like this—this is a little big for me."

Mickey raised an eyebrow.

Alexei shrugged. "Sometimes I talk too big. So sue me— no wait, forget I said that. I know your mom. I would like to keep the royal jewels." He grinned and grabbed his crotch. To us, he said, "They really are royal jewels. My family is descended from the Romanovs. The last Tsar of Russia? That was a long time ago, I don't expect you to remember. But no matter. My great-uncle continues to file lawsuits in the World Court, every session, for the restoration of the monarchy. No, I would not be the Tsar—not unless sixteen of my cousins died mysteriously first, which will not happen. I only hate four of them." He turned back to Mickey. "This won't be easy. You know that the whole Line is locking down."

"I know," said Mickey.

"It's going to be expensive."

"I have information. *Big* information."

Alexei pursed his lips and frowned to himself. He was thinking it over. He steepled his fingers in front of his chin and nodded thoughtfully. "How big?"

"The biggest. It *will* affect your business." To us, Mickey said. "Alexei is a money-surfer. In the truest sense. Do you know what money-surfers are?"

"Sure. Everybody does. A money-surfer is someone who rides the flow of money."

"That's right," said Alexei. "That is the common usage. But I am a traditional money-surfer, one of the best. Maybe *Mikhail* will explain later." He looked at his friend. "So? What do you want me to do?"

"Deliver the packages."

"You overestimate me, *Mikhail*. Didn't you have any ideas of your own?"

"Only one."

"*Ah.* What was your wonderful idea?"

" 'Call Alexei.' "

Alexei made a face. "That was *not* a good idea. Tell me, what is Alexei supposed to do?" He sighed. "I am sorry, *Mikhail*, I cannot help you with this."

"Listen, Alexei—Max here has pissed off one of the SuperNationals. Do you know Hidalgo? Yes, that one. He's apparently involved. He threatened Max—oh, not directly, of course—but there was no doubt about his intentions. This might very well be a matter of life and death."

Alexei glanced over at us again, with new respect. "I like you. You make powerful enemies." To Mickey, he said, "All the more reason why I shouldn't get involved in this."

"Yes, you should," said Mickey. "You really want to hear what I know."

"Don't do this to me, *Mikhail*."

Mickey leaned over and whispered in Alexei's ear. Alexei's eyes widened, and he pulled back to stare at Mickey. "You're crazy."

"No—*they're* crazy."

"They'd have to be—good God." Alexei put his hand over his mouth, shocked. It was like he didn't want to let himself say anything else. It took him a moment to find his voice again. "I have phone calls to make, lots of phone calls," he said. "I wish you hadn't told me—no, that's not true. I'm glad you told me. But now I'm obligated to do this stupid thing for you, aren't I?"

"That's why I told you." Mickey smiled sweetly.

"You have the soul of a viper. Your mother trained you well."

"I love you too, Alexei." Mickey glanced at his watch. "Come on. We'd better get going." Mickey slid his card through the table's reader. "Okay, we're paid. Let's go."

FLOWING UP

IN ONE OF HIS WEIRDER moods, Douglas once said that the best definition of a living creature is that it's a bag of water that moves by itself and makes more bags of water. Life is nothing more than a convenient way for water to get up and take a walk. Life is how water takes a vacation. Life is the way that water flows uphill. Et cetera, et cetera, et cetera.

But yeah, I guess if you think about it that way, it sort of makes sense. Life is water in a membrane, doing stuff. And anywhere that life wants to go, it has to take water with it. So it's the membrane that makes life possible.

Weird says a lot of stuff like that. He says good philosophy is the foundation of sentience, but good plumbing is the foundation of civilization. Once, he even said, "If you want to really know people, look in their sewers." That was good for three weeks of teasing him about going around looking down toilets as a way to meet girls. I stopped the joking only when he threatened to stuff me headfirst down the commode in search of intelligent life. That is, I stopped the jokes in front of his face, not behind his back—

At least until Alexei said something about showing us

what space sewers looked like—"Come, I will show you the plumbing." He pointed toward the ceiling. "Here we keep it in the attic." He led us toward a hatch opening into a service corridor. So I poked Weird and said, "Hey, we're going to get to know these people really well, right, Doug?"

"Bag it, Chigger." He said it without any apparent emotion. If he was too worried to be nasty, then the situation was serious enough to be *serious*. I shut up.

Alexei had pulled out his phone and was already calling people. Most of his calls were in Russian; he spoke in thick, rabid phrases, shouting almost hysterically at whoever was on the other end. Each time as he broke the connection, he smiled at us. "You've got to talk to them in their own language: Stupid. Is not to worry. They will do what I tell them. There is too much money at stake." He looked at Mickey. "This is going to be very expensive—for everyone. Especially for me. Not for you, though. You are already paid. The information you have given me—I will make millions of dollars today. Already I am having some wonderful ideas. *Mikhail*, I hope there is time for them all. I am most grateful that you called me—I will name my firstborn child after you, even if he is a girl." He popped his phone open and started hollering into it again.

Still roaring into his phone, Alexei fumbled a pass card out of his shirt pocket and used it to unlock a wide hatchway; we followed him into a service bay and boarded a cargo elevator. Alexei gestured impatiently at the walls, and we all grabbed handholds—he hit the Go panel and we rose "up" toward the axis, the innermost rings of the disk. As we rose, pseudo-gravity faded out. Dad and Doug and Mickey took turns carrying Stinky, who hadn't quite fallen asleep again, but was content to just rest in the arms of whoever was carrying him. In micro-gravity, he wasn't as much of a burden, but he was still an awkward bundle.

Alexei closed his phone and looked at Mickey. "I am going to make too much money today, *Mikhail*. I will have to give you some of it or my conscience will trouble me—not too much, though. I do not have a very large conscience. You will share some of it with your new friends, *da?* That gives me another idea—later." He opened his phone again.

"Mishka, when you get home to your kennel, don't let your mother bite you in the ass—listen to me, you son of a German whore—" I didn't know if Alexei was like all Russians, but he had a strange way of treating his friends. If those were indeed his friends. I wasn't sure.

When we got to the top, we came out of the tube into a narrow service corridor, the floor here had the steepest up-curve of all. The pseudo-gravity was too light for real walking, so we sort of bounced forward, caroming off the walls for a bit until Alexei slowed us down and suggested we conserve our energy. He pointed to handholds spaced along the walls. "Use those. Pull yourselves along. Pretend you're swimming. I will carry the little one—" I wished he hadn't said that about swimming. I was already having trouble remembering up and down. This wasn't as much fun as it looked. Stinky thought it was fun. He wanted to try bouncing by himself, but Alexei promised him that it would be more fun to ride on his back, so he decided to try that instead. How often do you get to piggy-back ride a Loonie in free fall?

We passed a whole bunch of KEEP OUT, THIS MEANS YOU! and AUTHORIZED PERSONNEL ONLY! signs, but Alexei ignored them. Whenever we came to a locked hatch, Alexei would pull out an appropriate clearance card and pass us through. "How do you have all these cards?" Dad asked.

"Ah, it speaks—" Alexei laughed. To Dad, he said, "What do you think I came here to study? Domestic Ecology. I am on a work-study plan. I earn my education with hands-on experience. I am three years here, I have clearances everywhere. I can go anywhere on the station. It is the perfect job for a young smuggler, *da?* Do not worry, Mr. Dingillian, I do not abuse the trust of my employers. At least, not very often. And usually only for a good cause. This is a good cause. Besides, if what *Mikhail* tells me is true, I think that my usefulness here has just ended. I am returning to Gagarin very shortly. I will visit my money."

"When?" Dad asked.

"Tonight," laughed Alexei. "On the very same elevator as you. We go out together. Ahh, here we are—"

Here was a thick hatch into a triple-sealed room—an airlock? Inside was a ladder up into a hatch in what would have been the ceiling, except there was so little gravity here, it didn't feel like a ceiling—except for the orientation of a big red arrow marked THIS SIDE UP in English as well as in several other languages.

Alexei passed Stinky into Mickey's arms and pulled himself up the ladder. At the top, he hesitated, scratching his cheek thoughtfully. He put his card into the reader and punched an entry code. The panel flashed green. He looked back down to us. "You must be very careful here. We are at the hub. The axis. The Line passes through a pressurized core. We run pipes and conduits and vents through the core all the way from Disk One to Disk Seven. It is the foundation for the next stage of construction—a common domestic ecology. But the core doesn't rotate, because it's connected to the Line itself. As you come through the hatch, it will look like the top side of the corridor is moving; it isn't—we are. It isn't fast, but it's fast enough to look scary. Just keep your head down, hold onto the railings, you'll be fine. I'll be right here to help. Any questions? No? Good. Let's go."

Alexei tapped the Go panel and the hatch slid open. He pulled himself up through the opening and disappeared for a moment. Then his head reappeared. "Hokay, Douglas, you come next please?" Douglas jumped and floated right up to the hatch, grabbing onto the handholds near the top. Alexei put a hand on his shoulder to keep him from sailing through. Douglas pulled himself up carefully and peered through the hatch. "That's right," Alexei coached. "Float through slowly. Hang onto this railing and just move down to make room." Douglas nodded and went through.

"Hokay, Charles—you come next. This is very easy, *da?*" I swallowed hard. For some reason, up and down and sideways had suddenly decided to stop being up and down and sideways and were all changing directions on me. I felt dizzy. I squeezed my eyes tightly shut. Sometimes that helped. This time it didn't.

"Charles? Are you all right—?" That was Dad. I didn't answer.

"*Charles—!*" That was Alexei. "Open your eyes and look at me. Do it *now!*" His voice was so hard it startled me. I opened my eyes. He was holding his hand out toward me. "Look at my hand, see? Just grab my hand, hokay? I'll do the rest."

Before I could shake my head no, or even as I did, I felt Dad lifting me up to take Alexei's hand. Alexei grabbed my arm and pulled me gently through the hatch. "See, that wasn't so bad—here, grab this railing and hold on. Douglas, hold him, please? Thank you. Move down now, just a bit. Make room for the others." I was still uncomfortable—almost close to tears, I didn't know why—but then Douglas put his arm around my shoulder and held me close and I didn't feel quite so bad anymore.

"*Mikhail,* I am ready for the little stinky one. Pass him here. That's it. Come to me, Bobby. Here, stick your head through. Look around—see? Nothing to be afraid of. The only monsters up here are your brothers. Hold onto this railing, please. *Mikhail—?* Send up Mr. Dingillian, please."

Dad came next, and Mickey followed. Alexei sealed the hatch behind him. Now, we were all clutching handholds on the inside of the steepest curve yet. Three meters away, the curved wall of the core whispered by. We could hear the air whooshing as it passed. We watched a steady progression of warning signs and arrows and numbers and access panels. There were tracks in the opposite surface, matching tracks in the wall we clung to.

Alexei looked anti-spinward expectantly, so I followed his gaze. I was still uncomfortable, but watching the moving ceiling sort of helped. I don't know why.

"Ahh," said Alexei. "Here it comes."

It was a bright red platform sliding toward us on the tracks. It slowed to a stop directly next to the access panel we'd climbed through. It had handholds and equipment boxes mounted all over it. All its corners were rounded, and most of its flat surfaces had bumper pads. There was a funny angular contraption in the middle, like a collapsible tower. Alexei pulled us all aboard, and then pushed a green Go button, and turned a dial. "We want the One-Gamma-Three entrance," he explained as the platform began moving spinward. "One is the disk we're on. Gamma is the cable. Three is the access. *Capisce?*"

We passed similar cars mounted on other tracks, on our side as well as on the rotating surface above / next to us; most of them were stopped and waiting, but our car sped up until we had matched speed with the inner wall. There was a panel there marked ONE-GAMMA-THREE. Alexei unfolded the collapsed contraption in the middle of the car. It was an extensible ladder and it went all the way across. "Hokay, let's go."

Alexei grabbed Stinky in a bear hug and started scrambling across like a pregnant spider. I shook off Dad's help, but not Douglas's. When we were all safely across, Mickey hit the release on the top of the ladder and it folded back down. Now the ceiling felt motionless and the floor was rolling past. Except it wasn't a floor anymore. It was just a rotating wall-surface, with a car tracking along beside us. Then the car began to slow, and pretty soon it disappeared around the curve behind us.

Alexei was already opening the One-Gamma-Three panel and pulling us through. First Douglas, then me, then Mickey—they passed Stinky through—then finally Dad and Alexei. Inside the core, I levered myself around to look and nearly lost it—"*Douglas!*" I wailed. My brother caught me and held me tightly with his right arm. "It's okay, Charles. I'm right here. I'm not letting go. Just hang onto me—we'll be fine. Really."

I buried my face in Douglas's shoulder. I could sense that both Mickey and Dad were hovering close, but I didn't want to have anything to do with either of them. Only Douglas.

What I'd seen . . . was the largest interior space I'd ever seen—well, maybe not *the* largest, maybe Terminus was larger—but definitely the *deepest*. It was like the inside of a giant pipe, filled with humongus wires, cables, tubes, conduits, vents, pass-throughs, catwalks, ladders, platforms, machinery, and *stuff*. And it all looked *up* and *down* and *sideways*—all at the same time!

"Are you okay, son—?" That was Dad. I didn't answer. Douglas pulled away just enough to look at my face. He tilted my chin upward so we were eye to eye and nose to nose. I couldn't remember the last time we'd ever been this close. Maybe we never had. "I'm not going to let anything bad happen to you, Charles. I promise."

"What's wrong with Charles?" I heard Stinky asking.

"Nothing. Please be quiet, Bobby. Charles has an upset stomach. He'll be okay in a minute. Go back to sleep." Douglas looked back to me. "Just tell me when you're ready."

I shook my head. I didn't want him to let go. I liked having his arm around me. I felt safe. I swallowed hard. "I don't want to lose you, Douglas," I whispered, so only he could hear. "Not to anybody—" I sort of nodded toward Mickey.

"You're not going to lose me. I'll always be your brother, no matter what."

"Is that a threat or a promise?" I half-joked.

He half-smiled. "Yes." He nudged me. "Come on, the others are waiting. And we don't have a lot of time. Are you ready?"

"Yeah. Just stay close, okay?"

"*Hokay*," he said. Just like Alexei.

THE OLD SWIMMING HOLE

IT WAS LIKE BEING ON the inside of a giant pipe that kept changing its orientation. But as long as I kept focused on the wall and pretended that I was swimming and it was the floor, I was okay. If I had to look away from the wall, for any reason, I pretended that everything else was *up*. It sort of worked, but I still felt dizzy.

Alexei pointed around the curve of the wall toward a cluster of pipes and a vertical platform on which there were some storage lockers. We pulled ourselves along a line of handholds, and when we got to the platform, we anchored ourselves against its railings.

"Do you see this pipe?" Alexei pounded on one of the thicker pipes next to us. "Put your ear next to it. You can hear the water rushing through it. Very useful stuff. We use it for ballast. We use it to balance the rotation of the disks. Sometimes we even turn it into oxygen to breathe and hydrogen to burn. And of course, we also use it for drinking and bathing and growing our crops. It is our lifeblood!

"Listen, you can hear it flowing—back and forth, up and down, in and out, all over the station—carrying sewage to the farms where it will be turned back into food, going to the distilleries where the sunlight will turn it into steam and the cold of space will turn it back into fresh water, three times over, and then it will rush back down here, flowing this way and that, nourishing the lives of all of us.

"Do you know what is one of the worst crimes you can commit here on the station? Interfering with the water. Because whatever else it is, water is first and foremost, the stuff of life—so you do not tamper with it. The flow of water—in fact, all of what we call the domestic ecology—is the property of the whole community here, and each and every one of us has a responsibility to the community. The way we keep the water flowing, that demonstrates how responsible we are to our people.

"But—" he interrupted himself "—these pipes are also very useful if you have to go somewhere and you don't want anyone to know that you are going or how you got there. And so, while we respect the water, sometimes we ride it too." Alexei opened one of the storage lockers. Inside was—scuba gear?!

"Huh? Are we going swimming?" Stinky asked.

"You? No," Alexei said. "Them. Yes." He pointed. We looked up—every direction was *up*—and saw four, no five, teenagers diving out of the center toward us. Three boys, two girls. They were wearing shorts and T-shirts and looked like they had fallen off a runaway picnic. They were laughing like they were diving into a party.

As they approached, they began waving and calling to us. They caught themselves easily on the platforms and ladders and railings around us, and they shouted things at Alexei in Russian that made him blush with embarrassment. They passed him a backpack and a pair of canteens. They had a third canteen of their own, which they passed around among themselves, each one taking deep swallows of whatever was in it. From the way they acted, I didn't think it was water.

Alexei took the flask when it came to him and took a deep swig of his own, then he pocketed it, much to their dismay. "You have all had enough," he said. Then he bawled them out in Russian. Or gave them instructions. Or told a dirty joke. Whatever. When he finished, they all laughed and started pulling on the various pieces of diving equipment.

Alexei explained, "These are my fellow students and colleagues. The swimming equipment is part of our service. Sometimes we have to inspect the pipes from the inside. Sometimes there are air bubbles. Sometimes we have to retrieve a broken robot or a piece of something that has caught somewhere. We do not have to do that very often. In fact . . . I can't ever remember having to go into the pipes at all for anything a robot couldn't handle. But, nevertheless, we have our responsibilities. We have to keep ourselves ready and able to handle any possibility, any emergency at all. So we practice and drill and keep ourselves focused on our responsibilities to the water of the community. Today—ah, today we get to put into practice what we have practiced. They shall be . . . the *decoys*."

"So this is how you do it," Mickey said. "I've always wondered about that."

"Wonder no longer," Alexei said. "Sooner or later, somebody was certain to figure it out anyway. No matter, I already have three other ways to move things from here to there—just not as exciting. I leave it to you to figure them out, *Mikhail*. I will bet you a day's interest that you cannot."

"I can't afford that bet." Mickey laughed.

Alexei laughed with him and clapped him on the shoulder. "You are smarter than you act. This is a good trait." To the rest of us, he said, "We have to assume you are being watched. At the very least, monitored through station security. There are those damnable little cameras everywhere. They saw us coming up the service elevator. They know that an access hatch was opened. That was why I used my *own* card. So they could monitor our progress. Very shortly, they will be monitoring the progress of five divers through the pipes—and one of them will be carrying my locator. Five divers, not six, we will keep them wondering what happened, *da*? They will meet the divers on the topside of Disk Seven. But by then, we will be somewhere else, and they will have lost us. I am too clever for my own good." To his Russian comrades, Alexei shouted, "What is taking you so long? Do you think we have all night? Look at the time. We have less than an hour—"

"Alexei," said one of the men, a dark brooding fellow with eyebrows like furry caterpillars. "The deposits are made, *da?*"

"*Da.*"

"This is good. We have made our own reservations, we will be on the one A.M. car. If what you say is true—"

"You have told no one else?"

Caterpillar-brow shook his head. "I think the word is already spreading. But no, we have told no one. Go now. Godspeed!" He glanced around. "Godspeed to all of you." Then he grabbed Alexei and the two of them exchanged kisses on each cheek, the way they do in Europe. I'd never seen men do that before, kiss each other—even friends. It sort of freaked me. I looked at Douglas and Mickey and tried to imagine them kissing. It didn't seem right, but it didn't seem as wrong anymore either. What the hell did I know?

AT THE CORE

WE WERE GOING UP THE Line—*by hand.*

From an Earth perspective, we were going up. From the Geostationary perspective, we were going sideways—starside—outward toward Disk Seven.

From our perspective, we weren't going any direction at all. Just *forward* along a never ending pipe. There was water on the inside of the pipe; we could hear it. There were handholds running the length. We were climbing to forever. I wondered how long it would take to climb the whole Line—

"How come we can't take a maintenance car?" I asked. "Look, there are lots of tracks along these pipes. And there's a car over there."

"The maintenance cars are monitored." Mickey said. "We don't want to leave any evidence of where we started and where we got off. Most of all we don't want anyone showing up to meet us. Just keep pulling yourself along."

Alexei showed us how to do it. "Don't try to hurry," he said. "You'll tire yourself out. Slow and steady does the job. Do like I do, hand over hand, counting like this—like music ... and one ... and two ... and three ... and four ... like that. That's how to make the best time over a distance." He added, "If you did this all the time, you would know how to go faster, but I need you to conserve your strength. We have a long way to go. Almost two kilometers. We can do it, but you must concentrate. Mickey, do you know a good song? Something to give us a pace?"

"Alexei, you forget who you're talking to. I couldn't carry a tune in free fall." And then, after Douglas and I finished laughing, he said, "No, I mean it. I can't sing. Douglas?"

Douglas snorted. "Chigger is the one in our family who sings. Charles?" He was right behind me. "How about a song?"

Without hesitating an instant, I began, *"It's a small world, after all—"* Four voices shouted for me to stop before I finished the first line. Two of the voices contained serious hints of violence, Dad's and Doug's.

"Now, I'm going to have an earworm, all night," Douglas muttered. "Whose good idea was that?"

"I think we should all save our breath for a while," Dad said, "and just concentrate on the job at hand."

The job at hand was the next handhold—and the one after that—and the one after that—I could feel the slap of the plastic handholds against my palms like a steady beat; it echoed up through my wrists, my forearms, my elbows . . . there was a rhythm to it. For some reason, I started thinking of a song that Mom used to sing to us when we were small. *"Oh, Lord, won't you buy me a Mercedes Benz . . . ?"*

A Mercedes Benz was some kind of car they didn't make anymore, but it didn't matter. The song always had such a plaintive quality, it might have been about my life. I didn't even realize I was singing it aloud until Douglas joined me on the chorus. I stopped, embarrassed.

Dad was right behind Douglas. He called up to me, "Charles—I didn't know you liked Janice Joplin."

"I used to," I said. "Until about four seconds ago." That came out a little nastier than I intended. "Why didn't you tell me about John Coltrane?"

"Huh?"

"The Coltrane Suite. You never sent me a copy."

"Yes, I did."

"I never got it."

"It came back refused."

"I didn't do that."

"It must have been your mom—" He stopped himself. "I'm sorry, Charles, I promised myself I'd never say anything bad about your mom, but there were times when she acted badly. I sent you a lot of stuff, a lot of music. She sent most of it back; she told me not to send you any more. She didn't think it was good for you to spend all that time locked up by yourself with your headphones on. I liked it that you were always so interested in my recordings. I think that's why she did it—to keep us apart, to keep me from using the music as a way to stay close to you. I'll get you another copy. I promise."

"Never mind. I don't want to hear it."

"Have it your own way." Dad sounded hurt. I didn't care. John Coltrane was just mine. Not his. Couldn't he let me have one thing that was just mine alone? Couldn't he let any of us have our own lives? He was always using us—like Stinky's monkey—without asking permission or telling us what was going on. He didn't trust us. So why should we trust him?

I felt Doug pulling himself up closer to me, alongside me. He looked at me oddly. "Chigger, we've gotta talk."

"There's been enough talk already," I said. "I don't need any more. Thanks."

Doug looked annoyed. "What's with you anyway?"

I indicated Stinky's chimpanzee with a backward nod; it was clinging happily to my neck. "I got a monkey on my back."

"In more ways than one," Douglas said. "I'm not going to talk to you when you're like this." He let me pull ahead so he could follow me again. Dad came after him. And we kept going.

We were in free fall. Or the next best thing to it. We were inside a giant cylinder filled with ladders and tubes and wires and stuff. We were at the geosynchronous point of the space elevator. We were pulling ourselves more than two kilometers along the handholds on the outside of a water pipe big enough to push a Volkswagen through. We were here because our parents hated each other, both of them certifiably neurotic, and because Dad had kidnapped us with the intention of taking us off-planet somewhere. To finance the trip, he was acting as a courier, and had hidden some illicit memory inside Stinky's monkey.

So of course there were people after us. Mom had sent lawyers, other folks were sending security agents, and still others might send some thugs to hurt or kill us. We'd been served with a subpoena, and we were running away from a court action. We were in a restricted access zone with a Russian smuggler—and we had no idea what he usually smuggled. And meanwhile, there were folks getting ready to break the Line free of the Earth, which would probably kill thousands of people and collapse the economies of a hundred different nations and at least a thousand different industries.

Dr. Hidalgo's sacred money would stop flowing just like a stopped-up toilet. Maybe it would back up and overflow and seek out new channels, and a lot of fortunes would be lost and new ones would be made, and all the ordinary people caught up in it would suddenly have their own set of problems. Ghu knew just how many millions of people might end up losing their jobs and their homes and their belongings. In some places people might even starve to death. There would certainly be riots and civil unrest and refugees and plagues and probably even a war or two. And that would trigger even more problems; and everything would just keep on going. On and on.

I guess this was what some people would call an *adventure*.

Thanks, but no thanks. I didn't ask for this adventure, and nobody had asked me how I felt about it. Just like the divorce. It made my stomach hurt and my chest felt like I had a knot in it. I don't know why people think adventures are so wonderful. Mostly they hurt, they're boring, and they're dangerous.

I concentrated on watching the handholds passing in front of me. I pulled myself steadily forward, left hand over right, right hand over left, and went back to wondering. If Judge Griffith were to take away the words *right* and *left*, how I would be able to explain the difference between one and the other.

MONEY-SURFING

EVERYBODY USES E-MONEY.

You slide your card through a reader and you're paid. The money travels from your card into the store. It's a stream of numbers representing a sum of money, and wherever it goes, it's still the same amount of money. E-money carries its own verification codes, so anyplace you can send a block of data you can send e-money. You can send it across a wire, or you can pipe it into a card, or you can put it on a beam of light and send it off to Betelgeuse—like that crazy artist did last year. Or you can stuff it in the back of a toy monkey. But however e-money gets sent, as long as it decodes authentically when it arrives, it's *money*.

Weird says that at any given moment, twenty percent of the world's wealth doesn't exist. It's nothing but bits and bytes on its way somewhere else. I always thought that money had to represent something—like kilowatt-dollars are backed by electricity and potato dollars are backed by potatoes; but Weird says that e-money is backed by e-balances and e-potentials and e-futures, which are sometimes backed by e-stocks and e-bonds, and sometimes even by digital resources, but it's all so detached from the real world now that it really doesn't have anything at all to back it, except the whole world's mutual agreement. We all pretend that it's real and we pass it around like it's real, and once in a while, we turn e-dollars into plastic-dollars or chocolate-dollars or sugar-dollars, and sometimes even into paper-dollars or gold-dollars. The gold-dollars are the best; Dad showed me one once, in a museum. But it isn't real unless you make it real.

Eighty percent of the world's economy uses e-money now. It's almost impossible not to, unless you're bartering raw cocoa or something like that. It's estimated that four trillion dollars of e-money changes hands every day on the North American continent alone. I have no idea what it's like worldwide. But Weird says that if you could shut off all the electricity in the world at the same moment, you could destroy the world economy, that's how much money is in transit at any given instant.

I didn't fully believe that, but Weird said it could happen. If they break the Line, the world would never recover. But I didn't understand how that was so. All the buildings would still be there, all the people, all the crops and factories and stores and products in the stores. Why couldn't people just keep working anyway? And besides—wasn't there some kind of backup system to keep e-money from being lost in transit?

We'd studied e-money in school, but I'd tried hard not to pay attention and mostly succeeded in getting all the way through the semester without learning very much about it. It didn't seem very interesting at the time. But the important thing about e-money is that every transaction needs to be authenticated by the International Transfer System, which is kind of like an electronic post office for money, every transfer is insured.

Every time money is transferred from one person to another, it goes through an ITS node, which verifies and audits the exchange; this is particularly important when you need proof of payment for legal reasons. But the ITS also charges you one-twentieth of a percent—that's a nickel for every hundred dollars being transferred—which isn't all that much, I guess, because most people hardly notice it. But it's called the "transfer tax," because the more money you move, the more you pay.

If you move $2000, your transfer tax is a buck. But if you're a SuperNational, and you're moving around hundreds of millions of e-dollars, you're going to notice the e-tax real fast. If you want to move a *billion* dollars from here to there, it's going to cost you half a million in transfer charges. Of course, if you have a billion dollars, you can afford to spend half a million whenever you feel like it, but that's probably not the best way to *stay* a billionaire.

If the average daily flow of money is four trillion dollars, the government should make two billion dollars a day in e-tax alone. More than 70 trillion dollars a year. Almost enough to service the interest on the international debt.

Actually, the international authority only makes 1.25 billion dollars a day in e-tax. At least 750 million dollars moves through private services. Not everybody wants to pay the transfer tax. And not everybody wants the government auditing their finances either.

So anyone who has money that they want to move from one place to another without leaving a trail sends it through a transfer service, which is just like an anonymous remailer on the net. It strips the ID off the money and sends it on.

The e-money gets decoded into a service account, and a corresponding transfer is authorized to the recipient. The entire process is automatic. But for the few seconds or minutes it takes to send the money on, it's earning interest for the transfer service. That's why they're called money-surfers, they're riding the flow.

Most of the private services charge only a minimal fee, like a buck a transfer, no matter how much money is moving. Some of services are even free, if you're moving more than a million dollars a week. If you're a money-surfer with millions of dollars a day moving through your service accounts, at any given moment, you probably have a couple of million dollars in your pocket—even if it's somebody else's millions, you're still being paid interest on it. It's called your "average daily balance." A money-surfer with good clients can live quite well off the interest. It's like owning a perpetual motion machine that makes money just by sitting next to a river of it and sticking a finger in.

Not everybody can be a money-surfer, though. It can be dangerous. Two of the private services were hit very badly by a virus that scrambled some of their incoming data, and another company was hit with a counterfeit e-check. They still aren't talking about how that was done. The one that was hit had been "double-dipping"—transferring the money to a second account before sending it on, so it was collecting twice the interest. There wasn't anything really unethical about it, and it added only two or three minutes to each transfer, but somebody didn't like it, that was for sure. Anyway, there are a lot of companies providing transfer services, and some of them work through international pipelines—connected series of accounts—making it impossible to trace an exchange of money, even if you had a dozen international subpoenas.

According to Mickey, Alexei was an interplanetary money-surfer. That meant he had to be at least a millionaire—maybe more. That's why I began to wonder if there was more to this than Mickey was saying.

See, Alexei was helping us break the law. If we were caught, he'd go to jail too. He didn't have to take this kind of risk.

So why was he doing all this for us?

And just what was in the monkey anyway?

☾

WORDS

IT TOOK US MORE THAN an hour. We stopped once to pass a canteen around and catch our breaths. This canteen had water in it and a nipple over the opening; I sucked at it thirstily. Doug whispered to me, "Slow down, Chigger—don't pull a Stinky." He was right. I passed the canteen on. It was a very short rest; as soon as everybody had had a drink, we were on our way again.

At the top, or the far end, there was a wall blocking further progress. We had to climb up through a narrow tube and through a series of thick air locks.

"Okay, comrades," Alexei said. "This is where you must each make a prayer to Saint Vladimir—" We were at the final hatch.

"Saint Vladimir . . . ?"

"I made him up. He is the patron saint of smugglers. I smuggled him into heaven. Now let's see if he is appropriately grateful." Alexei took out his clearance card and swiped it through the reader slot. He inhaled. He exhaled. The panel turned green, and when he tapped it, the hatch popped open.

"Thank you, Saint Vladimir. I shall light candles at your

altar," Alexei said to the ceiling. "As soon as I can find candles. And build an altar." We passed through—into the top or bottom of a brightly lit shaft lined with machinery. It was deep and the walls were lined with tracks and service bays. On one side, we saw seven or eight elevator cars, each one docked and surrounded by lights and equipment and service gear. None of them had their cabins spinning; all had their lights on.

"Ahh," said Alexei. "I have done good. Very good. And Saint Vladimir has done good. I was afraid I was going to have to replace him. See there? We are almost at the beginning of your journey. This way, citizens. We must not be seen."

There was small chance of that. There weren't any people on the outside of the cars. There were two spider-jeeps inspecting hulls, but they were all the way down at the bottom of the bay.

Nevertheless, Alexei led us around to the backside of a thick service pipe, where we would be out of sight, and we lowered ourselves down it. Bobby was clinging to Douglas's back and the monkey was still on mine.

Halfway down, Alexei and Mickey stopped to whisper hurriedly to each other. Mickey pointed. "That one. Number 1187. According to the tickets, that's the midnight car."

Alexei shook his head. "Are you sure? It looks like it's in the wrong position. There are too many cars ahead of it."

"That's what the tickets say. Wait a minute—" Mickey pulled his phone out of his pocket and spoke softly into it. He listened for a moment, then nodded, closed the phone and put it back in his pocket. "They're sending extra cars out to Whirlaway. VIP traffic." To our puzzled looks, he said, "I might be fired, but I still have friends."

"Hokay. Let's go." Alexei pointed. "We go around here, go across this catwalk, and enter through the left-side hatch. Any questions?"

"Why aren't they spinning?"

"They only spin them for passengers. If they were spinning, we couldn't do this; all the access through the transfer pods is too tightly controlled. Hokay, enough talk. Mickey, you lead."

We entered 1187 without incident. It was a lot like the car we'd ridden up in. We pulled ourselves in through the left-side hatch; it was the cargo hatch, the bottom. I wondered which way it was going to spin—clockwise or counter-clockwise? Would it make any difference?

Mickey led us directly to our cabins; Olivia had booked two, and there was a connecting door between them.

We pushed and pulled ourselves into the biggest one, the suite, and bounced into chairs. Mickey showed us how to release the seat belts, and we belted ourselves down. Douglas wrapped a blanket around Stinky, who promptly curled up and fell asleep wrapped around his monkey. The monkey snored softly for a moment or two, then fell silent.

Mickey glanced at his watch and grinned. "We made it. With time to spare. Now all we have to do is wait for Mom."

Alexei was already pulling rations out of his backpack. "I thought you might like a snack while you wait. I have cheese, fish-sausage, bread, grapes, little tomatoes, carrots. Eat hearty. *Bon appetit.*" He bowed from the waist, difficult to do in micro-gravity. "I must return now—they will be looking for me. I must not disappoint them. Otherwise, it spoils the game. Besides, I need to collect some things. Including my alibi." He handed the backpack to Mickey. "*Mikhail*, please make sure my father gets this. If I am not able to deliver it myself. Hokay? Thank you." And with that, he was gone.

"Where's he going?"

"Back down."

"The same way?"

"He can do it in fifteen minutes. He was a finalist in last year's no-grav Olympics. It's those long arms of his. And all the practice he gets." Mickey explained, "He'll probably go back to the ice cream place, or walk around the promenade for a while, whatever it takes, until he's sure that whoever is watching knows that he's not with us anymore. Then he'll disappear again. At least, that's my guess. Charles, do you want some grapes?"

"No thanks." I pushed the plate away. "All the grapes I've ever gotten have been sour."

"Yes, and you've done a fine job making sour whine." It

was the first time Mickey had ever said anything rude to me. I looked at him surprised. He looked right back at me. "Don't you ever put a cork in it, kiddo? *Do you know that you are no fun to be around?*"

"So what?"

"So look around you and stop acting like a spoiled brat. Your family is coming apart—"

"It came apart a long time ago."

"*Shut up, stupid.* Try listening for a change. You might learn something. In case you hadn't noticed, your brother, Douglas, is having a very difficult time of this. And your dad isn't doing too well either—he hasn't spoken two words to anyone except you since we left my mother's. And you shut him down. The only reason Bobby hasn't thrown a tantrum is that we slipped a sedative into his chocolate soda. We should have done the same for you. You're not doing anything to make this easier for anybody."

"Nobody's trying to make it any easier on me," I snapped back.

"Excuse me—?" Mickey pushed in close, getting right in my face. "Douglas wasn't there for you when you got free-fall panic? Your dad didn't lift you up when you needed it? Your dad hasn't been trying to reach out to you all evening? Or was I hallucinating? You're acting like a selfish dirtsider, Charles. And I don't like you very much, right now."

"So fucking what? None of this would have happened if you hadn't—"

"Don't *go* there . . ." he warned.

"Mickey, please—" That was Douglas. "There's more to this than you know." He stepped / bounced over to Mickey and put his hand on his shoulder; they looked at each other and something unsaid passed between them. Mickey looked frustrated, but he nodded and backed off. Douglas turned to Dad then. "Okay, Dad," he said. "What's in the monkey?"

Dad shook his head. "I wish you hadn't found out about that."

"Yeah, well—it wasn't too hard to figure out. Is there anything else you want to tell us?"

Dad shook his head. He looked beaten, frustrated, angry, unhappy. "No, there's nothing else. I just thought—that maybe we could have some time together that wasn't a fight."

"Why would you think that?" asked Douglas. "Every time we get together, it's a fight. That's all we ever do. Why would you think this time would be different?"

Dad looked across at Doug and his expression was as straight as I'd ever seen. He spoke slowly. I guess it was hard for him to get the words out. "I thought that because it would be . . . the last time we'd all be together as a family . . . that maybe we'd all try to make it something good to remember."

"Why should we? What do we owe you? Or Mom? You've both been using us—and using us up. Between the two of you, Mom and her tirades, you and your passive-aggressive bullshit, you've turned Stinky into an incontinent little pissant, and Chigger—well, he's well on his way to becoming a sociopathic hermit with surgically attached earphones. I'm sorry, Chigger, but Mickey is right. You can be a royal pain in the ass sometimes."

Of all the things that anyone had said to me—even the load of crap Mickey had just dumped on me—what Doug said was the one that hurt the most. It shriveled me instantly. I'd never *really* thought about Doug's feelings before; I'd always assumed he didn't have any feelings at all. Seeing him angry like this, I felt so bad about every nasty thing I'd ever said to him, I wanted to cry, but I didn't dare, not now, so I turned away from him and wrapped myself up in a ball on the couch. Between Mickey and Doug . . . I wished I was dead.

Now Doug turned back to Dad. "And me—? Well, just look at me, Max. I'm your son. This is how I turned out. A big fat nothing. With the social skills of a virus. I don't know how to talk to people. That's why I hide out in C-space. You should've seen how clumsy I was when I tried to talk to Mickey. I don't even know how to flirt. I'm pathetic. I hate myself because I'm so geeky. I still can't believe that Mickey really likes me. I keep wondering what's wrong with him." Mickey started toward Douglas at that, to comfort him I guess, but Douglas put up a hand to stop him. He wasn't through talking. "Chigger is right," he said. "I *am* a geekoid from hell. We're all of us fucked up, Dad—and this . . . this isn't an answer. It's more of the same. It's you running away again. Only this time, you want us to run away with you. How can we run away with you when it's *us* you've been running away from all this time?"

I couldn't believe what I was hearing from Douglas. He was almost in tears. But he just kept on and on, letting it all out, all at once, and Dad—poor, stupid Dad—he just sat there and took it. I uncurled myself and sat up again—

"They say that parents are supposed to prepare kids for adulthood—well, I'd say we're pretty well prepared now, Dad, aren't we? We've learned all the different ways to run away." Douglas stopped, exhausted. He just floated there limp. Finally, he drifted back down into a chair—right toward Mickey's lap. He bounced off Mickey and started to push himself up again, but Mickey pulled him back down and held him with one arm firmly around his waist. Douglas looked uncomfortable for a moment, but Mickey whispered "shhh" at him, and Douglas finally let himself relax on Mickey's lap. He leaned his head back and closed his eyes for a moment, exhausted. Tears were running down his cheeks and I felt so sorry for him I didn't know what to do. I'd never seen him like that before in my life.

"Charles?" Dad looked at me. "Do you have anything you want to add?"

I thought about the opportunity. Yeah, I had a lot to say. But it wasn't necessary anymore. "No. Doug said it all."

"Is it my turn now?" Dad asked. "Do I get to say anything?"

I shrugged. "I don't care." Douglas just put a hand over his eyes.

Dad took a breath. He was gathering his strength, and his words. Then he said, "You're right, Douglas. Everything you said. You're right. And yes, I *was* trying to kidnap you. And yes, I knew it would hurt your mother and I didn't care anymore. At this last court hearing, this last nasty custody fight, I finally stopped caring about her feelings—yes, after all this time, do you know I still love her? *Loved*. It's finally over. I finally gave up—and gave in to the urge to hurt back. Yes, I was selfish. So what? I'm fifty-two years old and I'm tired of having to be Mr. Nice Guy every day. I'm tired of making payments—I want something in return, something that's mine. Yes, I got impatient—I got tired of working and working and working while everybody else around me is riding the money-flow. I want to eat food that doesn't taste like wallpaper. I've *earned* it."

Dad stopped to catch his breath. He looked across the room, as if suddenly remembering who he was talking to. "I remember when you were born, Doug—when Charles was born too. And Bobby. How proud I was of each of you, how much I cherished you. I used to wake up in the morning, promising myself every day that I'd be the best dad I could for my boys. And I really did try. I really did. Now I wake up every morning wondering how I screwed up so badly. And what I could do to make it right. And it always came back to money. I don't have any. I'm a million and a quarter in debt. And no matter how hard I work, I just keep getting deeper and deeper. And nothing is fun anymore. Not even the music. Everything is a chore. Sometimes even taking the next breath is a chore.

"So when they offered me this chance to be a courier and get off the planet and make some money—and give my sons a second chance too—I didn't have to think about it too hard. It was a way out. I was drowning. What would you have had me do, Doug? Charles?" He added, "I don't know what's in the monkey, I don't even care, but someone is paying for this trip. Whatever it is, we'll deliver it and we'll be done. Then you can do whatever you want to. I'm through trying. I'm beaten."

Doug didn't say anything to that. Neither did I. There wasn't anything to say. And I was through trying to figure things out. I looked at my hands and clenched them into fists of frustration. I couldn't even figure out my left from my right.

CRIPPLED INSIDE

WE ATE, WE DOZED, WE waited. Pretty soon, the car started sliding along the track to the departure bay. We felt it thump into position, and then we heard the soft clunk of the transfer pods moving into place. A little after that, the car started spinning and the pseudo-gravity came on. A while after that, we heard people moving around outside in the corridors.

When he deemed it was safe, Mickey ducked out of the cabin. "I'll be back as fast as I can. I have to get your tickets validated. Otherwise, this cabin will show up as empty and they'll give it to someone else." To Douglas, he smiled. "Save my place, huh?" And then he was gone.

I broke the silence. "Can I call Mom?"

Dad looked at me, startled. He started to say something, then thought better of it and closed his mouth instead. "Do what you wish, Charles. You've already made it clear that I can't control you." He sounded like he hated me. Well, at least that was honest.

I went to the phone and punched Mom's number. The screen showed a map of the route-finder as the system tried to locate Mom. First it went to El Paso, then San Francisco, then Vandenberg, then—stopped. Instead, a notice appeared, flashing in several languages. "We apologize for the inconvenience. Weather conditions have temporarily disrupted all communication services. Please try again later."

"Hokay," I said, and flicked the phone off. I sat down again. I was on my own. Douglas was going his own way with Mickey. Dad had signed off on the whole family. Stinky had his monkey, his thumb, and his dreams. And Mom was temporarily out of service.

Mickey came back in, waving our boarding passes. "All right, we're clear."

"That was fast," Doug said, "How'd you do it?"

"It was easy. A friend of mine is working the desk. I told him we had VIPs traveling incognito, they were already aboard, but we needed the paperwork handled, and he'd be doing me a great favor if he'd check in the tickets. By the time I finished explaining, he'd already done it. He said, 'Give my best to Alexei.'"

Doug smiled. "Why do I have the feeling that some money has been spread around?"

"Because it has. The information I gave Alexei? He's put all his assets into lockdown, and now he's peddling a very delicious rumor to some of his very best clients, plus lockdown storage for their volatile liquidity. By tomorrow, he could be a billionaire, just in percentages alone."

"He's going to start a financial panic—" Dad said.

"He's counting on it. Panics are profitable to guys like Alexei. They don't care which way the money flows—as long as it flows."

"That's disloyal," Dad said grumpily.

"To whom? Earth? Alexei isn't from Earth. He's from Luna. He's being loyal to his family in Gagarin."

"By breaking the law? By hurting Earth?"

Mickey shrugged. "What law is he breaking? And why should he try to help Earth? Earth isn't trying to help Luna—or anyone else. Never mind." Mickey looked disgusted. "You'd have to get your mind out of the dirt to understand."

"All the economies are linked. If you pull one down—"

"No, they're not," Mickey said. "Not anymore. You can thank the SuperNationals for that. There's only one economy—and they push their money from place to place, whenever they want, regardless of who it hurts. What Alexei is doing is taking their money away from them. Some of it, anyway."

"Like Robin Hood, eh?" Dad looked skeptical.

"Whatever," said Mickey. "I don't expect you to understand, and I'm not going to waste any more time explaining it to you."

"I know about the political situation," Dad said. "And the rest of it. The planet is dying. Everybody knows it. The human race has eaten it down to the bone and it's still chewing. Did you check the news this morning? It's now *official.* Africa is having a 'Population Crash.' India too. And China next. And it's still spreading. That's why we're here. Just like everybody else who's jumping off the planet." Dad looked more frustrated and angry than I'd ever seen him. "And just like you said, the lower half of the Line is shut down to everyone except corporation personnel. So why shouldn't the people who've been pushed down into the dirt by the SuperNationals all their lives feel resentful? I do."

"Speak for yourself, Dad," said Weird.

"Douglas!" Dad looked at him warningly. "I've tried very hard to understand your . . . situation. I think you should recognize how hard it's been for me." To Mickey, he said, "I've been appointed the villain by everyone in this situation—by you, by Charles, by Douglas, by my ex-wife, by the law. Once in a while, I'd like someone to say they're trying to understand *my* feelings about all this. I'm tired of being the target, that's what this is about. I'm tired of having to listen to other people tell me why I can't have what I want. It's my turn now. Watching Alexei take what isn't his and live like a—a grasshopper while the rest of the ants are starving for crumbs is supposed to make me feel better about Luna? Or Earth? Or anyone? I don't think so."

Douglas finally let his own anger show. He said, "Well, maybe if you'd managed things a little bit better—"

"I did the best I could—"

"Obviously, it wasn't good enough—"

"It would have been, if Charles hadn't opened his big mouth—"

Boom. The banana-split time bomb had finally gone off. *He blamed me.*

"—I had it all figured out. And everything was working. Get on this elevator, get on that elevator, and by the time anyone knew where we were, it would be too late to stop us, and then Charles had to ruin it. We could have been halfway to the moon by now—"

"That isn't fair, Dad—"

"*Nothing* is fair anymore, Douglas. That's what this whole trip has been about. Escaping the unfairness." He put his head in his hands. "All I wanted, all I hoped for, was a little understanding, a little cooperation from you kids. I did it for you!"

"You did it for yourself," corrected Douglas. "Just like I did it for myself and Charles did it for himself. None of us knows how to do anything for anyone else—"

"Excuse me—?" I said. Very quietly. "Excuse me?"

It was the quiet tone that did it. They all looked at me curiously. "Each of us has now had a fight with every one else in the room. Except Mickey and Douglas. This isn't fair. Mickey, Douglas? It's your turn to say nasty things to each other now." One thing about growing up with Weird, you learn how to do sarcasm real well.

Both Douglas and Dad shut up. They looked at each other. Mickey looked to Douglas. Douglas looked at me angrily. Stinky snored. Mickey turned and went back to the chair. He looked like he was trying to make a decision. "Is anyone hungry? No? All right, why don't I make up the beds? We're all tired. I'll be back in a moment." He stepped out of the cabin, leaving the rest of us to sit and glower at each other. I settled my headphones over my ears and dialed up something very distracting. John Lennon's bitter period, when all he could do was write songs about how wrong everybody else was. *Crippled Inside.* That was a good one. Nice and loud. The monkey crawled into my lap and hugged me. I wondered who'd programmed that, but I didn't push it away.

WORKING LATE

MICKEY CAME BACK WITH AN odd expression on his face.
"Come with me," he said. "All of you. Quickly."

"Huh? Why?"

"Just come—" He was already picking up Stinky. I grabbed the monkey. Douglas shouldered the backpack. Dad picked up his worries and we followed Mickey out the hatch and up the corridor to the transfer pod. Mickey wouldn't answer any questions. "I'll explain later," was all he said.

The transfer pod dropped us down to the boarding level. Actually, there are two boarding levels. There's the public boarding level and the Very Important Person boarding level—Mickey took us to the VIP level.

We stepped out of the hatch into—

I didn't see the room at first. It was about the size of a classroom or a lounge, I guess, but directly in front of us was Judge Griffith in her wheelchair, and next to her, but not too close, there was Olivia, looking unhappy, and a couple other people I didn't recognize, but very official looking, and also that stupid lawyer, Howard. He still wore the same stupid suit that didn't fit right, only now he looked like he'd slept in it, and he had a very smug look on his face, like he'd caught us with our pants down and our hands on our dicks. I was tempted to give him my own farkleberry.

"Ahh," said Judge Griffith. "Thank you all for joining us. Mickey, did you have any trouble?" Mickey shook his head. "The Court thanks you for your efforts." Douglas glared at him, but Mickey didn't meet his look, so Douglas stepped over and took Stinky out of his arms, then he moved away from Mickey, as if he didn't want to know him anymore. The fuse was finally lit on that argument. Mickey looked miserable. I pretended to be interested in the monkey.

"All right, if everybody will take their places, we can get this business handled once and for all." Judge Griffith wheeled backwards, moving out of the way. She gestured with her gavel; she held the head of it in her fist and used the handle as a pointer. The chairs and the tables of the lounge had been moved into positions like a courtroom. "Olivia, if you'll sit over there on the left. Mickey, you too. The Dingillians—thank you. Howard, I want you on the right. Court officers, here beside me. And . . . yes, that'll do it, thank you."

Dad whispered to Olivia, "What the hell is going on? What did you do to us?" Olivia just shook her head and pointed us toward the chairs. "I can't advise you," she whispered. "You're on your own now." Dad looked as angry as I'd ever seen him in my entire life. Angrier than that even.

Douglas laid Stinky down on a nearby couch. The rest of us sat down in chairs that were much too comfortable for a legal procedure. It was hard to believe we were actually in a courtroom. But Judge Griffith put those doubts to rest immediately. She wheeled up to a small table that was to serve as the bench; her clipboard was already open and propped up so she could see it. She reversed the gavel in her hand and rapped it sharply on the table. She glanced over to her assistant. "Are we missing someone?"

The woman nodded. "Godot called. He'll be late."

Judge Griffith raised a questioning eyebrow. "I assume he has a good excuse?" She glanced at her watch. "Was the shuttle delayed?"

"The shuttle docked on time, the paperwork was delayed.

Last I heard, he's waiting for customs to clear."

"Damn nuisance," Judge Griffith said, obviously annoyed. "Never mind, we can still take care of the preliminaries. And if he can't get here before we finish, then the hell with him. This Court is not on call. At least, not in this case." She turned forward again. "The Third District Court of the Orbital Space Authority, serving GeoSynchronous Station and Allied Domains, Judge Georgia Griffith presiding, is now in special session, this session being mandated by the attempted flight from jurisdiction of the following individuals . . ."

Olivia stood. "Beg pardon, Your Honor, but no one has actually fled jurisdiction yet—"

"Don't nit-pick, Counselor. We caught them with the tickets in their hands. Don't act like an Earth-lawyer or we'll be here all night. I promised you we could resolve this quickly, and we will. If you and Howard will both keep your big mouths shut. First of all—"

Now Dad stood up. "Your Honor? If I may? Ms. Partridge no longer represents us—"

"Yes, yes, I know all about that dodge. I used it myself when I was a cub. Who do you think taught it to Olivia? Sit down, Mr. Dingillian. We have work to do here." She looked at Howard. "I suppose you want to have your say too?"

Sarcasm was wasted on him. He stood up, talking. "Thank you, Your Honor. I appreciate the opportunity. I think that the actions of the defendants clearly demonstrates their willful disregard for the authority of this—"

"Sit down, Howard. I don't need to hear it from you, either." She sighed and looked exasperated. "Listen up, folks— I don't like working late. I'm pissed at the lot of you. You've acted like spoiled brats and if I could think of a good reason to justify tossing all of you into the cooler for a week or two, I'd do it. Except that would give me the problem of finding custodial authority for the minors involved, and while I suppose I could release them to the custody of the oldest brother—" She stopped herself. "Hmm, that's not a bad idea, it would resolve everything . . . well, almost everything. Never mind, just don't anyone tempt me." She glared around the room, as if daring anyone to speak.

"All right," she continued, with a dark glower in Dad's

direction. "We're here because Max Dingillian and his three kids somehow ended up on the midnight elevator to Farpoint. I presume the destination was Whirlaway. Correct? This, in spite of the fact that a court hearing was ordered for nine in the ayem, tomorrow morning. So I am left with the not unreasonable assumption that you, sir, Max Dingillian, were attempting to evade the authority of this court. Not that you could have. I'd have transferred authority—a single phone call down to the end of the Line—and you'd have been detained there. I doubt that the shift in venue to Farpoint would have resulted in a different outcome. Regardless of the distance, and sometimes the expense involved, starside courts have demonstrated a remarkable and refreshing consistency."

She leaned forward in her chair, aiming her remarks directly to Dad. "Up here, attempting to evade authority usually gets you a trip groundside. However . . . in light of several recent judgments where groundside courts have held the Line authority liable for expenses and damages when individuals are returned to Earth with resultant detriment, we have become extremely reluctant to expose ourselves to that liability *unless* we are certain that we will not have to bear the cost of the bounce-back. I am concerned that this case may have some exposure in that direction. So in that regard, the Court *chooses to ignore*—for the moment, anyway—the evidence of your attempt to evade jurisdiction. Sit down, Howard! I'll get to you in a moment!" She turned back to Dad. "At the very least, I should hold you in contempt of court, Mr. Dingillian, but it is not in the best interests of your children to do so, and it does not serve the goal of a speedy resolution. Let it be known, however, that the Court views your conduct with extreme displeasure. Let me translate that for you: you've exhausted whatever good will you had here. Do you understand?"

Dad nodded. "I understand completely. And I thank you for your . . . uh, mercy, Your Honor."

Judge Griffith ignored Dad. She turned to Howard-In-The-Wrinkled-Suit. "All right, Howard, now you may object. . . ." Howard started to stand up, shrugged, sank back down in his seat, spreading his hands helplessly.

"Right," Judge Griffith agreed. "Objection overruled. Thank

you. The Court appreciates your efforts to help move this process forward as fast as possible." She turned to Olivia. "Counselor, you no longer represent the Dingillians, is that correct?"

"That is correct." Olivia's voice was unemotional. Detached.

"Nevertheless, you were planning to leave on the midnight elevator with them. Is that correct too?"

"Yes, Your Honor. That is correct."

"Do you have an interesting explanation for this?"

"Conflict of interest. My son has a relationship with Douglas Dingillian."

"*Had*," corrected Douglas. Judge Griffith gave him a curious look, but otherwise ignored his interruption.

"Did you advise the Dingillians to evade jurisdiction, Counselor?"

"Of course not. I'm an officer of the court. That would be unethical."

"Nevertheless, was it among the options you discussed?"

Olivia nodded reluctantly. "Yes, it was."

"Well, Olivia," the Judge continued, "we have here the evidence that you booked the tickets yourself under one of your shadow accounts. So even though you recused yourself from this case, you still managed to be a participant in an action that would have damaged the court's ability to function. The Court finds you in contempt and fines you . . ." The judge consulted her clipboard, tapping at its surface as she looked something up. ". . . one thousand chocolate-dollars." Olivia didn't react to that. Judge Griffith continued, "Sentence suspended in recognition of your assistance in arranging this special session."

"Thank you, Your Honor," Olivia said quietly.

"The same thing I said to Max Dingillian goes for you too, Counselor. Your store of good will is exhausted in this court. Remember that."

Now, Judge Griffith turned to Howard-The-Smug. "Any objections? No? Overruled anyway. Don't worry about your store of good will, Howard. The Court's opinion of you remains unchanged." To the rest of us, she said, "The issue here is simple, and if we can resolve it in the next two hours"—she glanced at her watch—"then the Dingillians, or at least Max Dingillian, depending on the ruling of this court, can continue their—*or his*—journey." By the emphasis she put on "*or his,*" she made it very clear that she had not yet made up her mind whether Dad was going to go to the moon with us or *without* us.

She looked to me. "Charles?"

"Huh?"

"Please come forward. Leave the monkey. Sit over here on this chair, will you? Thank you. Do you swear to tell the truth, the whole truth, and nothing but the truth?"

"Sure," I said. "I mean, yes, I do."

CLOCKWISE

JUDGE GRIFFITH TURNED HER CHAIR so she was facing me. "All right, Charles—is that what you like to be called, Charles?"

I shrugged. "My family calls me Chigger."

"Is that what you want me to call you?"

"It's okay," I said, half-heartedly.

"I'll call you Charles," she said, nodding. "It sounds more respectful. Now . . . do you remember the riddle I asked you at dinner?"

"About how do you tell a Martian the difference between left and right?"

"Yes, that's the one. For the record, would you restate it?"

I took a breath. "You asked how to explain left and right without using the words *left* and *right*. How would you demonstrate or explain the difference? What are the . . . the defining criteria? Is that the right way to say it?"

"Yes, it is. Very good, Charles. That's even better than I said. So, have you thought about the problem?"

I made a face. "I haven't been able to think about anything else. That's really a tough question."

"Yes, it is." She grinned right back at me. "The first time I heard it, I couldn't get it out of my head for months. So do you have an answer?"

"I'm not sure. I mean, I'm not sure if it's the right one—" But before I could say anything else, Howard-The-Rude stood up. "Your Honor? With all due respect, may I ask what the purpose is of this line of discussion?"

Judge Griffith looked annoyed at the interruption. But she turned to Howard-The-Ugly and replied, "Yes, you may ask. The purpose of this line of inquiry is to determine the depth of thought that Charles Dingillian is able to bring to a problem. There are questions that we need to ask him. We need to know what kind of credibility his answers have. Will he tell us what he thinks we want to hear? Or will he tell us what he's really thinking? That's what's going to determine a large part of the Court's decision here. Any further questions, Counselor?"

Howard-The-Stupid didn't look happy with Judge Griffith's answer, but he sat down anyway. "No more questions."

Judge Griffith turned back to me. "All right, Charles—I'm sorry to have to put you on the spot; try to pretend it's just you and me talking about this riddle over dinner again, okay?"

"Okay."

"And it doesn't matter if you have the right answer or not, Charles—that's not the point. In fact, I'm not even sure there is a right answer, there may not be, so don't worry if you didn't get any answer at all, that's not important. I just want you to tell me the way you thought about it."

"But I did get an answer—" I said.

"You did?" She looked surprised.

"Uh-huh."

"Well, if you did, then you're the first. I never did."

"Oh, well—um, I dunno. Maybe it isn't obvious. You don't live on a planet, so maybe that has something to do with it. See, first I thought that you could tell the difference by the sun. Turn and face the direction the sun rises. The hand pointing south is your right hand, the hand pointing north is your left hand. But then I realized that the Martian would have to know north and south for that answer to be any good. And that depends on which way the planet is spinning, doesn't it? North is the pole that when you look down on it from above, the planet is spinning counter-clockwise. So you need to know clockwise to know north, don't you? And if the Martian doesn't know clockwise, then the answer doesn't mean anything at all to him, does it? So I have to find a way to tell the Martian about left and right in a way that doesn't depend on any Earth definitions at all."

"Very good, Charles. Go on."

Dad was looking at me oddly. Douglas was sort of smirking, as if he already knew how hard this riddle was. Stinky sat up, rubbing his eyes. He looked around once, then laid back down again. Douglas put his jacket over him.

I looked back to Judge Griffith and held out my hands in front of me, palms open and facing away, thumbs sticking out at right angles. "Then I thought that maybe my hands might be a clue. See my left hand? My index finger and thumb make an L—L for left. But that doesn't count either, because a Martian isn't going to know what an L is. You need a way to describe an L, and you can't really do that without first having the definitions of right and left, can you? How do you say a left-pointing right angle? So that doesn't work either. That was when I got really really angry at you." I curled my fingers into fists and pantomimed pounding on a table and growled through my teeth.

Judge Griffith smiled and nodded, "I remember that feeling."

"But that gave me part of the answer." I stretched my arms out in front of me so she could see my fists. "It's in your fingers, see? Look down at your fists. The left one is clockwise." I traced it with my right index finger. "If you start at the outside, with the tip of the thumb and follow the spiral of your fingers all the way around to the tip of your index finger on the inside, then you see that the left hand is the hand that curls clockwise in while the right hand curls counter-clockwise out. And that's the only way they can be."

"That's *very* good, Charles." Judge Griffith was looking at her own fists. Around the room, almost everybody else was looking at their fists too. Olivia, Mickey, Douglas—even

Howard-The-Clumsy. "That's the best answer I've ever heard."

"Except . . ." I added, "That's not the whole answer. Because the Martian still has to know clockwise"—Howard groaned; I ignored him—"or you have to be able to define clockwise for him. See, all that this answer does is move the problem into another . . . um, what's that word that Douglas uses all the time? *Domain*—that's it. This answer only moves the problem into another *domain*. You still have to define clockwise and counter-clockwise."

Howard-The-Impatient stood up then. "Your Honor," he said, with obvious annoyance, "I think you've made your point. Can we be done with this and get on with our business?"

"We are getting on with it, Howard. And *I'll* decide when we're done." She waved him down impatiently and turned back to me. "And did you figure it out, Charles? How *do* you define clockwise?"

"Well, first I thought about clocks, obviously—but maybe Martians don't have clocks. But they could have a sundial. You could tell a Martian that clockwise is the way the shadows turn—except it's reversed in the southern hemisphere. There's no way to tell the difference between northern and southern. It's the same as left and right. Again. So I've got to find something that's always clockwise no matter how you look at it."

"And, did you find anything?"

"Well . . . I thought about Neptune and Uranus, both of which are laying down on their axis. If there was a planet that always kept one of its poles toward the sun, then the sun would always see it spinning the same way, counter-clockwise. But both those planets are like Earth. Half their year, the north pole points toward the sun, the other half the south pole points toward the sun, so there aren't any celestial objects you can use."

"So you didn't get an answer?"

"No, I got two answers. But . . . well, you'll see. The first answer is to point to the Southern Cross and say, 'That's south and this is the southern hemisphere.' Or you point to Polaris and say, 'That's the north star. This is the northern hemisphere.' But that only works where you can see the sky."

"And what's the other answer?"

"Periwinkles." Douglas looked up sharply at that—I guess he was surprised that I had actually listened to what he had said back there on that Mexican beach. "They're a kind of seashell," I explained. "They always know which way to turn. Clockwise."

"In both hemispheres?"

"I think so."

"Hmm. That's very interesting. I'll have to look that up. Those are good answers, Charles. You get an A." Judge Griffith looked impressed.

"Uh-uh," I said. "I think they're C+ answers."

"Oh? Why? They answer the question."

"Yeah, but they all depend on being able to point to something else. You can't talk about right or left or clockwise or counter-clockwise, unless you can point to something else. Otherwise, there's no way to define one hand from the other."

Judge Griffith smiled. "I believe that you have just stumbled on the essential existential dilemma."

"Huh? The what—?"

She answered slowly and carefully. "The only way we *ever* know anything about ourselves is by measuring ourselves against something outside of us. Do you understand what that means?"

"I think so," I said, remembering something Weird had said once. "Everything's connected to everything else. If we don't have any connections, we're lost. We can't even tell which way is up. But—?"

"Yes?"

"That means that there isn't anything absolute, doesn't it? That everything is just sort of 'agreed on.' Like we all voted on which way is north and what time it is and what words mean. It's like looking down and finding there's no floor."

"Exactly," said Judge Griffith. "There is no floor. And we're all living in a universe of agreements. That's why we have courts—to sort out all the different *dis*agreements where they rub up against each other. If we had absolutes, Charles, we wouldn't need courts, would we?"

"Mm." I had to think about that one for a minute too. "I guess not."

"So let's get this one sorted out now. You've done very well, Charles. Very well indeed. The Court thanks you. You've shown me what I needed to know. You can go back and sit with your family now."

"Yes, Your Honor." I went back and sat next to Douglas. I picked up the monkey again and held it close. It hugged me again. I didn't know whether to be annoyed or not.

GODOT

J UDGE GRIFFITH LOOKED TO HER assistant. "Any word yet?"

"The last of the passengers have cleared customs. Godot is on his way up. Five minutes."

"All right," said Georgia. "Fifteen-minute potty break." She banged her gavel once and wheeled toward the restroom, her assistant following.

Dad leaned toward Olivia. "Who's this Godot?"

"I don't know," Olivia whispered back. "That's what the judge calls anyone she has to wait for." She added, "I'm sorry we got caught—but I don't think Georgia had any choice in the matter."

"We—? You got a suspended sentence. I'm likely to lose my kids—! There's not a lot of 'we' in that, Olivia! You turned us in, didn't you?"

"I didn't have a choice, Max." She sounded just as frustrated as Dad.

"Oh, terrific. You told us to go out on the limb—and then you sawed it off."

"I don't think you should say any more," Olivia said quietly, with a meaningful nod toward Howard-The-Brooding.

"You've put us in a really bad situation, Olivia."

"I'm sorry. I miscalculated."

"Apology noted. Now what are you going to do to help clean up this mess?"

"Nothing. I can't! I'm not your lawyer anymore, Max."

Dad shook his head in disgust. "I can't believe this. Why did I trust you?" He sank back down in his seat, not looking at Olivia anymore. She looked just as unhappy. Now all that was left was a fight between her and Mickey, and we'd be complete. Everybody would have fought with everybody. I couldn't think of anyone else we could fight with—

And then Godot arrived.

Godot was Doctor Bolivar Hidalgo. And following him into the room was . . . *Mom?!* And that other woman behind her.

Just about everybody came to their feet. Douglas, Dad, me—even Stinky woke up, rubbing his eyes again, this time, crying, "Stop waking me up!"

Mom went straight to Dad. She moved across the room like a missile—and slapped him across the face. Hard. Dad was knocked back a step; he put his hand to his jaw and blinked. "It's good to see you again too, Maggie," he managed to say.

And then Stinky saw her for the first time and yelled, "Mommy!" And flung himself into her arms like a screaming monkey. He grabbed hold so tight, she almost fell backward. "Mommy, Mommy! Are you going with us?"

"I came to take you home, sweetie—"

"But I don't wanna go home! I wanna go to the moon!"

She stroked his shaven scalp. "What have they done to you, baby?"

"It's a moon-cut!"

Mom gave Dad a dirty look and moved away from us, cooing softly to Stinky and patting his head. Now it was Doctor Hidalgo's turn. He waddled over and bowed to Dad. "My compliments, *Señor* Dingillian."

Dad just glowered.

Dr. Hidalgo pretended not to notice. Instead, he took Dad by the arm and made as if to lead him off to a corner. "Can we talk?"

"You can talk," Dad said, not moving. "Do I have to listen?"

"It would be better if we could talk alone . . . ?"

"Anything you have to say to me, you can say in front of my children, Dr. Hidalgo. I'm not going to hide anything from them. It's their lives too."

Douglas and I exchanged a look. We came and stood next to Dad. The monkey climbed up onto my back and made faces over my shoulder. Doug hissed at me, "Turn it off, Charles," so I did.

We followed Dad and Doctor Hidalgo over to a corner of the lounge. Doctor Hidalgo plopped himself down onto a chair and started talking immediately. "It's a pity you didn't accept my earlier offer of help. It would have simplified matters a great deal. For all of us. I told you that there were people who would act against you. You should consider your wife's oh-so-convenient presence here as evidence of their commitment. If you think about the organizational effort involved and the money it takes to get someone onto a shuttle on such short notice, you might begin to understand just how important your package is. It's important enough that a great deal of money is going to be spent on the effort to intercept it and prevent its delivery. Are you convinced yet?"

"What I told you before still stands," Dad said.

"It affects the lives of your sons. How do they feel about it?"

"Whatever my Dad says, goes for me too," I blurted. "Right, Douglas?" I poked him.

Douglas didn't need to be poked. "We're a family, Doctor Hidalgo. We might be having problems right now, but that's our business, not yours. No matter how bad our family arguments might get, we still don't sell each other out." -

"Admirable. Very admirable." Doctor Hidalgo grunted his approval. "Not very smart, but still admirable. The smart man recognizes when he can't win and cuts his losses early. So . . ." He levered himself to his feet. I figured he must have massed two hundred kilos. He sure looked it. Even in low-grav, he was having problems getting out of a chair. "I guess we have nothing further to discuss. Let the games begin." He waddled back to the other side of the lounge.

Dad looked to me and Douglas like he wanted to say something. But there wasn't anything that needed saying, so he just clapped Doug on the shoulder—he was closer—and said, "Let's go."

IN COURT

JUDGE GRIFFITH CALLED THE SESSION back to order with three sharp raps of her gavel on the table. "All right, people, we've got a lot of work to do and not very much time in which to do it. I've made a promise to some folks here to be finished before midnight so they could catch an elevator, and I intend to keep that promise. Would everybody please take their seats and settle themselves quickly?" Judge Griffith nodded to her assistant. "Joyce, please make a note of our new arrivals. Godot is here. Finally."

Mom and the woman who had followed her in, I guessed she was the woman from San Francisco, sat down with Dr. Hidalgo, on the other side of Howard-The-Malignant. She leaned over to confer with him. They shook hands quickly, so I guessed this was their first face-to-face meeting. She held Stinky in her arms, but he appeared to have fallen back asleep. He woke up just long enough to stick his tongue out at Howard, then he laid his head back down on Mom's shoulder again. Whatever they'd given him, I wanted a lifetime supply.

Judge Griffith was already moving along. She meant it

about finishing quickly. "Dr. Hidalgo, the Court appreciates your interest in this case; however, if it is your intention to complicate matters with extracurricular issues, let me warn you ahead of time that the Court will take a dim view of any such matters that do not *directly* affect the issue at hand."

"Your Honor." Dr. Bolivar spread his hands wide, in an oily gesture. Obviously, someone's snake was squeaky. "I am here only as a friend of the Court. I simply wish to see justice done."

The judge snorted. "Bollie, you and I both know that I have a low threshold of bullshit. And you and I both know that you have no interest in anything except your own stomach. You brought the boys' mother up for reasons that have nothing to do with justice or friendship. The Court will *tolerate* this only so long as it does not impinge on the ability of this Court to function. Consider this a warning. Your friends have no authority over this—" She waved her gavel at him.

Bolivar gave her his smarmiest smile; he nodded politely and sank back into his chair. It groaned.

Judge Griffith turned to Mom now. "Mrs. Dingillian—"

"Campbell. It's Campbell now. I've gone back to my maiden name, Your Honor."

"Fairly recently? Ah, yes, here it is. Thank you for the correction." Judge Griffith made a note on her clipboard. She frowned to herself, took off her glasses, polished them with a handkerchief, and reseated them on her nose. I got the feeling that she did not do it because her glasses were dirty. Finally, she sighed to herself in resignation. She looked over to Mom and said, "Ms. Campbell, the Court acknowledges your interests in this hearing. Just so you'll know—and you too, Mr. Dingillian—I've spent the past several hours reviewing the records of your divorce and custody hearings. I wish I could say it makes for interesting reading. Unfortunately, it does not. It is a tiresome and petty matter, and I think both you and your husband have a great deal to be ashamed of. You for what you did, he for the way he reacted. This is not a case where one side is right and the other is wrong. It is a case where both sides are wrong—and this Court has no interest in trying to determine which side is more wrong. That way lies madness. At this point, the *only* issue here is the welfare of the children. Everything else, I will leave to you and your respective lawyers to battle it out until hell freezes over, or you both drop dead of exhaustion, whichever comes first—and for the children's sake, I hope it's soon. Just so there's no doubt in your minds, I hate cases like this. I hate the people who create cases like this. I hate what it does to the children."

Judge Griffith leaned forward now, putting her elbows on the table in front of her and folding her hands together under her chin. "I want to make it clear to everybody that this is the basis on which I'm going to make my decision. I've already heard all of your arguments. They're all in these records I had piped up the Line. And I very much doubt that there is anything that either side has to add, and it isn't going to serve any of us to take it out of the box and exercise it again. Additionally, whatever moral or legal or emotional advantages either of you felt that you could make a reasonable claim to in an Earthside court, those advantages do not obtain here. This court is interested in one thing and one thing only—the welfare of these children. The Court does not like being put in this position, but the Court has no choice, because events have clearly demonstrated that *neither* of the parents has provided an appropriate commitment to the welfare of these children. Therefore—"

"Your Honor, I object to that—" That was Mom, leaping to her feet.

Judge Griffith sighed. She could see where this was headed. "Ms. Campbell?"

"I am *not* a bad parent, and I do put my children's welfare above everything else—"

Judge Griffith tapped her gavel gently to interrupt Mom. "Spare me the organ recital. Your husband came home and found you in bed with someone else. I was raised old-fashioned, Ms. Campbell. Maybe you think that what you did was a generous and unselfish demonstration of commitment and dedication to your family, but *this* court is having a very hard time viewing it that way. This situation—this entire avalanche of errors in judgment—was all triggered by that first little pebble. Now, maybe they do things differently on Earth, but up here when two people make a promise to each other—especially a promise to love, honor, and cherish—there's a reasonable expectation that both parties will make some effort to keep that commitment. And when there are children involved, well then the commitment to the children and their well-being has to outweigh everything else. Your children didn't get to vote on this situation—that's why the Court is involved now—to vote for the children."

"Your Honor," Mom started to protest, "with all due respect—we *had* a working custody arrangement, until *he*"— she waved her hand angrily at Dad—"went and violated it! All I want is for you to return my children to me so we can go home!"

"Sit down, Ms. Campbell. That's *not* going to happen. At least not because you or anyone else demands it. You pushed your husband into this situation. It's all here in the history." She tapped her clipboard meaningfully. "You kept challenging his visitation rights every chance you got—you gave him no rational choice. That doesn't excuse what he did, but neither did you provide an environment in which your separate disagreements could be worked out rationally. And for the record, let me stress this again: this Court has absolutely no interest in providing an arena for one more round of legal spouse-bashing. If you want to hurt each other, if that's the kind of postmarital relationship you both want, that's fine with me—I'm just not going to let you use my court for it.

"We're going to resolve this once and for all. At the end of this session, if you or your husband have issues that are still unresolved, then sign up for one of those silly courses you folks downside love to do. I can recommend a dozen good ones—there's the one where you call each other names, there's the one where you whomp each other with plastic clubs, there's the one where you process out all your bad feelings, and so on and so on and so on. Do any of them, do them all, I don't care. But stop using your children as weapons against each other!"

Judge Griffith poured herself a glass of water. Her hand trembled slightly as she drank. She put the glass back on the table and looked from Mom to Dad and back again. "In other words, Mr. Dingillian, Ms. Campbell, based on everything that has happened so far, this Court cannot justify awarding either one of you custody of these children. Do you understand what I am saying? The decision cannot be based on your credentials as parents. Neither of you deserves that consideration. This Court is going to have to look *elsewhere* for guidance in this decision. Fortunately, I think I have a way to resolve this. Now, when you get back to Earth, you may both feel perfectly free to find a court that will return a ruling more to your liking, but right now, you are here in my jurisdiction, and what I say here carries the weight of law. Any questions? No? I didn't think so."

She looked around the room as if daring anyone else to speak. No one wanted to. So she rapped her gavel sharply. "Douglas Dingillian, as you are only two months shy of your eighteenth birthday, this court sees fit to declare you an independent adult. You are hereby granted autonomy. You are no longer under the custody of either of your parents. Do you understand?"

Douglas nodded. He looked a little scared, but he nodded. Mom looked like she wanted to say something, but held her silence. Dad looked to Doug, but Doug wouldn't meet his gaze.

Judge Griffith continued. "You are free to return to Earth, either with or without your mother; you are free to continue your outbound odyssey, either with or without your father. However, before you make *any* decision, we still have the matter of the custody of your brothers to resolve, and the Court will appreciate your input on that."

Douglas nodded again.

Now Judge Griffith turned to me. "Charles, the whole point of that little exercise earlier was so I could find out how you think about things—how deeply you consider a question—and I have to tell you, I'm very impressed with you. I don't think the people around you know you very well. You're a very thoughtful young man; at least, that's my experience of you. I tell you this because I want you to understand, ordinarily I would not ask a thirteen-year-old to make the kind of choice that I'm about to give you. But under these circumstances, I think this is the best way to do it—and I'm satisfied that you're up to the challenge. So here's the question—"

I could already see it coming. And I was already formulating my reply.

"—Do you want to go back down the beanstalk with your mother, or do you want to continue outward with your father?"

I didn't have to think about it. I'd already been thinking about it long enough—ever since Dad went *boom*. I stood up. "Neither," I said.

Judge Griffith shook her head, smiling gently. "I'm afraid that's not an option, Charles."

"Yes, it is," I said. "*I want a divorce.*"

THOREAU'S AX

ALMOST IMMEDIATELY, BOTH MOM AND Dad were on their feet, shouting: "Your Honor—you can't allow this!" "Charles, have you lost your mind?" Douglas looked surprised, though he shouldn't have been. Even Stinky was awake now. "Whatever Charles gets, I want one too!" he yelled, screeching above the tumult. Judge Griffith banged so loudly with her gavel that the head popped off. She had to wait until her assistant, Joyce, went and got it and brought it back to her.

"Everybody settle down, dammit!" she shouted over the noise. "And *sit down!* I'll handle this." She banged a few more times until everyone sat down again, then she turned back to me. "Charles—" she started to say gently.

I didn't let her finish. "I want a divorce," I repeated.

Judge Griffith looked very unhappy. "That does complicate things, doesn't it?" she said. "I wonder who could have put that idea into your head."

"You did," I said, bluntly. "Over pizza."

"So I did. Well shame on me. I must learn to watch my big mouth. The karmic chicken has come home to roost.

Charles, do you know what's involved in that kind of action?"

"Yes, actually, I do. At least as much as I could find out from reading about it."

"Somebody should hang a warning sign on you, Charles: 'Caution, contents will probably explode in your face.' " She smiled wryly, to let me know she was joking, but I could see she meant it too. Well, so what? I *did* want a divorce. "I'm probably going to regret asking this," she asked, "but *why* do you want a divorce?"

"Do I have to have a reason?"

"Not really. You and your brothers are the only ones who *didn't* promise to love, honor, et cetera. And if that's not a promise you want to keep, you shouldn't be held in a situation where it's a requirement. But it would help if you did have a reason. Otherwise, children would be announcing right and left that they want a divorce every time they get sent to bed early."

I pointed at Mom. I pointed at Dad. "Those are my reasons."

The judge nodded. "Those are two pretty good reasons. And considering everything else that's happened, the Court would ordinarily be inclined to grant your request—but let's look over the edge of this cliff for a while before we jump, okay, Charles?"

"Sure," I said. "Whatever. But it's not going to change my mind. I've been thinking about this for a long time. Not because you mentioned it. I just never knew how to do it before."

"Charles—" Mom called across the room "—you don't have to do this. If we could just sit down and talk things out—"

"Leave him alone, Maggie! Haven't you done enough damage already!" Dad shouted across at her. "Look at the poor kid! Charles, I'm sorry for what I said back there—"

Judge Griffith rapped her gavel only once. Without even looking up: "Any more outbursts and I'll put the both of you in jail. In the same cell!" The threat worked. They both sat down again, glowering at each other. "Howard?" Howard-

The-Troll looked up. "Are you still representing the interests of the mother?"

Howard looked to Mom, she nodded, and he said, "Yes, Your Honor."

"Would you like to question Charles Dingillian?"

"Uh—I haven't had time to prepare."

"Neither has anyone else here. Perhaps giving lawyers time to prepare is why justice always takes so long. Maybe in the future, in the interest of producing results, I should deny all recesses and continuances. Don't panic, Howard, it's a joke."

Howard-The-Repulsive came over and stood in front of me. "I know you're impatient to have the privileges of an adult, Charles. I remember being thirteen once—I was a kid just like you. We might have liked each other. We might have been friends—"

"I don't want to be your friend, *Howard*. I want a divorce."

His expression hardened. "All right, let's approach this another way, *Charles*. You're having doubts about this, aren't you?"

I shook my head. "No, I've been thinking about it for a while. I can't see anything better to do."

"Ahh," said Howard-The-Smarmy. "Maybe you haven't asked yourself all the questions you should have. Let me ask you this one. Do you think running away is going to solve anything?"

"Some people do."

"Yes, I know. Do you?"

I knew what he wanted me to say. I mean, everybody knows the right answer to that question. No. Running away never solves anything. But . . . sometimes running away buys you time to think. And that lets you solve stuff. Doesn't it?

He held my eyes with his. He didn't look nasty. He looked like he was trying to be friendly and it was a strain. He said, "Charles, do you think your parents have a responsibility toward you?"

"Yes. Everybody knows that. That's what they teach us at school. Don't make babies unless you're also willing to make a lifelong commitment."

"Good. Do you think you have a corresponding responsibility to your parents?

"I don't understand."

"Well, your parents worked hard to give you a home and an education and take care of you. I know that it hasn't worked out the way you think it should, but don't you think that your parents have your best interests at heart?"

"Your Honor—?" That was Olivia. "I realize that I no longer represent this client, but as a friend of the Court, I must object to this transparent attempt to manipulate Charles Dingillian through the use of guilt."

"The Court appreciates your concern, but I think young Mr. Dingillian is quite capable of sorting this out for himself. Nevertheless, Howard, would you please lower the level of rhetoric here . . . ?"

"Yes, Your Honor." He turned back to me. "My point is, Charles, that you've taken a lot from your parents. You owe them something in return. Do you think this is the right way to repay it?"

And when he put it that way, something clicked. "Can I ask you something?"

"Yes, Charles—what is it?" He seemed genuinely interested.

"Well, when I was in school—I don't know if it's the same way up here—we had classes about social responsibility. My teacher taught us that everybody is part of society. We all depend on each other in lots of different ways. We all make work for each other, so we need each other for jobs. And we all make messes—like garbage and pollution and sewage and crap—so we all have to clean up after ourselves. And sometimes, like during flu season, we're all infectious. And stuff like that. And even if we like to think that we're individuals, we really all depend on each other all the time. My teacher said it was Thoreau's ax."

"I beg your pardon?" said Howard-The-Puzzled. "Thoreau's ax?"

"Yeah. Thoreau was this guy who thought it would be a good idea to go out in the woods to Walden Pond and commune with nature. He thought worldly goods distracted people and kept them from really finding themselves and getting in tune with everything good."

"Yes, I know who Thoreau was. What about his ax?"

"Well, that's the point. Where did his ax come from? If he wanted to build himself a shelter, or chop a tree for firewood, or stuff like that, he needed an ax. Where does the ax come from?"

"From a . . . blacksmith," offered Howard.

"Uh-huh. You got it. Thoreau was a dope. You can't just go off and live by yourself. You need the products of other people. Everything you need to survive, all that comes from other people. They contribute to you. And you have an obligation to contribute to them too. In whatever way you can. That's the social contract. And even if you think you're not obligated, you really are, because just like Thoreau, if you're going out to the woods to live, where are you going to get your ax?"

"Judge Griffith is looking at her watch again. What does this have to do with your situation?"

"Well . . . I can see what's going on. Some kind of evacuation. People who can afford it are leaving the Earth. Like guests leaving a party after they've trashed the house. They're taking their money and they're going up the Line to the moon and everywhere else. Isn't that right?"

"Yes, Charles. I won't lie to you. There are people who are afraid of the possibility of war and disease and economic turmoil—"

"That's my point—if you grownups can't keep your promises, if you can't keep your part of the social contract to the whole planet—if grownups are running away from the problems they made, then how can you ask a kid like me to stay behind with the mess? I don't know that running away solves any problems, but I don't see that I accomplish anything useful by staying either."

For a moment there was silence in the court. A lot of people looked real uncomfortable. Dad. Mom. Judge Griffith. Olivia. Mickey. Howard. Dr. Hidalgo. Finally, Judge Griffith said, "I think he's pretty well nailed the lot of us to the wall."

But Howard-The-Merciless wasn't finished. He said, "I can think of a reason to go back."

"What?"

"Because you love your Mom."

I looked over at Mom, she looked hopeful. Her eyes were shining. I looked to Dad, he looked kinda proud. I looked at Douglas, who flashed me a quick nod and a smile.

"Yeah," I said to Howard-The-Duck. "That's a good reason." Mom smiled at me—until I added, "But it's not good enough. Not anymore," and her expression collapsed into grief. I should have stopped there, but I didn't. "I love my mom. I really do. I love my dad too. But I don't like being in the middle anymore. Love's a good reason for lots of stuff—but not for doing something stupid. And going back to either of them is the stupidest thing I can think of."

Howard sat down, defeated.

LAWYERS AND AGENTS

JUDGE GRIFFITH GLANCED AT HER watch and made a face. She turned sideways in her chair to face me. "Thank you, Charles. That was very nicely argued. Have you ever considered becoming a lawyer?"

"Only once. Dad threatened to strangle me in my sleep."

"And he's probably right. Never mind. Do you still want a divorce?"

I nodded. "Yes, Your Honor. I do."

"Hmm." She frowned. "You know, I can grant it, right here and now. It's irregular, but so is this whole situation. So it wouldn't be out of line to resolve it with an unorthodox decision, particularly in light of some of the other pressures on us." She sighed, glanced at her watch again, and began to explain. "But I'll tell you honestly, I'm very reluctant to just bang the gavel and be done with it."

"Why?"

"You see, Charles, we have a problem here. You and I in particular. I can declare Douglas an adult, because he's only two months shy of his majority. And I can ask you what you want to do, because even though you're not yet old enough to be independent, you're still old enough to have a say in what happens to you. And if you want a divorce, I can put you in Douglas's custody. But I can't give the same choice to Bobby, can I? Do you think he's capable of making an informed decision? Do you think so, Douglas?"

Douglas and I both shook our heads.

"So you see the problem here. We have to make a decision about what's best for your brother, you and I and Douglas. I already know what your mother and father are going to say. They're going to fight over custody of Bobby, even more ferociously, because he's all that's left; so I need to hear what someone else thinks—someone else who knows your Mom and Dad, and nobody knows them better than you and your brother. So what do you two think I should do? Charles? Douglas?"

Douglas and I looked at each other. I searched his face for a clue, even a hint, of what he was thinking. He shook his head slightly—a signal to be careful? Or that he didn't know, either?

"Well . . . first of all," I said slowly, "I want to go with Douglas." I looked to him for reassurance. He gave me a quick nod of okay, and I smiled tightly and blinked fast before any tears could come. I was surprised I'd said it, and even more surprised he'd agreed.

"What happens if Douglas chooses to go someplace you don't want to go?"

"I can't think of anyplace like that, Your Honor. I want to stay with my brother. We're family. We've always been together. I know how to live without my mom and without my dad. I've been doing that almost all my life. I don't know how to live without my brothers, and even though Douglas can be real weird sometimes, I still want to go with him."

"You're sure about that?"

"As sure as I can be."

"Hm. Well. I see." Judge Griffith mulled that over. "I could probably do that. As I said, I can grant Douglas acting custody over you, subject to the approval of the jurisdiction you end up in; in the absence of any other contesting relatives, they'd probably confirm it. Your problem is going to be—or rather, it'll be Doug's problem—supporting yourselves. I understand that you're looking for an indenture, Douglas?"

"Yes, ma'am."

"Mm. Be careful. Make sure you have an agent review the contract. But you should be able to get an indenture that covers Charles as well. He can take on a delayed indenture that doesn't kick in until he turns eighteen, and the two of you should be able to find a colony that can use a couple of fairly intelligent warm bodies. So it's doable, and I can sign off on it. But that still leaves the problem of your younger brother . . . ."

"Yeah, Stinky's a problem," I said. "But he's *our* problem. Douglas and I have spent more time taking care of him than Mom or Dad."

"Are you suggesting that you and Douglas also take custody of Bobby as well?"

When she put it that way . . . I had to hesitate. But Douglas didn't. He stepped forward. "Ma'am, I'm not saying it'll be easy. In fact, it'll probably be the hardest thing I've ever done. But I've been thinking hard about this—not just tonight, but for several days now. I think it'd be the best for Bobby. I think it'd be best for me and Charles too."

A DECISION

JUDGE GRIFFITH SIGHED. SHE WAS doing a lot of sighing tonight. She steepled her fingers in front of her mouth and thought for a moment. "You have your tickets?"

Mickey stood up then. "I have their tickets, Your Honor. And unless they've cancelled my contract, I am the agent of record for this family. I can guarantee delivery to Luna and a high probability of an acceptable contract. I have three possibilities already. We have insurance in place against failure to contract, so the family will not end up a drain on the resources of any starside facility."

"Fair enough. Is it my understanding that you are also emigrating, Mickey?"

"Yes, Aunt Georgia."

"I'm going to miss you, sweetheart. Is it your intention to accompany the Dingillian family?"

"Uh—" Mickey looked to Douglas, uncertain. Douglas . . . hesitated, then nodded. Okay, so that fight was over. "Yes, Your Honor."

"Are you willing to accept co-responsibility with Douglas Dingillian?"

"Uh—yes, I'm prepared to accept co-responsibility up to and including such time as I can guarantee financial security through an appropriate colonial contract, and for as long after that as the Dingillians are willing to accept my support."

"Mickey?" The Judge looked at him sternly. "You just met these folks—what is it? Two days, three days ago? Are you willing to take on this kind of a commitment on such short notice—especially now, after you've seen them at their worst?"

"Aunt Georgia, I admit that there's a lot of dirtside crap going on. But I think these are good people. And they wouldn't be in half the trouble they're in if it hadn't been for me. . . ."

"And your mom," Judge Griffith added.

Mickey shrugged in acquiescence of the point. "The thing is, I like them in spite of themselves. I owe them. I want to do it."

Judge Griffith cleared her throat gruffly. "Well, that sort of settles that. The younger generation has come of age. All that's left for us old broads is to find a nice warm grave and get someone to throw some dirt over us. Olivia, you did a good job on this boy. He has a conscience." To the rest of us, she said, "All right, I'm now prepared to hear arguments from the parents. I assume you are both going to protest a ruling of divorce here—?"

Both Mom and Dad stood up at the same time; they both said yes. In unison. It was the first time I'd ever seen them agree on anything. They looked at each other in surprise. Dad made a waving gesture at Mom. "You go first."

Mom didn't spare any words. If there's one thing Mom can be counted on for, she lets you know what she's thinking. "Is this the way justice up here works? Is your culture up here so morally bankrupt that you have to steal other people's children—?"

"That's the way, Mom," Douglas said. "Butter her up. Make her like you."

"Shut up, Douglas," Mom snapped at him. "I heard about your—misadventures. I can't tell you how disappointed in you I am."

"Then don't try," said Douglas.

"Douglas," said Judge Griffith. "It's your mother's turn. Sit down, please." To Mom, she said, "I assume you have an argument to present?"

Mom turned to Howard-The-Repugnant. "You're a lawyer! Do something!"

He shrugged, looked through his briefcase, pulled out a folded paper, and passed it to her.

"Huh? What's this?"

"My bill," he said. "The minute you walked in the door, you destroyed my case. Not being here was your best chance. As long as you were still groundside, I could make the argument that the children were being taken away without your opportunity to be present and have your side of the issue heard. It would have justified pushing the case into a Liaison Court, which handles mixed jurisdiction disputes. But now that you're here, this constitutes a fair hearing, and all I can do is restate what's already in the record. There might be a couple other things we could try, but the end result is going to be the same. And the judge has already made it clear she's not going to tolerate any delaying tactics. So there's nothing I can do here, except enjoy the show—and that's exactly what I am doing. Please pay that within thirty days." Howard leaned back in his chair, grimly satisfied. He looked almost human.

Olivia grinned over at him. "I may have misjudged your intelligence. You finally found a way to avoid losing a case—stay out of it. And present a bill anyway. My compliments, Counselor."

"Belay that noise, Olivia." This was punctuated with a rap of the gavel. I was beginning to wish I had a gavel of my own. It was a great way to get people to pay attention. I wondered how hard it was to become a lawyer. Probably not too hard, if Howard could be one. "Ms. Campbell, do you have anything else to say? Anything to justify awarding you custody, that is?"

"Your Honor, I already have custody. You have the case in front of you. The El Paso District Court awarded me custody of my children. These hearings are illegal. This is a kangaroo court. You have no authority over me or my children. I demand that you affirm the rulings of the groundside court."

"Thanks for the demonstration of how to put the tact into tactical, Ms. Campbell. But even if I liked you, you'd still be wrong. This hearing is *very* legal. I suggest you ask your attorney—I assume Howard is still acting as your representative, despite his apparent dereliction of responsibility—but ask him anyway. Ask him to explain the limits of groundside jurisdiction and the more far-reaching authority of starside courts. Because, up here, life is maintained at such great expense, we have to hold ourselves to a much higher standard of integrity than most folks from dirtside. What I am telling you is that the authority of this court is absolute in these matters. You are certainly free to take this case to the World Court, and I'll be disappointed in you if you don't, but once I make my ruling, it's going to be implemented immediately, and so far, I haven't heard anything from you that has given me reason to reconsider my intentions. In fact, the more you talk, the more you confirm my decision."

The woman next to Mom stood up. "Your Honor, may I speak?"

"Why not?" Judge Griffith sighed. "Everyone else is going to insist on having their say tonight. Your name is . . . ?"

"Bev Sykes, Your Honor. I think you can understand that my partner, Maggie, is justifiably upset about this situation. She came to San Francisco for a much-needed vacation; the next thing, she's in the biggest crisis of her life—"

"It is a crisis which she helped create, Ms. Sykes. No one is innocent here. Least of all you, if I read this history right."

"The point is, Your Honor, that what you're proposing to do is overturn a stable situation—"

"I've seen absolutely no evidence of stability in this situation, Ms. Sykes."

Mom spoke up again then. "Perhaps if you'd ever had children of your own, you'd understand—"

Oops.

Judge Griffith's face darkened. "I had two daughters of my own, Ms. Campbell. They died in the Line accident of '97. That's when I got this chair. Do either of you have anything useful to add?"

Mom and the other woman whispered together for a moment, then they both shook their heads and sat down. They looked very unhappy. I almost felt sorry for them, but I wasn't going to change my mind, and I didn't think Doug was going to either.

Judge Griffith looked to Dad. "Mr. Dingillian, you had something to say?"

Dad stood up. He took a breath. He seemed strangely calm. "Thank you, Your Honor. I want to apologize for my conduct in this whole affair. I made a serious error in judgment. I've hurt my children. I've made a lot of trouble for everybody. That I did so out of my love for my sons and my commitment to their well-being does not excuse my actions. I know that."

Judge Griffith was studying her watch. "Get on with it, please."

"Yes, Your Honor. The point is, whatever you decide, I'll still be the boys' father, and Margaret will still be their mother—regardless of how you assign custody, we have the right to spend time with our children. And if our children want to spend time with us, they should have that right as well."

"The Court is already taking that into consideration," Judge Griffith said, typing something into her clipboard.

"Well, that's my argument, Your Honor. If the children end up in a location so far removed that visitation is impractical to the point of being impossible, then those visitation rights are effectively denied."

Judge Griffith raised her eyebrow. "In view of the circumstances which forced this hearing, the court finds it profoundly ironic that you should be making that argument, Mr. Dingillian."

Mom snorted. Loudly. I knew that snort.

Dad remained nonplused. "Nevertheless, Your Honor—if it was wrong for me to consider denying my wife access to her children, and it was, I admit it, but if it was wrong for me to do so, then it is equally wrong for the court to allow a situation to occur where visitation is impossible."

"Now that's a good point," Judge Griffith said, gesturing with the gavel. "But it seems to me that if visitation with your children is important enough to you, it's your responsibility to make sure to keep yourself near to them. The problem in this family is that both you and your wife have been attempting to make visitation impossible for each other, either by legal means or by moving the children around. And the Court finds that behavior an intolerable state of affairs. Not because it is unfair to either of you, *but because it is unfair to the children.*

"You both claim that you are interested only in the well-being of your children, but you have both put enormous emotional burdens on them. Your children need a place to heal, a place to recover from their parents. Considering the abuses of the visitation process in this case, the Court is not inclined toward allowances for the needs of the parents. I won't rule out visitation rights, but I'm not going to make visitation rights as large a part of the final decision as it was downside. Anything else, Mr. Dingillian?"

Dad looked beaten. He shook his head and sat down.

"All right, then." Judge Griffith rapped her gavel. "Here's my ruling. It is the decision of this court that Douglas Dingillian is to be regarded in all rights and privileges as a legal adult. It is the further decision of this court that Charles Dingillian is granted a summary divorce from both of his parents and given to the care and custody of Douglas Dingillian, contingent on the co-responsibility of Mickey Partridge. Charles, this divorce is contingent on review by the legal authority of whatever jurisdiction you and your brother settle in. So choose your destination carefully."

"Yes, Your Honor."

"In the matter of Robert Dingillian, the court recognizes the long history of custody disputes in this case, and acknowledges the already established legal rights of both parents . . . and sets them aside. The welfare of the child always takes precedence. Because the parents of Robert Dingillian have not demonstrated, in the opinion of *this* Court, sufficient commitment to the child to put their own disputes aside, the Court is left with no alternative but to remove the child from the custody of the parents and place him in the care of his elder brother, Douglas. This is also contingent on the statement of co-responsibility from Mickey Partridge, and final review by the legal authorities of your ultimate destination. Mickey, I mean it, choose *carefully*. This concludes the business of this Court. And if there are no further objections, I declare this hearing adjourned—"

THE McGUFFIN

BUT **BEFORE SHE COULD RAP** her gavel on the table, Dad stood up. "Your Honor? Point of order? Um—may I ask for clarification, please?"

Judge Griffith hesitated, the gavel poised above the table. "Go ahead."

"My sons are free to use the tickets I purchased for them, if they wish to. Is that correct?"

"Your sons are free to choose their own destination. Yes, they can use the tickets you paid for. The Court has not terminated your access, only your custodial authority."

"I understand that, I'm just trying to get clear on where the line is drawn. Am I *also* free to use the ticket I purchased for myself?"

"Yes," said the judge. "You are."

Over on the other side of the room, I heard Mom gasp. "I can't believe this—"

Both Dad and the judge ignored her. Dad asked, "Even if it means traveling together with my sons? Your Honor, you do understand that if my sons use their tickets to go on to Luna, we'll be sharing the same cabin . . . ?"

"Mr. Dingillian, the Court has no objection to you traveling with your sons. You *are* entitled to visitation rights. But you no longer have any custodial authority over them. That's the limit of this ruling—"

"Oh, great!" said Mom. "We're right back where we started! He has no custodial rights, but he still ends up with the kids! What kind of a kangaroo court is this?" She turned to Hidalgo. "You said you could help me! This is the way you help people?!"

Hidalgo wasn't stupid. He didn't even try to calm her down. He was already pushing himself ponderously to his feet, raising his hand for attention. "Your Honor, there is one other matter left unresolved. If I may beg the Court's indulgence . . . ?"

"Just a moment, Dr. Hidalgo." Judge Griffith turned to Mom. She finally laid her gavel down. "Ms. Campbell, please understand, you have the exact same rights—or should I say, lack of rights. If you wish to travel with your children, you may do so as well. Under the same terms as your ex-husband."

"Oh, yeah, right! With what money?! I don't have a SuperNational credit card—I can't go to the moon!"

"Somebody paid for two tickets on the express shuttle . . ." Judge Griffith left the second half of that thought unsaid. Mom fumed and sputtered, but the judge was already moving on. "All right, Bolivar. You paid for two tickets to this circus—let's hear what you have to say." She glanced meaningfully at her watch.

"It is the matter of *Señor* Dingillian's financial status. If you will consult your own records, you will see that this man does not have the resources to have paid for even one ticket up the beanstalk, let alone four."

"So?"

"So if he is going to the outbeyond, the Financial Responsibility Act requires proof that he is leaving behind no significant debts."

Dad stood up. "Your Honor, there is documentation on file with the Emigration Authority to demonstrate that not only are all of my outstanding debts paid off, but that there is a fund in escrow to handle any future claims that may arise. Additionally, there is Emigration Insurance to cover any contingencies that exceed the funds in escrow."

Judge Griffith was sitting at her table with her hands folded in front of her chin again. She looked from one to the other, more amused than anything else. "Is there a point to all this?" she asked.

"With the Court's indulgence," Hidalgo said, "I would like, at this time, to present documentation that *Señor* Dingillian's trip has been financed by certain SuperNational interests, and that in return, he is functioning as a courier for them—"

"So what?" said the judge. "We have private couriers going up and down the Line every day. Many people finance their emigration that way. There's nothing illegal about it."

"Your Honor, may I please direct your attention to Section Four of the Line Authority Transportation Act? There are a number of restrictions on private courier service. It is illegal if the item being transferred is contraband or stolen property, or if the intent of private service is to avoid legal obligations, such as liens, claims, custody, or taxation. If a courier is suspected of carrying items in violation of Section Four, the Line—that's you, Your Honor—has the authority to investigate and, if appropriate, require divestment of any and all packages."

"I see you've done your homework, Bollie. As usual. So what is it that Max Dingillian is carrying that you want to get your hands on so badly that you're willing to pay for two premium-class round-trip shuttle tickets?"

"Your Honor, it is not for myself that I act, it is on behalf of the—"

"I've heard the speech, Bollie. More than once. Just tell the Court what the McGuffin is."

"Your Honor, six days ago, Stellar-American Resources transferred an extremely large amount of money into a Canadian-Lunar transfer account. The account is a pipeline that may be accessed freely both on Earth and on Luna. It is commonly used for holding funds being moved off-world. Stellar-American Resources has three transfer accounts of their own, all bonded and monitored, which they normally use for off-world access. That they are suddenly using this account to transfer an extremely large resource suggests that they are attempting to avoid transfer taxes, as well as legal scrutiny. Not even the company's own stockholders are aware of this transfer—"

"But you are?" Judge Griffith noted with mild sarcasm.

"There are people who tell me things, Your Honor. Be that as it may, however the information comes to light, there is certainly enough to be suspicious about. And it is my solemn duty to call this to your attention. My people believe that *Señor* Dingillian is carrying one of three password-checks necessary to complete the transfer of funds. The other two may have already arrived on Luna."

"Just how much money are we talking about, Bolivar?"

Hidalgo pursed his lips and looked extremely uncomfortable. "It is over three trillion dollars, Your Honor. Perhaps as much as ten. The money came out of nine thousand different accounts that my people regularly watch, and at least ninety thousand more that we have not yet found a way to monitor. For this much money to move off of Earth so abruptly—"

Judge Griffith rapped her gavel. "The money flows, Bolivar. The fact that you don't like where it goes doesn't make the river a crime. This isn't a McGuffin at all. It's the stuff that dreams are made of."

"Your Honor, I respectfully request the Court to require *Señor* Dingillian to divulge the truth about what he is carrying. If it is a legal transfer, then I shall apologize profusely for taking up his time and the Court's. But if *Señor* Dingillian is carrying a check of such enormous size, I am certain that there are law enforcement and tax agencies both groundside and starside who will want to check that no laws are being broken by such a transfer." Hidalgo folded his hands across his paunch and waited.

Judge Griffith frowned. "I understand exactly what you're trying to do, Bollie. But what you're asking is generally beyond the reach of this Court. I can ask Mr. Dingillian to reveal what he is carrying, but absent any evidence of a crime, he isn't required to violate his own privacy. If there is no evidence of wrong-doing, I can take no action."

"I understand, Your Honor, but I believe it is in the interests of justice to compel such performance as is appropriate."

"Mm. Yes. Bollie, I know you—you always want the best justice money can buy. So be it." She turned to Dad. "What are you carrying, Max? You don't have to tell me, but if it'll get Bolivar Hidalgo off your back . . ."

Dad shook his head and spread his empty hands wide. "Your Honor. *I'm not* carrying anything. . . ."

The way he said it—with an unspoken *now* attached to the end of the sentence—was enough to raise Judge Griffith's eyebrows. "Have you already delivered it?"

"I have not delivered anything, Your Honor." Again, the same unfinished tone. If you didn't know Dad, you might not catch it, but if you were smart . . . like Judge Griffith, you could hear that what Dad *wasn't* saying was almost as important as what he *was* saying.

Judge Griffith hesitated. I could see she'd figured it out. But of course, being a judge, she'd probably learned how to figure out when people were telling the truth or not. And then, too, she might have had some game of her own working. . . .

"Well, then," she said. "If you're not carrying anything—this Court has no further business with you."

"Your Honor!" That was Hidalgo. "Ask him who paid for his tickets and what he had to do in return!"

She appeared to be mulling it over. I glanced over at Doug, he looked to the monkey in my lap, I shrugged and looked at the ceiling. Dad looked back and forth between us, carefully blank. Despite the judge's decision, Stinky was still asleep in Mom's lap, and I wondered if we were going to be able to get him away from her.

Judge Griffith unfolded her hands. "Dr. Hidalgo, I think you're asking me to go into an area that is beyond the scope of this session. I told you earlier that I would not get into any inquiries that did not bear directly on the custody of the Dingillian children. I'm not going fishing for you. While the matter you have raised is certainly an important one, we cannot pursue it here. If you wish, you can pursue this in another court." She started to pick up her gavel again—

Almost as soon as the judge had begun speaking, Hidalgo had nudged Howard, who began fumbling in his briefcase.

Now, as Judge Griffith finished, Howard leapt to his feet. "Uh, not so fast, Your Honor, I have a warrant here—"

"And you're just serving it now?"

"I hadn't expected that it would be necessary."

"Pass it up."

Howard-The-Unkempt gave the paper to Judge Griffith's assistant, Joyce, who passed it to the judge. She unfolded the paper and studied it thoughtfully. She scratched her eyebrow with a fingernail while she read. "Well, this appears to be in order," she said finally. To the rest of the room, she announced, "This is a Line Authority search-and-seizure warrant for the property of Max Dingillian. I'll spare you all the whereases. You're accused of transporting contraband."

Dad stood up, "Your Honor, all I have are the clothes I'm wearing. If the court will provide me with something to wear, I'll be happy to give you these clothes."

"It's not that easy, Max. I'm authorized to detain you."

Dad shrugged. "Go ahead, Your Honor." He held out his wrists, as if awaiting handcuffs. "Take me away. I don't have anything—"

"Wait a minute," I said. I stood up, still holding the monkey. "Dad is telling the truth. He isn't carrying anything. I am. He gave it to me. I put it in the monkey."

Dad and Douglas both stared. "Charles—!"

I was already prying the back of the monkey open. I pulled out the bottommost memory bar and carried it over to Dad. "Here," I said. "Give this to the judge."

Dad looked at the memory bar, looked at me, looked at Olivia—she was carefully blank—then handed it to Joyce, who handed it to Judge Griffith, who turned it over in her hands, examining it. "You were paid to transport this?"

Dad looked to Olivia, looked back to the judge. "Yes, Your Honor. I was paid to transport that."

"Well then, the warrant is satisfied." Judge Griffith passed the memory bar to her assistant. "Joyce, seal that. It's not to be released to anyone." To Doctor Hidalgo, she said, "If it can be demonstrated that the intention of this warrant was to disrupt a lawful business enterprise, not only will I hold you in contempt, I will fine you for the full amount of damages. And you too, Howard. Let it be noted that this Court does not approve of the mischievous abuse of litigation."

"Your Honor," Howard-The-Illegitimate said, "we would like to request that the . . . uh, monkey be confiscated as well. In case there are other memory cards—"

"Nope. The monkey doesn't belong to Max Dingillian. It belongs to Robert Dingillian. Sorry, Howard." She raised her hands in mock helplessness.

He sputtered. "But the warrant—!"

"The warrant says nothing about the property of *Robert* Dingillian. And as he is no longer under the custodial authority of Max Dingillian, we cannot even use that umbrella. Hm, I see you forgot to add an *a priori* clause that would have allowed me to grant your request. You should be more careful when you draft these things, Howard. You left a loophole big enough to be an escape hatch. Given the wording of this document," she waved it at him, "this Court has no authority to seize the property of any other Dingillian. And I will not act beyond the authority of this document. If I did, the next judge up would have ample grounds to invalidate the warrant anyway. So consider that I'm doing you a favor. If you want the monkey, go get another warrant."

I couldn't help myself, I surreptitiously switched the monkey on—and whispered into its ear. It leapt down from my lap, ran over to Howard-The-Stupid, and gave him a double-chocolate, hot-fudge farkleberry with whipped cream and a cherry on top. Plus a noise like an elephant fart. Then it came scurrying back to me. Howard looked like he was going to explode.

Keeping her face carefully blank, Judge Griffith picked up her gavel and rapped it once. "We're adjourned." She looked at her watch. "And just in time. You have an elevator to catch, Mickey. Get your butt in gear. They're holding the gate for you—"

GOOD-BYES

AND THEN A LOT OF stuff happened all at once. Dr. Hidalgo waddled over and stood in front of Dad. "You have been very lucky, *Señor* Dingillian. Very very lucky. I hope for your sake and your children's sake that your luck holds out."

Dad shook his head and laughed. "And you've been very stupid, Dr. Hidalgo. Very very stupid. You never figured it out, did you?"

Dr. Hidalgo raised an eyebrow. "Enlighten me?"

"You and your people—I was never carrying anything. I was a *decoy*. Do you really think they'd trust that much money to my care? Even I'm not that stupid. Whoever it was—and even I don't know for sure, you probably know more than me—they wanted you looking in the wrong place. So they hired me. And I guess it worked. While you were busy chasing me up the Line, you weren't hassling a whole bunch of other folks."

"That's an assumption on your part."

"Maybe so, maybe not. But I got my job done. Thanks again for dinner." Dad offered his hand.

Surprisingly, Dr. Hidalgo took it. He held Dad's hand in

both of his. "You may yet need my help, *señor*. I do not think you know what you are playing with. You keep my card. You call me if your new friends don't work out. *Adiós. Vaya con dios*." And he turned and waddled over to confer with Howard-The-Unhappy.

Dad turned to look at me. And Douglas. We were whispering together. Dad must have seen the look on my face. And on Douglas' too. He said, *"What?"*

And I said to Douglas, "You tell him "

And Dad said, "Tell me what?"

So Douglas swallowed hard. "You sure, Charles?"

"Yes." I nodded.

Douglas turned to Dad. "We don't want you to come with us."

Dad looked confused. He looked from me to Douglas and back again. So I added, "Judge Griffith said we don't have to take you if we don't want to. Well . . . we don't want to."

Dad went pale. "Charles? Douglas? Are you sure—?"

"We have to go, Dad." Douglas hugged him quickly. "Maybe we'll see you on the moon. I hope so."

I went to Dad to hug him too, but I didn't say anything to him. He looked like he'd been stabbed—and was still waiting to fall down. He didn't hug me back, so I let go and followed Douglas over to where Mom was standing. She was holding Bobby, rocking him back and forth on her shoulder.

Joyce, the bailiff, followed at a respectful distance. Mom had picked up Bobby and was holding onto him as hard as she could. She glared over his shoulder at Douglas, and at Joyce too, and she held onto Bobby for the longest time, holding him, stroking his head, whispering into his ear, telling him over and over how much she loved him and how she was going to come and get him, not to worry—but at last, Douglas bent down to take him, and she let him slip out of her arms. Tears were running down her cheeks and I was starting to feel real bad about this whole thing. Doug bent his head to kiss her, but she just turned away.

So Douglas turned away from her and she was standing there by herself, just looking at me—and I didn't know what to say or do. She walked slowly over to where I was standing alone, and when she spoke it was like being dragged naked over nails. She just shook her head and asked, "Why, Charles—why?"

I shook my head helplessly. "I—I'm sorry, Mom. I didn't do it to hurt you."

"Was I really that bad a mother to you?"

"Mom, you're angry all the time—"

"Well, don't I have good reason to be? The way you treat me. The way your father treats me."

"Mom, this isn't about you—"

"Well, then *who* is it about—? Answer me that!"

"Mom, you don't listen! You don't *ever* listen—you're not listening now."

"Charles, I have a right to know. You're breaking up our family—"

"No, Mom. It was already broken. You and Dad broke it up a long time ago—"

"Is this really what you want—to hurt me like this?"

I wiped the tears from my cheeks. "Mom, what I want most"—it hurt to say it; my voice cracked—"what I want most is . . . to get away from you, right now. I can't stand it when you talk to me like this. It isn't *my* fault!"

"Go ahead, then! You're just like your father, you little bastard! I hope you're happy!" And then—she slapped my face! For an instant, I saw stars.

I didn't know what to do or say. I was too shocked. She hadn't ever hit me before. I couldn't believe it—everybody was staring at me—so I just turned to go—and then she was grabbing at me, crying, "Oh, God, Charles—I'm so sorry, I didn't mean to do that! Charles, please—wait! Wait! Charles!"

There was one thing she could have said that might have made me stop, and I was listening as hard as I could to hear her say it, and maybe she *was* saying it in her own way, but I was listening for the words, and she never said them. She never said the words. So I kept going.

And then Doug put an arm around my shoulders and I started sobbing as we followed Mickey to the hatch of the transfer pod. I looked back to see Dr. Hidalgo and that Sykes woman rushing to Mom's side, and then Doug steered me into the waiting pod and then the door closed and they were gone—

"So what happens now?" I asked, still wiping tears from my eyes.

"I have an idea," Doug answered, shouldering Bobby with one arm, and hugging me with the other. "Let's go to the moon."

JESSE BETHEL HIGH SCHOOL
1800 Ascot Parkway
Vallejo, California 94591
(707) 556-5700